THERON GIBBONS

ILLUSTRATIONS BY CHRISTY A. MOELLER-MASEL

This book is dedicated to the people who had faith in me.
Theron L Gibbons

Other dedications from the Author

Tremendous Thanks to Christy A Moeller-Massel for her incredible talent and support.

~ and ~

To my editor, Mireille Gibbons-Schmidt, for her passionate devotion to the cause.

BIT
AT
LARGE

The contents herein are a work of fiction. Names, characters, places, and the incidents within this book are all imaginary creations of the author. If there is any similarity to actual events, people living or dead, organizations or locales past or present, or to some other causal, ethereal, or material aspect of reality, it is purely coincidental, and neither the author nor the publisher intended such a corollary.

Elucid Press
PO BOX 15971
Phoenix, AZ 85060

Visit us online at:
www.elucidpress.com

First Paperback Edition   Circa 2,000 AD

ISBN 0-9678345-0-3

Chapter 1

I punched the Doctor when he smacked Tiffany to encourage respiration. Of course, my hand passed right through his skull, doing no damage except to give the doctor a slight creeping itch on his forehead. Everything starts with the birth of a child, and Tiffany's birth, which I attended despite my not being officially attached to her, was a bloody and spectacular mess.

When I was finally put in formal charge of Tiffany, she had just been kidnapped. Stolen as an infant from a foster home in southern California, Tiffany was well on her way to being a $400,000 profit for a slave trader from Southeast Asia. I would have intervened, because I've been given the auspicious duty of being her Guardian Angel.

I would have done anything to put her back in the foster home, with her happy parents. Though small by angel standards, it was a darn sight better than being sold into slavery. Father Wisdom, however, had other plans for the girl. No matter what I argued in her favor, he wouldn't change her fate. He wouldn't let me rescue her.

On distant shores, where law was controlled by force and money, the slave merchant sold her to a rich and violent opium trader. From what little I could understand of their conversation, Tiffany's fate had already been determined. She would be raised as Roan's concubine. Three days after Tiffany got settled in with a wet nurse, Father Wisdom came to visit me. Father had always been such a terribly impressive man. His shocking white hair stood out like a lion's mane, and his face looked like worn, crumpled parchment. He wore a flowing white set of robes, simple and uncomplicated.

He was very different from mother, who tended to wear nothing but her leathery wings. Tester, my mother, and Wisdom, my father, were Avatars of the angels. Both had come down as husband and wife to set the example for angel kind. I often wondered why they'd had me as a child, because they had so many childish angels to look after. Since he was there, and I was concerned about my girl, I had to convince him that Tiffany would be better off elsewhere – a difficult task considering his omnipresent existence.

"She's not safe in that house. It has too many shadows, and too many bad people in it." I tried to sound angry, but ended up pouting.

"She's safe for now." Wisdom said.

My father, ever understanding, put a loving hand on my bare shoulder. We sat in the rafters, studying the dish placement as it was spread onto the traditional knee-high dining table. I looked at my toes, trying to fathom her safety. Time shifted unexpectedly, as it often does for angels on assignment. Tiffany, now a supple three-year-old, scrubbed the floors with her nursemaid. The years continued to pass sporadically, my attention peaking when Tiffany needed me, diminishing when my presence held no purpose.

By her twelfth birthday, Tiffany had learned her place and duties as a concubine, studying books and being educated in the ways of womanhood and medicine. Her skin and body type would keep its youth well into menopause. Because of her profession, the effects of weather and daylight would hardly be a factor in her appearance.

When Tiffany actually got to meet me face to face, she was very close to thirteen. Because of her sheltered life, there was little opportunity for me to intervene. She was, as Wisdom had said, in no immediate danger. By the time she turned twelve, she was short, sassy, and incredibly smart. When she went out of the house, which was rare, her blond hair shown in the sun like chaffed wheat.

Though still a little girl, she could speak three languages, and was too well trained in the ways of persuasion. As a concubine, she learned a specialized talent for persuading men to think of themselves as sexual overlords and her as their servant. Every moment that passed forced me to consider my duty.

The daughter of the avatars, I had been raised as an angel. I felt it my duty to serve the wishes of my parents, and yet I felt also a strong, almost overwhelming urge to take Tiffany any place else. I had one thing on my mind – Tiffany must be free of such hardships, must be free to become that which her heart intended.

There were several problems with my strategy. First, being as young as I was, I had limits. Most of my power came from my parents. And Tiffany wasn't exactly educated to live under normal conditions. Being the concubine to a rich and abusive opium smuggler gives a girl little opportunity for social advancement, but as soon as I could convince my parents, I was going to bust Tiffany out of that place. Maybe sooner, if I could justify freeing her as a means of protecting her mind and spirit.

Roan, an amber skinned American who had moved to Asia to cash in on the illegal medical industry, was her master. Fortunately for Tiffany, Roan only had relations with the girl, if only because I ensured his lonely life. If the opportunity arose for Roan to end up with another lady, I saw to it that she'd suddenly hate him and seek out somebody else before things got out of hand. No need for Tiffany to be getting sick, after all.

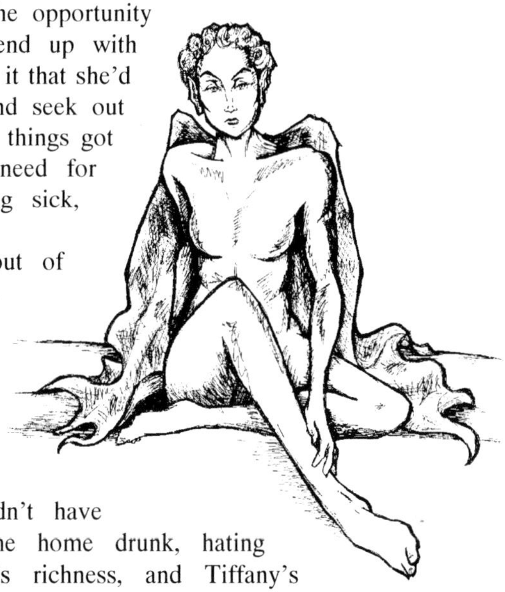

Keeping Roan out of strange women's beds was the easiest task I could do – Roan really wasn't much to look at. On nights when even the prostitutes wouldn't have him, he would come home drunk, hating himself, thanking his richness, and Tiffany's unwitting loyalty to him. He could be abusive with Tiffany. When he got too harsh with her, I would step in and manipulate his mind a little, to keep him from hurting her. It was my one pleasure.

There were the evenings that Roan acted almost like a gentleman. On these evenings I could almost understand Tiffany's misplaced affections. Perhaps, at times, she enjoyed her job a little too much, but I would bash anybody who'd condemn her for it. Though I'm a very young angel, barely thirteen, I've watched some humans go through their many lives, and believe me, they've all done some pretty wicked things that bring no pleasure to anybody.

One day, while Tiffany scrubbed the wood floors in the business room, Mother Tester called me away from my post. The second avatar of the angels, Tester was a creature of dark skin, black horns, and I'd never seen her wearing clothes. I'd been worried that I might be put on another assignment. I dreaded that thought. Tiffany was my girl, and nobody was going to take her form me.

As if sensing I was in a bad temper, Tester was late. She left me waiting by a tree in the woods while she tended to other business. She'd called me from Tiffany's side, and now she had me waiting for her. I sat down for close to an hour, for her to finally come back and tell me what was so important that I had to wait for her for so long. Of course, by the time she finally did show up, I'd fallen asleep in a patch of sunlight.

"Why, if it isn't my little Buddha, thinking away the day under such an old tree." Tester said, waking me up with a gentle nudge of her big toe.

I looked up from my catnap. Mother smiled savagely, her eyes studying me in ways that always left me wondering if she weren't mentally dissecting me. Tester was something to envy, with her long, silken legs with muscles both feminine and fully developed. Such was her nature, to test the ethics and dignities of humankind. But she didn't test me like the other angels. Being the daughter of the avatars did have some perks. She was still pushing me gently with her toes when I finally looked away.

"I'm awake already, you can stop with the kicking. What's so important that you'd dirty your hands coming to Earth just to talk to me?"

"Can't a woman visit her own daughter without a reason?"

"You never have before." I said.

"Well then, I wouldn't want to disappoint you. You're growing fat and lazy watching that little concubine. So I'm giving you a task worthy of a higher angel – one that will knock a few pounds off that plump body of yours. Hope you've enjoyed your vacation, because your new assignment is a serious one. You have to stop a war."

I flexed my wings, trying to puff them out in the humid, stagnant air.
They were dark folds of hairless skin. Nothing could make them look like the feathered wings of the transcendent angels.

"Why can't one of the older angels do this job and leave me to the simple tasks?"

I made one more wasted effort at trying to look imposing, finding it hopeless. I just wasn't like my mother. I let my wings sag and met Tester's gaze, my own eyes defiant. Her breasts, like mine, were small, her body a little more ideal than my own – and her horns actually exposed above her hair. Some angels, by the way, do have horns, because sometimes people need nightmares. She seemed to be thinking of the appropriate answer.

"They've sealed their fates already. It's up to you to determine your personal destiny now."

I wanted to scream out that nothing could be more important than taking care of Tiffany. The thought of having to do something that might separate me from the girl I'd spent so much time with made me angry. I bit my lip, frustrated, then realized that even Tiffany's one life might have less value than thousands of lives lost in battle.

"What war?" I asked, humbled.

"Father can explain it to you much better than me." Tester smiled, and I chilled about thirty degrees. "Go to Otherspace and speak to him. He'll explain the severity of this mission."

I felt myself shift reality and when my senses cleared, I was in the city of Transcendence, located at the heart of Otherspace. Otherspace, the home of the angels, is said to have been created by the merging of conscious thought and children's dreams. Though my native home, I'd had little chance to visit it since I grew up big enough to be put to work. The laws of physics shifted slightly, and I resisted the urge to puke.

Otherspace was a beautiful cosmic plane, where time was relative to the evolution of a person's thoughts, and gravity was a vector relative to what way your feet were pointing. Transcendence, the city of all

Angel-kind, seemed carved of silver, gold, and glass. In Transcendence a lower angel such as myself was rare, and a young child such as myself practically nonexistent.

My body, covered only by my leathery wings, was out of place. With my dark skin and kinky crown of hair, I was in direct contrast to most of the transcendent angels. With their white robes and feathery wings, they looked and acted so smug. A reflective aurora passed by me, a spirit of some deceased soul about to merge with Wisdom's consciousness.

I could see by my reflection in that pristine soul that I wasn't the only one who felt I was out of place. From behind me it reflected the arrogant stares of my fellow angels, though they were so uniform in appearance and dress that they blended into their surroundings. It also pointed out another commonality among the upper echelon of angels: They were all a bunch of stuffy bureaucrats.

With the other angels staring down their noses at me, I felt my confidence dwindle. I felt like my namesake, something tiny drifting through an unfathomed, infinite heaven. I was out of place but stuck in the middle. I moved through Transcendence at a quick pace, waiting impatiently for Father to notice me.

Being such an infinitesimally small Bit in an Otherspace full of ancient, powerful angels far older and more experienced than myself, I doubted I would come to his attention any time soon. The force that created the entire universe and all of its intricacies could easily lose track of me, even if I was his daughter.

Fortunately, a diversion happened without my ever having to cause it. Perhaps Wisdom had planned it that way all along. He is, after all, capable of a sense of humor. In this case his sense of humor was incarnated in Fluff. I'd known Fluff all my life; he's the second youngest angel beside myself. He's a good two thousand years older than me, but he still acts like a kid. He caught me from behind, spun me around, and hugged me close. He rubbed his ideal little face against mine, whispering greetings. His breath was like mint, and unlike a lot of the transcendent angels, he didn't have wings.

"It's so good to see you again. How are things in Realspace?"

"Just wonderful." I said sarcastically. "There's going to be a war, you know." He took my hands and spun me around as fast as he could, making me giggle with glee. My feet came off the ground, and my wings snapped back. I started laughing and at the same time asked him to stop.

He was the only child-like angel to reside in Otherspace, which was fortunate for perhaps everybody near him. The boy acted like a golden retriever on uppers, only with more energy. Before long I found myself pushed into a heated wrestling match. Mostly he was tugging me and harassing me into losing my considerable cool, and I was trying everything I could think of to shake him off before I got in trouble.

Trouble and Fluff, however, were merged at birth. I fought a losing battle, bumping into the tall angels and creating a little too much hoopla in their spotless and unchanging little afterlives. Somebody must have complained, because Father intervened. In a flash of brilliant light, Fluff and I found ourselves at the Heart of Transcendence, zapped there by one of the hierarchy of angels with greater authority.

"The girl's here on business, so leave her alone."

Wisdom's voice, ever understanding, ever calm, was dismissive. Properly scolded, Fluff stepped away from me and raised his arms, vanishing in a burst of light. Wisdom turned his full attention to me, and I felt even smaller than I had just a few moments before. Father's gaze, ever loving, seemed to bore straight through me. I shifted my weight from foot to foot, waiting for him to explain Tester's previous comments.

"As it so happens, the fate of the universe sits on your shoulders, and yours alone. It will take courage, pride, devotion, and sacrifice to save what's been created and survived until now." I wondered what could possibly interfere with Wisdom's Dream.

He answered, thus saving me the embarrassment of asking. "Alas, dear, it is not what, but who. I created the universe, started it rolling, and let it go. Occasionally I've had to take some physical form to see that the whole ball of wax doesn't roll off track, but only when corruption's involved. Sentience exists on a thousand million worlds throughout the universe, but no two races have such a potential for violence as the seventh and fifth magnitude right now."

I looked stunned. The human beings of Earth were the fifth

magnitude, and another alien sentience was the seventh magnitude. The two shouldn't have met for a thousand years or more. I let my wings fall gently around my body, trying to hide my ignorance. I couldn't remember the name of the race that was the seventh magnitude.

"The Seventh Magnitude are the Scandivats, and you're really too young to remember everything we've taught you. It's the corruption of one human, and not many, that's brought this problem upon you. In thirty-three years, all life on Earth will be in jeopardy. You have twenty-seven years to make Tiffany worthy of being the governor of the Forever Children. If you fail, you'll have to become the governor, and fulfill Tiffany's destiny. If she fails, you'll be Earth's last chance."

While I was trying to remember who the Forever Children were, Wisdom explained. "The Children that protect the worlds from harm. The ones who formulated Otherspace so angels could live separate from the rest of Humanity. There was a whole chapter in your history book on them. With your memory, Earth may be lost already."

"No it isn't, I was there just yesterday." I said, confused.

"I was being humorous. Fact is, the Forever Children's old governor has been assassinated. One of our Forever Children may have been killed as well. The salvation of the Scandivats now relies on you."

I felt terribly stunned, as if I was about to faint. "I don't want this job. Give it to somebody older, you've got a million angels here, and some of them may even be able to dust off their wings and do a better job."

"I asked everybody. Every one of them said they were too busy. Because you're my daughter, I get to tell you what to do. Remember, now, that you always promised to do what's right."

"I did?"

"Yeah."

"Stupid promise." I kicked at a puff of ethercloud. "I still don't know why one of the big boys can't get off their lazy butts and do this. I've got Tiffany to think of, and I can't possibly hope to save an entire universe alone."

"You won't be totally alone on this. Those who've enlightened themselves will help you. And there's always mother and me, and Fluff's got a part in this too. Your mission begins at dawn tomorrow.

When Tiffany wakes up, you'll do what's necessary to see to her safety, and you'll watch and wait until it's time to help her escape. Because of the damage to my universe, my options are growing more limited every day – and you're my strongest asset."

I felt my consciousness shift, and I started to shift out of Otherspace, back into Realspace. Wisdom was playing the part of the doddering old man who was powerless to help, when in reality he had the magic to make everything right.

His last words were curious. "Be careful when you wake up tomorrow, because you'll be an angel in human form."

Chapter 2

The next morning, my body was physical, making me vulnerable, but I still had my angelic abilities, making me – at least in theory – dangerous. I could choose who would see me and when. I would still be capable of all kinds of miraculous things that are written about in ancient texts stored in Transcendence's Historical Library. Of course, I'd never had much luck at doing any of that angelic stuff. I dozed off in my advanced angelic capabilities class. The teacher was mundo boring.

I flexed my wings, not really feeling all that different than I did before. This illusion of a body didn't show my wings – I looked like a normal little girl resident to whatever part of Asia Roan lived in. I looked through the window of the house, observing my precious Tiffany. She was busy helping an older woman make breakfast. Both of them hummed cheerily. It amazed me how happy Tiffany was despite the cruel truth that was her life.

"Something really disturbing is about to happen." I said to myself. It didn't take angelic intuition to know that, merely a highly tuned sensory system. A star ship had set down about a mile south of the Roan's poppy fields. To get from one place to another, star ships had to travel through Otherspace, and the process created enough of a disturbance that angels such as myself could feel them even at a distance.

I heard a click just as a hand went around my neck and face. So much for those keen angelic senses. The man smelled of poppies, soil, and sweat. A worker, undoubtedly, had caught me spying and wanted to earn points with Roan. I let myself vanish into nothing, and slunk invisibly out of his grip. The man, probably assuming himself delirious, went back to work rather than tell anybody.

I returned to watching Tiffany do her chores, squinting to see through my own reflection. Roan stumbled lazily down the stairs, his black smoking jacket, hanging half open, exposing his pudgy belly. Within moments his meal was before him and a small pot of heated sake sat at the left of his tray. As she passed him, he patted Tiffany's rear, saying something imposing and boorish about her. True to her training, she smiled at him adoringly. I resisted the urge to vomit. Roan was in his late thirties.

"The head guard's earned a night in the temple."

"I don't like Lupan." Tiffany said, sniffing.

"It's not for you to say." Roan said, his tongue clicking an obvious warning.

"At least make sure he bathes." Tiffany was arrogant, scrubbing the dishes as she spoke.

"You have to clean the sheets either way, what should you care?"

"I do care. That should be reason enough."

"I should've known a white girl would be a little snotty. That's why I paid the big bucks to get you."

Tiffany actually smiled in response to this, and I began to wonder if her concubinage was beginning to wear on her psychology a little. The scene transfixed me. Curious about the conversation transpiring between master and servant, I hardly noticed the wood boards creaking behind me. Lupan walked past my invisible self and into the dining room. Speaking in a less educated tongue, a language of harsh, simple words, Lupan announced visitors.

"They're not our usual customers, Lord. Should I send them away?" Lupan was quite impressive, in a raw, testosterone and sweat sort of way.

"Are they government? Do you think they pose a threat?" Roan asked in a whisper.

I could see Lupan straining his mind, trying to find an appropriate answer. "Any unknown is a hazard. They're not government forces. One man carries a pistol, but seems to be a merchant. The other is his strong arm, and he carries a sword and a box." Lupan kept his eyes to the front window.

The local government preferred Roan to the monks he'd slaughtered in conquest, when he was only fifteen. There'd be no threat from the local government, as long as the right people got their cut of his profits. The national government simply didn't have the resources to needed to route out such a powerful, dangerous man.

"Bring them in, maybe they're new customers."

Roan dismissed Lupan and snapped his fingers. Tiffany set two seats and two places at the woven reed, knee high table. Ten minutes after the conversation with Lupan, the visitors were seated across from him, each sitting on their knees. I crept in just behind them, ready for action. One looked like a local. He had two swords strapped to his back, and was carrying a box on his head. The other was a human from another planet; his clothes gave him away.

I liked the off-worlder almost instantly. His heart seemed good and his smile sincere. As they sat and talked, his attention turned to Tiffany on many occasions. I walked casually into the room, completely invisible to everybody – worrying about Tiffany. Her fate, it seemed, was yet to be determined.

"Now that breakfast is concluded, I would like to get down to business."

Roan smiled, "Ah, a customer. We have very high grade this year."

The older man looked for a moment as if he were insulted. "I've come to buy her."

Roan looked sidewise at Tiffany. Her back was turned, and she had frozen slightly, intently listening while trying not to look like she was intently listening. His eyes returned to Jodiah's.

"The girl isn't for sale. She seems too young for you, old man. But if the price is right."

Roan snapped his fingers, and I had to concentrate to keep from becoming visible. Tiffany turned, facing Jodiah, her face hidden in the shadow of her hair. She put her hands to her dress, pulled loose the first knot holding her dress in place. Jodiah motioned for her to stop.

"She's for my son. He couldn't make the journey, but he needs a wife. I'm not a bargaining man, but I'll show you what she's worth to me. My associate has brought her price."

The man carrying the box must have been about ten times stronger than he looked, he removed hundreds of pounds of gold from the box, and there was little evidence that he'd had help carrying it from the ship. The small box held perhaps fifty bars of gold, each having to weigh at least five pounds apiece. It piled over the table until the table bowed and splintered under the strain. My own eyes widened at the sight, and I secretly wished somebody would think I was worth so much.

"It's All I brought with me, and all I'm willing to pay." Jodiah said.

Roan, his medium brown eyes glowing with greed, looked at the small pyramid of gold as if it were something divine.

"Shit of God." He exclaimed in a quiet whisper. "She is yours."

Tiffany turned, her eyes filled with rage and hatred. "I'm not. I'm yours."

"Quiet girl." Roan rose, dwarfing Tiffany completely. "This is business."

"I'm yours." Tiffany said, a little louder than before. Her head had raised a notch too high – her eyes could be shined in the light.

"Defiance." Roan smacked my girl hard across the face, and I had to resist the urge to pluck his eyes out. I let things play through, because once she was with the merchant, Tiffany would be out of Roan's wicked influence forever. I smiled, both at the though of Roan blindly scrabbling for his bloody eyes on the dusty wooden floor, and at the thought of Tiffany finally being free.

"Don't damage her, or I might put a prompt end to this transaction." The tone of Jodiah's voice implied that he would not let Tiffany be harmed. His hand rested on his pistol, confirming his intention.

Tiffany let her head fall in humiliation. I whispered in her ear, as only angels can, "Go along with the new man, you'll see that it's the right thing to do." Tiffany might have been too upset to hear me, and to be honest I'm really not all that much a telepath. Her mood stayed dark, she felt betrayed, and suddenly less human than she'd thought she was just moments before.

"Actually, there's no reason why I shouldn't have both your gold and the girl, except that I'm a man of business. She's yours now, I'm sick of her anyway." Roan dismissed them, studying the gold closely.

Without even saying good-bye, Jodiah left with Tiffany between himself and his bodyguard.

I followed them beyond the temple walls, into the relative safety of the forest. The men didn't speak, and I was forced to keep hidden. Tiffany said nothing, her eyes filled with tears. Neither Mr. Sevenson nor Jodiah touched her. Occasionally, when she strayed, Mr. Sevenson would give her a dirty look so she would move back between them. I followed close behind, caught sight of the archer almost before Mr. Sevenson.

"Down." He said, throwing himself across Tiffany. The first arrow pierced his chest, high on his right side.

I launched my body into action, thinking the arrow had been intended for Tiffany. Mr. Sevenson lay over my girl; the bandits reloaded and launched another series of arrows into the men. Each arrow was a threat to Tiffany, and I felt justified to act. I took my true body, and in doing so became a visible target.

"Leave them alone." I said, flicking out my wings so I'd look more threatening. I bared my teeth and claws, but the man with the bow didn't seem impressed. He snapped off an arrow, which I caught in midair and broke with one hand. I rushed the man, intent on teaching him a lesson, only to find Tester in my way. Time froze for everyone but me. My mother looked at me with a mix of worry and anger.

"My girl." I said.

Mother shook her head and ticked her tongue. "You won't be much good to her if you end up dead." Tester pointed behind me.

I saw, frozen in that instant, an arrow, pointed straight for my back. I nervously moved aside. "Use your mind, not your emotions." Tester vanished.

The arrow whizzed past me and out of sight. Feeling cowardly, I became invisible one more time. The archers slowly approached the fallen men, setting aside their bows for small daggers. There were only two attackers, and now that I was calm again, I could sense none in the forest around me. They almost got close enough to use their weapons, when Mr. Sevenson snapped out of his fallen position and killed them both in a single swipe of his sword. Neither had time to counter. He winked at me, and I was startled. He shouldn't be able to see me.

Mr. Sevenson went about the business of trying to free the arrows trapped in his body. The shafts kept slipping from his grip, lubricated with his blood.

"How can he see me?" I wondered – those stories of seeing angels close to death usually only applied to one's own guardian.

Tiffany looked down at him. "What's your name?" She asked.

"Lim."

"If we could stop the bleeding we might be able to save him." Tiffany said.

"I can't help you here, can you get back to the transport?" Jodiah asked. Arrows had pierced Jodiah's arm and hip. Breaking the arrow in his hip off so it would be out of his way, he limped to Lim.

Lim fell to one knee, then forced himself upright. Jodiah carried him until his strength gave out. When Jodiah slipped, Lim fell all the way to the ground. Lim had saved her life, but his fall had finished him, shoving an arrow through his heart. Jodiah recited a prayer over Lim's body. Ignoring his own wounds, he rushed onward, dragging Tiffany harshly by the hand.

"Come girl, we can't help him and it's not safe here."

Tiffany no longer tried to stray into the forest. Branches nicked her body and her feet were bleeding before Jodiah resorted to cradling her in the elbow of his good arm. When they were finally aboard the transport and sealed safely in its helm, the ship shot out of atmosphere and vanished from sight. I followed them with angel sight until they crossed into Otherspace, but I didn't leave the body behind.

There was no danger to Tiffany from the trader. Her wounds would heal quickly in Otherspace, and I could follow them once I finished my investigation. Something was strange about Mr. Sevenson; his soul still lingered in the corpse. I walked back to him, thinking that at the least I would bury him.

"Are they gone yet?" His voice was a hoarse rumble.

"They're gone."

"Good, I was starting to get cold. And these arrows hurt." The man forced himself upright, pulled the shafts from his ravaged body. The blood flowed anew as his heart began beating, then he healed. "The real Lim Sevenson should be thankful." He shifted shape and size. His face became that of a boy, his brown eyes glowed vibrantly.

"Well, don't just stand there, the ship's probably to the other side of Transcendence by now."

"Fluff. How'd you do that?"

Fluff, his usual happy self again, sniffed arrogantly, ignoring my question. "You're awfully human for an angel, losing your temper like that."

"Whatever." I said, exasperated, hugging Fluff close in my wings. "Why are you here? Did Mama send you to help me out?"

"The one Tiffany was bought for is mine. They don't tell me anything, except that the two of them are supposed to save each other, and hopefully the galaxy, as far as I can tell."

Using my one exceptional talent, I shifted us into Otherspace. I took Fluff's hand in mine, using my wings to drag him along faster than he could have gone alone. Fluff, being absent of wings, was a little weaker than myself where interstellar travel was concerned. We angels have to pass through Otherspace to get to distant places in the universe, just like star ships.

Space travel is all about finding a war out of space, or so I'm told. Otherspace is outside of normal space, and so it is the perfect jump point for ships and humans alike. Jodiah's ship materialized in Realspace, near a small lunar world covered in a primordial forest.

I let Fluff go as we entered the atmosphere of that world, and let him fall gracefully to the surface as I glided down behind him. As we neared the surface, Fluff and I heard a proclamation and several profane words.

"Trespassers." A farmer yelled. The sharpened prongs of his pitchfork were pointed at us.

Rather than get pricked, we vanished, and the man scratched his head, dropping the pitchfork back into toil. Laughing at his apparent confusion, we followed the ship's ion trail to a house at the edge of the city. This city was special; it had things unique to an intergalactic port of call.

"It's safe to come out of hiding for awhile. This city is full of alien life, and we shouldn't stand out too much."

I took my true form, naked except for my wings, and Fluff took his own, more human form. He wore a black shirt and trousers, the clothes of an unarmed knight. I found it almost comical, especially since he didn't look a day over twelve. Sometimes I'd fool myself into believing Fluff was as young I was, but then he'd say or do something to remind me just how many thousands of years he'd been an angel.

The ship settled into its metal nest, waited patiently for my girl and her new master to open the hatch. Her face had healed and her feet were covered in felt slippers. Her eyes were sparking violently in the sun. As always, we watched from the shadows, this time from a street corner. A small boy wheeled himself in his chair, his dark face as bitter as Tiffany's. His body looked healthy, but my angelic senses told me his back was broken.

He'd need extensive physical therapy to regain function in his legs.

"What happened to the boy?"

For the first time in my memory Fluff seemed completely serious. He coughed politely.

"I let him get hurt when I should've been watching him. That's why I was in Transcendence, I needed time to think things through. They forced me back to my guardian post to work with you. I can't heal him, can you?"

"I'm not exactly designed for healing. Tiffany's a healer. She has to want to heal him, though, and she hates him."

"Pity. Perhaps there's no hope for either of them."

"You better get them to like each other." Tester said from behind me. Wisdom was with her, in the form of a beggar. They were standing on a street corner, about thirty feet from us, and they seemed to stand out. He was actually collecting coins from the city dwellers, none of which could see Tester.

"Credits for the poor." He shook the cup, giggling with glee. "I could get used to this. Listen to them jingle. Like little bells."

Tester grumbled something indignant. "You're always playing. Must I be the serious one all the time?"

"Hush now, you don't want the natives to know our little secret do you?"

"They can't see or hear me, crazy old man." Tester said. Her eyes locked with mine. "What are you going to do about Tiffany and Kotian?"

Wisdom turned his attention to Kotian and Tiffany. "If they can't work together, magnitudes five and seven will be destroyed." He sounded very matter of fact. If he weren't jingling his coins playfully, I might have been worried.

I tried to imagine a force able to destroy two entire sentient races. "Okay, we'll do our best." I said, but I was speaking to thin air. Tester and Wisdom had vanished.

Fluff looked at me, and I at him. "Let's give them a few days to adapt. Tiffany is a concubine, she'll do her job and hopefully she'll get to like Kotian in the process."

I brought my attention back to them.

Tiffany sputtered arrogantly at Jodiah. "I can't believe you bought me for a cripple."

"I can't believe you bought me a slut." Kotian spat back.

"I'm not a slut, I'm a concubine. A job of skill and integrity. A duty of sacrifice, devotion, and service. I'm the best trained concubine on Earth." Tiffany stuck her nose up, looking away. "My old master knew how to treat a woman."

"Yeah, with a swat on the ass and a sharp tongue, no doubt." Kotian laughed bitterly, his face a twist of arrogance that matched Tiffany's almost perfectly. "She's no woman, father, she's younger than I am. But since I own her, might as well put her to good use. Go clean my room. Wash my clothes. When you're done, bring me dinner. You can find the kitchen on your own."

"Jodiah paid for me, and only he can order me around." Tiffany said, looking away.

Tiffany ignored the boy and his father as she was led into the main household by a robot servitor, a hovering cube of metal and glass summoned by some unseen means.

Jodiah dealt with his son as soon as Tiffany was out of sight. "She'll be your wife, not your slave. Do you have to mistreat her so?"

"You brought me a whore to be my wife, and you wonder why I'm angry."

Jodiah raised his hand to smack his son down. "If you weren't my son, I'd beat you senseless."

He let his hand drop and left the boy to his sulking. Kotian had a forgiving father. I would have bitten him on the nose.

"Don't worry," Fluff said, as if reading my thoughts. "I'll give him a good going over."

"I'll take care of my girl."

Fluff turned visible and stepped up next to Kotian. With a solid thrust, he kicked the wheel chair on its side.

Kotian's voice was a menacing disgust. "What are you doing here? I told you to go away."

Fluff wasn't much nicer. "Would've listened, but you're not my boss, you're my friend."

"Some friend you are, kicking me over like this."

"If you make the girl your friend, she'll never leave your side. She knows loyalty better than anybody."

"Her kind of loyalty is prostitution."

"She's here against her will, but of course, you wouldn't take that into consideration." Fluff said.

Fluff helped Kotian back into his chair, and set him upright. After that, the two were sociable, if not outwardly friendly. Fluff dusted Kotian's shoulder off and unbent his wheel break. I realized then that Kotian's family wasn't a terribly rich one by galactic standards. The two glowered at each other, until finally Fluff turned away.

Chapter 3

I should have known that I would be ill received. Fluff tried to warn me, but I wasn't really listening. I was too busy losing myself in his gorgeous brown eyes. Somehow I had fallen in love with him. Even so I did have some serious concerns. Age was one. And his station in the angelic hierarchy was significantly higher than my own. He was really smart, too. He always remembered everything. Meanwhile I just muddled along, going on instinct and hoping for the best.

I hoped that Fluff knew what he was doing with his boy. I was in way over my head with Tiffany. I didn't know I would be working with Fluff, and I certainly didn't know he had ever failed an assignment. I also never anticipated that his boy and my girl would hate each other right from the start. The two were totally caustic, all one needed was the other and there'd be a near explosive reaction.

"So why did you come back anyway?" Kotian said to Fluff. I felt a spiked weight in my heart, whatever Fluff had done, he'd hurt the boy bad.

"Orders from high up. Guard Tiffany with your life. Maybe, if you try really hard, she might like you."

"Do I have any say in the matter?" Kotian said bitterly.

"You never have."

"Fluff." I called to him.

"What are you waiting for?" Fluff pushed me away, toward Tiffany.

I had, quite by accident, become visible to Kotian. He looked at me, anger in his eyes, and we both knew who served whom. "She's one of your kind, isn't she?"

While Fluff explained my presence to Kotian, I went to Tiffany's bedroom.

"Who's there?" Tiffany looked around. She was more sensitive than I anticipated. This would definitely get ugly. I paced some more. She could sense me but not see me, and it was making her look paranoid to the robot servitor.

"Listen to me, I'm a friend. I've been with you your whole life."

I showed myself in all my angelic glory, and Tiffany let out a surprised scream, putting her back to the wall. As I approached her, she started kicking at my shins, bruising her toes while bruising me. My trademark temper kicked in, and I froze Tiffany's body and mind.

"Calm down." I told her. "I could never harm you. I'm your best friend."

"Friend." Tiffany said, glowering. "Let go of me, demon."

"Better let me handle this for a moment." Fluff said to me, so only I could hear.

I shooed him away and focused on Tiffany again. "The girl needs broken. Listen, I've hoped and prayed for your happiness your whole life, and what have you become for it? A spiny little brat, that's what. That's a beautiful boy out there that's been arranged as your husband. You won't be his servant, but his equal. Imagine it, actually having human rights."

I slowly released my mental grip on Tiffany. Once she calmed down, she walked straight up to me and punched me in the nose. "Don't ever do that again."

Blood trickled down my face, and I was properly chastened. "I won't. I promise." I said quietly. I never could understand why human beings freak out when they see me. When I look at myself in the mirror, I feel pretty. Not gorgeous like my mom, but quite attractive.

"He's a cripple," Tiffany said.

"When you were a child, you found a sparrow with a broken wing. You nursed it back to health. Remember how it flew again, when everybody told you to let it die? I was there, I was the one who was convincing you otherwise, your imaginary friend nobody believed in. Make him your new sparrow."

Tiffany smiled, and I felt the weight of her perceived betrayal slide off my shoulders. "And I could make him my new master, in the end."

"If it pleases you, but you don't need a master anymore. You're free, and Jodiah bought your freedom."

"No, he bought me."

I took a deep breath, tightened my wings against my back, and took Tiffany's hands in mine. I envied that human girl more with every passing moment, and yet I knew it would be many years before she realized her own self worth. Soon I would be only an observer again, and hopefully Kotian and Tiffany could work things through without too much interference from me. I stepped out of the house, leaving Tiffany alone.

Fluff materialized next to me, and I took his hand. "Do you think our children will survive whatever Tester and Wisdom have planned for them?"

"I don't know if they were ever meant to." Fluff said. Fluff and I snuggled for a moment, as angels often do.

"Let's watch them closely, I don't want to lose Tiffany." I said.

While watching them I did something I hadn't done in a terribly long time. I fell asleep, and so did Fluff. While Fluff slept, and Tiffany argued with herself, trying desperately to make a firm decision and act on it, Tester sneaked up behind me, scaring me so bad I sat straight up and banged my head on a banister.

"Why do you always do that?" I said, my head and pride both bruised.

"You scared that poor little girl half out of her wits." Tester said, ignoring my question.

"Yeah, and she bloodied my nose for it."

Tester looked at me as only a mother can – guilt crept in through the pores of my skin.

"She needs to be strong enough to survive, strong enough to fight an angel and win. If she's not as strong as I described, she won't stand a chance against her future. Good of you to focus on her healing abilities, but you crushed her soul so completely that she couldn't even think of fighting back, and you and I both know that's unacceptable."

"I know mother. But I thought –"

Tester was the most beautiful woman I had ever seen, even though right now she had a devil's tail curling around her left leg. Seeing that it was making me uncomfortable, she absorbed it into her skin.

"Stop thinking."

"Yes mum."

Tester did something that surprised me. She hugged me, close and tight. "You're my precious little girl, and you're doing well. I love you."

Her love was something wonderful. Tester kissed Fluff on the forehead and left him sleeping. With Tester gone, I stayed close to Tiffany. She'd walked out of her room, back outside where Kotian was waiting. She was a proud woman, with the determination to adapt to the changes.

She sauntered right up to Kotian, putting her hands on his shoulders and kissed him. "So, Sparrow, you still think I'm just a slut?" She asked, running her fingers down the back of his neck.

"I was just angry. Father acts so weird. I mean, how many fathers buy their sons a girl for his thirteenth birthday?" Kotian said.

I wanted to say that the number was significant, but I remained silent. Angels really would be annoying if we just spoke out any time we wanted to. "Why are you in this chair?" Tiffany asked.

"I was shot in the back. The doctors say I can't walk, not even with surgery. The damage was simply too severe."

Tiffany frowned, and I had to frown with her. She had studied medical texts as a concubine. Part nurse, part lover, mostly servant, Tiffany had chosen to be the best concubine possible. She looked at his back. The bones seemed intact to her eyes. If they had healed, Tiffany knew the nerves could be retrained.

"It could take years to recover without surgery, but I think if we work at it you will walk again."

Kotian looked at her, stunned, and chose verbal aggression as defense against intimacy. "So, you're a concubine. Wanna have sex?"

Tiffany smiled, as only a concubine can, and Kotian blushed. "Since your father paid for me, you will have to ask his permission."

Fluff woke up from his lazy sleep and watched the rest of the scene with me. He smiled, "They make a cute couple, don't they?"

I had to agree.

"Sparrow is a cute pet name." Fluff said.

"It's sickening, makes me want to puke." I said. "Tiffany's creative, isn't she? Now what do we do?"

"What we always do. Stay invisible, watch, and give guidance when needed." Fluff said. "My boy blames me for his accident, and he's right. I hope this makes it up to him. It took a great deal of persuading to get Tester to let your child be at his side."

I didn't wonder why I'd been left out of the information loop. Being the youngest and least experienced, my angelic rank is pretty low. I mean, the angel to the Buddha is supposed to be no better than the angel to a twelve-year-old concubine, but aristocracy exists even in angelic circles.

Fluff and I waited impatiently while Tiffany and Kotian grew up. For three years we watched while Kotian grew stronger. Tiffany gently taught him to use his body again. The first year he was able to move his legs. The second, he walked, though only with braces. By the third year he was able to walk and run. He had healed, often frustrated, but always supported by Tiffany, into a strong young man.

In the three long years that followed, Kotian never had the guts to ask his father permission to sleep with Tiffany. On his sixteenth birthday, he stood before his father, sword and pistol at ready, and asked the question.

"I would like to know if you would give Tiffany permission to make love to me."

"She's your girl, why are you asking me?" Jodiah wondered curiously.

"Since she's still a concubine, she insists that I ask permission of the man who owns her before I take her as my wife. You haven't been sleeping with her, have you? She teases me."

"Of course not. I would think that three years without sex would break her of such habits. Hmm . . ." Jodiah wrote a note.

"Take this to her. You've been teaching her to read as well as speak our language, I hope."

"Yes." Kotian said. It was a half-truth. Tiffany was a quick study at languages. She'd been correcting Kotian's class assignments for nearly two years.

Though a handsome youth, he'd never actually grown tall, and he would look like a baby for quite some time. I kind of admired it, probably because I myself am stuck looking like a permanent teenager.

I read the note in passing, surprised at what I saw. It read "The below person has been relieved of her duties as a concubine and now has all the rights of a citizen of our world. She is free to succeed or fail at her own choosing, and to choose a mate. Permission is no longer needed nor is it implied for any services rendered." It was signed and dated.

I giggled, because I knew how Tiffany would respond. She would tease him, and then ignore him completely for the next several years, then get married and have kids. Fluff disagreed with me, and we started placing bets.

"All right, looks like Koti's finally going to get some action, maybe even get married. Cool."

I shook my head fervently. "You don't know my girl very well, do you?"

"I've watched her for three years. She wants him."

"Bet you." I countered.

"All right. What are the stakes?"

I paused. I never expected Fluff to take me up on it. "You're serious? I was only kidding."

"I still say I'm right. Your mama would agree with me."

"Don't you go talking about my mama." I warned, shaking my fist playfully, letting little angel sparks flit around it. "I love you." I said, surprising myself, and Fluff as well. Three years with somebody or a lifetime, either way love is strong.

I took his hand. “Maybe, in another time, when our duty is complete –”

“Are you two talking about your own matrimony or theirs?” Tester caught me by surprise, and I pulled my hand from his.

“Umm, I dunno,” Fluff said, sounding confused, then added with a nervous kind of stutter, “Ma’am.”

“Just don’t let it get in the way of your duties. Remember how important their success is.”

Tester faded from view. She had never actually taken her physical form, just sort of bobbed in as a thought. I shook with relief, because I wasn’t in any kind of trouble.

“Guess we wait until something happens.” Fluff said, putting his hands behind his back. His pale cheeks were red as cherries. “Is she always so overwhelming?”

“Yes. Does Kotian know you’re an angel?”

“No, he thinks of me as a friend from an alien species,” Fluff said.

“I haven’t told Tiffany, but she seems to think I’m some evil spirit destined to haunt her. She calls me Demon Girl.”

“It could be worse, she doesn’t actually hate you.”

Chapter 4

Everything begins with the birth of a child. This, of course, is one of the most significant laws of nature. The entire universe would cease to be if every creature and star quit making more creatures and stars. But I never expected it of Tiffany. The girl got pregnant. No real surprise there. Happens once every sixty seconds on Earth, every five minutes elsewhere in the galaxy. By grace's light, Fluff vanished first, fading from my sight. Then my own sight started to go dark with sparkles all over it. My skin tingled with electricity. Tiffany was pregnant, and somehow I'd become that womb-trapped infant.

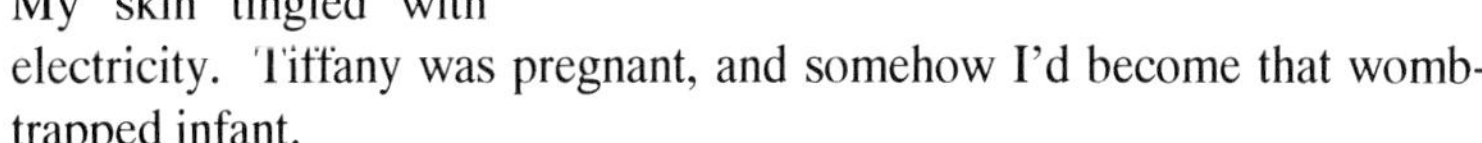

"Fluff," my thoughts reached out past the warm fluid around me. My memories of being an angel were being torn from me. Breathing water seemed as natural as flying. For the briefest moment, Fluff's thoughts touched mine, distant, but reassuring. Confident as always, his thoughts weren't as fearful as mine. Another voice filled my mind. It took me a moment to recognize it.

"Remember." The voice was strong, confident, and powerful. Father Wisdom's voice took my fear and left love in its place.

I wouldn't forget the important things. And even across the great space between an ocean, my bond to Fluff would stay strong.

Wisdom's last words were also a command. "Sleep until it is time. Rest until you're needed."

I slept in the body of a growing girl, thinking like a child, acting like one, worrying about nothing but learning and playing, though usually not in that order. Tiffany was a doting mother, Kotian a caring father, and nothing seemed to matter much. I felt as if I'd done it all before, a nagging déjà vu that haunted me throughout my childhood.

A year after my first menstrual cycle, I was walking alone, forgetful and dazed, but something was nagging at me with greater intensity. Then one day, a bee sting woke me up. While I was busy sucking the poison out of my aching skin, I remembered who I was and what I was destined for. Pulling the stinger free, I rubbed the painful welt and set a quick pace to the nearest beach.

Still dazed, I found a small boat and set myself adrift. The current grabbed that boat and pulled me out to sea. I drifted for what were mere hours to me, wondering how long I could go without food and water. It took a cargo freighter six weeks to cross Friol's ocean. Filled with alien craft, its purple waters and gray skyline showed no details, not even a hint of distant shores.

Some force drew me across the ocean at great speed. But time was tricky, because what were days felt like hours, and there were many nights as well. I passed through ships as if I wasn't anything but a ghost. Every night, I fought to remember a little more, but I only knew that I was in search of somebody. At one time I'd loved him. He'd been born a human just like I had. He may not have loved me, probably didn't love me. I thought of my mom, missing her.

Tiffany, so smart and dangerously beautiful, was already thirty, and I knew that she would worry over me. When I was growing up, I felt so slow, stuck on the ground, though it seemed irrational to think I could fly. Mother had to be careful when we were out, lest I try to jump off a ledge. At the same time, she seemed to understand me, as only a mother could. This would worry her to no end.

Some time later, a landline started to grow from the horizon. I didn't even know what I was supposed to remember. The boat drifted onto a beach, and I stepped out, still searching the recesses of my mind. If I'd been gone for as long as it seemed, then most people would think me dead. Mother would still be worried. I was, after all, only fourteen. She loved me. I knew that I loved him, the boy I had crossed an ocean to find. I stepped onto the strange shore, my dark skin the color of the sand beneath my feet. This surprised me; the sand elsewhere had been nearly white. I looked up and down the shoreline, wondering what exactly drew me here.

"Fluff." A gentle thought bounced around my mind, finding its way to my lips. I tried to fathom the word, the name. I know it wasn't the fluff my friends all took to escape the world for awhile. Fluff was Friol's premier designer drug. It was so widely used because it was both harmless and non-addictive. This Fluff was a person. Friol had 200,000 humans and over ten million sentient entities living on its surface and within its orbit.

I was but a speck on a speck, I knew it was a hint to another name, my other name. I didn't feel safe on the dark, sandy beach. As I walked the shoreline, passing bums and loafers, I tried to find the man named Fluff. We were supposed to be working together on some project, but I couldn't remember more.

Two men walked in the shadows, following me like wolves. They seemed intent on taking something from me. Perhaps they were after my virginity. Maybe they just wanted to roll me for my purse. I didn't care; I quickly walked away from them. They jumped me before I could get out of reach.

My temper flared as they grabbed me and forced me to the sand. If I had wings they'd both be dead. They had me though, and if I'd ever had wings, they weren't helping me now. One forced my arms behind me, pinning me so I couldn't move. The other reached for my face to slap some of the fight out of me. I spat and hissed like an animal, the second smack was harder. Then a flash of light blinded me. When my vision cleared, the air was torn open by vicious flashes of silver, each followed by a piteous scream.

I looked up, "Fluff."

His sword flashed twice more, each blow slashing a hand clean from its owner's arm. The men scrabbled away, screaming in agony.

"You hurt them." I scolded.

"They're scum." He wiped his blade on his trousers before putting it back in his scabbard.

I noticed only after Fluff pulled me close that my blouse was torn, that hands had gone after more than my purse. I felt so tired. His hug filled me with light.

"I've been waiting for you for days. How has transition been?"

I looked blankly at him, wondering what he was talking about. A voice filled my mind. Remember. I couldn't remember yet, it was a pointless order.

"I came here." I said, hoping that it explained everything.

"It is as I was promised." He kissed me gently on the forehead, then took my hands. "Only you don't know what's going on yet, do you?"

I shook my head, confused.

"Close your eyes."

I did, he put his hands to my temples. "You must remember, it's all got to be in there somewhere."

I yawned and stretched, and I felt totally free. Only I still didn't have my wings. I was merely human and still as clueless as before.

"Too many years asleep." I said.

"I missed you." I kissed him in earnest. I was hopeful, but he seemed hesitant.

"I missed you too. You know about Forever Children, right? You remember what we are."

"We're angels, I think." I was still feeling a little groggy.

Fluff dug his bare toes into the damp sand. He was almost a man, but looked little more than a boy. I was aware of my own youth, but somehow he seemed younger, if only at heart. A look of relief crossed his eyes. “Yes, we’re angels. A man is supposed to find us and tell us what’s happened while we were sleeping.”

“Know what happened?” I said, the haze of sleep almost past.

“No, but it must be something big to send two angels into human form.” His eyes glazed over for a moment, then he smiled brightly. “My sword flashed brilliantly back there. Those men suffered well. Pity they couldn’t learn from the pain.”

I looked at him, surprised. Fluff the human was a little different than Fluff the angel. How I knew this I wasn’t yet sure. We watched the suns set behind a mighty gas giant. We held hands and it felt wonderful. I was surprised when, as the bums left the beach for the tide, Fluff put his head on my shoulder. I tried to ignore him, looking north, and swore I saw somebody become solid, become something from nothing. I smiled, waved a hand, as if I had known this man all my life.

Fluff’s head popped back up. “Wow, a ghost.” He said, shivering instinctively.

The man looked ancient, but happy. “I’m Level Ringbreaker, new Governor of the Forever Children. I’m afraid I’ve been killed already, and this is the last contact I can make with the living before I merge with the life force in Transcendence.” He put a hand to my cheek, sending chilly little ghost tingles all through my body.

“So they sent you two. Good, good. Smart, young, and cunning. Just who I asked for, too. My predecessor sent one of my precious Forever Children to a world where a sentient species had just evolved a conscience. That was fifty years ago. Somehow, and I don’t know how because it’s never happened before, they killed my precious child. A new leader, who calls himself the Changeling Lord, is preparing to conquer Earth. The Scandivat Nation is a powerful force to reckon with, when it’s at war. You two, with the help of Tiffany, must to stop them.”

The ghost left us. “What about your parents,” I said.

Fluff smiled coyly. “They’re of no consequence. My mother was a prostitute, my father a customer. I grew up an orphan. I’ve this mission, and my sword. The truth must be routed out.”

"Do you remember ever having met a Forever Child?" I asked.

"Neither of us has ever met one. They tend to be reclusive."

I recalled only a little about the Forever Children, the souls of worlds, the caretakers of life, the travelers who could go from one sun to the next by merely thinking about it. I knew I could do it, but I felt blocked. My mind felt stuck in place when before I had only known freedom.

"I can't transcend," I realized suddenly. "My wings are gone."

"Not forever, when it's time you'll get them back. Don't worry, we'll find a way. In the meantime, we've got to find more information on this Changeling Lord."

"Do you think the Changeling Lord could have killed the Forever Child?" I said.

"I don't know, never heard of it. The Forever Children are supposed to be nature spirits – killing one would be next to impossible. I wonder where we go now?"

"Mother will know."

"Yes." It was Tester's voice, and her body came after it. "You're in physical form now, daughter, but it's good you remember." She put her hand on my head. Her soft fingers felt good. "I tricked you, didn't I, yet you feel no deception."

"I'm human now, and more. Fluff and I are still as ignorant as we were before. Tiffany was supposed to be the hero of this story, so why am I her daughter?"

"Insurance. Her only hope is in finding a data crystal. This one is special though. It has entire human lifetimes stored on it. With that knowledge, she'll become the new Governor and immortal servant of the Forever Children. Your job is as it always was, to protect Tiffany and see to it that she fulfills her life's work."

"Is this one of your tests?" Fluff asked.

"This is real world stuff, with real world consequences. Earth will be destroyed, and so will Friol and countless other worlds, should you fail. Humans are very influential in this part of the galaxy. Without their influence, entire races might go to war that would otherwise have remained peaceful."

I wondered absently about my human form. "I don't have wings."

"You have to walk before you can fly. And you will fly again, daughter. I have to leave you on your own now, and I can't promise that I'll be able to come back. You have your memory back, after all, so stop complaining."

"Yes mother."

"Stop being submissive, dear. No time for that now. An armada is on its way, will be here very soon. Get off planet any way you can." Tester vanished, and I knew I wouldn't be hearing from her any time soon.

Fluff turned pale, looking like he was about to feint. "We can't stop an invasion, can we?"

"No way. I think we're too far from Tiffany to get her off planet." I looked at the sky, my angel sight finding the invasion force. The numbers were unimaginable. "Wow, I got some of my powers back. That armada's moving slow, and far off, a week away at most. It's got some dark haze around it, making it hard to see. If we stick around here, we'll be killed for sure."

"Not if we get a ship." Fluff looked sly, like he was planning something.

It took us a week to formulate a plan. With Fluff's cunning and my fear induced adrenaline rush, we managed to break into the police impound yard and were looking for something to suit our needs. The enemy had already begun their attack while we searched for suitable transportation. I don't know how, but I could feel people dying.

"What about Tiffany and Kotian?" Mother and Father, I thought inwardly.

"We really need to worry about ourselves." Fluff caught a policeman off guard, knocked him in the skull with the butt of his sword.

With a practiced efficiency that made me nervous, Fluff tied the cop up and set him against a parts barrel. When I realized just how proficient he was, I began to appreciate his skill, and him, in a stronger, more caring light. The man seemed familiar, but my absent mind kept me unfocused. Fluff looked up from the policeman to me, saw the admiration in my eyes, and looked away. My heart felt as if it had just been run over.

Chapter 5

"I think I found our ship." Fluff said, turning a corner at the end of a row of impounded wreckage. He'd frozen in his steps, staring around the corner. Whatever he was looking at had him thoroughly excited. He motioned intensely for me to come have a look. "It's perfect." He said, several times. We could hear the beginning sounds of battle in the distance.

The invading force dropped to the surface, small strike fighters working their way across the city in violent sweeps, leveling buildings and blowing civilian and defense ships from the skies. Walking to the corner, I focused on the only ship in a row of wreckage that looked like it could fly.

I studied the ship critically. "It's a pirate ship. And it's heavily armed. We don't have a crew to fly something this big."

The ship was built like a water ship, was essentially an armored boat that could fly. Fluff smiled savagely. "It's not like we're going into battle." He giggled with anticipation. "Not yet, any way."

Time was running out. Argument would have to wait. As we entered the ship, I thought about the man we'd cuffed and left in the shadows. "What about the cop?"

"We'll take him with us."

Fluff ran back into the impound yard, grabbed the cop by the feet, and dragged his body through the ship's hatch. I saw his face and his name badge as I sealed the hatch, and my mind finally made the connection. Lim was already waking up. He looked at me, mildly surprised.

"Welcome aboard, Lim Sevenson." I said.

Lim recognized me immediately. "What're you doing here? Why did you tie me up? Where's that rogue who sucker punched me?" Lim demanded, still struggling. "You haven't gone wild on me, have you?"

"I haven't gone wild." I said, untying him. "We didn't want to hurt you, but we didn't have time to argue. The planet's under attack. We stole a pirate ship and are headed for safe space. Fluff's at the Helm. We're going to try to run without a fight."

I quickly led Lim up to the Helm. The sky darkened to black as we broke atmosphere. I could see the enemy through every port, ignoring the pirate ship, at least at the present. Lim commented on it. "We'd better get out of here, and fast."

Fluff looked over his shoulder. "Can't believe you let the cop go." He said, adjusting his course.

"By some unbelievable coincidence, he's a friend of the family."

"Tester's work, no doubt." Fluff returned his gaze to the controls.

I felt the ship shift course again, and Fluff continued to work at the controls.

"Why have we changed course?" Lim looked over his shoulder, eyeing the weapons console.

"There's a civilian craft caught up by the enemy. They intend to rip it open and take it for scrap. We need to free it."

I looked at the resonance image, magnified five thousand times on the sensor screens in front of me. Three Scandivat craft had a small merchant ship tethered between them, and were busy trying to quarter it. The tethers vibrated with the strain, flashing in a steady, calculable rhythm. We had to set that ship free before they tore it to pieces, but as usual, Lim had his own opinion.

"We can't win a fight against three of those ships. We'd best just fend for ourselves."

"I don't intend to fight. I intend to hit and run." Fluff flipped what must have been the thruster handles full forward.

We drew closer, and the image of the ship became clearer. "Tiffany's on that ship." I said.

"Are you sure?" Fluff asked, adjusting a trim screw on one of the thruster handles.

"Yeah, it's one of Jodiah's cargo ships."

Lim squinted to see the image more clearly. "I can see his Blazon on the side."

"Get over to weapons. Try to snap those cables. We'll give the ship a chance to jump to Otherspace, and then we'll follow in its wake. Bit, you have to flip the weapons safety switch to activate the weapons station."

"Bit?" Lim said curiously. "Since when did you change your name?"

"It's always been my name." I jumped to the weapons console. Having grown up on planet, I couldn't figure the weapons controls out. "I can't do this. Lim, put the weapons to use."

I slid from weapons to life support, something a little more my speed. I studied the sensor readings on the other ships. The sensor readings didn't look promising.

"They won't make it into Otherspace on their own. The Scandivats have some kind of dislocation field around them."

"Then we'll just have to activate plan bravo." Fluff said a little loudly.

He gave Lim the signal to fire.

Lim proved quite resourceful. Three tether cables snapped in four shots without damaging any of the ships. The Scandivat craft, no longer having the ropes to hold them in place, shot away in individual directions. Fluff, in a flash of brilliance, locked tether onto Tiffany's craft. Then, using superior engines, our ship, as yet unnamed, dragged the civilian craft into Otherspace.

Once in Otherspace, Fluff and I took our true forms, something I wasn't quite ready for. As angels we were still children. I held his hand, and he squeezed mine back. My clothes vanished as I became an angel, and only my bodysuit remained. Keeping my bodysuit wasn't my decision, but rather an odd anomaly of Otherspace.

Their own clothes, during the transformation, could harm Angels and other creatures that shift form when entering Otherspace. In Otherspace, being injured was supposed to be impossible, so special laws were created for such an awkward situation. Thus the reason that everything but my bodysuit completely disappeared.

"I thought it might be a dream." I flexed my wings experimentally.

Fluff knew better. He looked at Lim, who had drawn his pistol, ready to kill us both. "You aren't Gracie. I've never seen you before in my life."

"It's me," I insisted, trying to calm him, putting my hands up defensively.

"Get away from me, demon."

I stepped back, afraid of what a bullet might do in Otherspace. It probably wouldn't have done anything to me, though it definitely would have stung as it passed through me. Not being one to endure unnecessary pain, I didn't want Lim to fire his pistol.

Lim studied Fluff closely. "Don't know you either. No doubt you're partners."

I flashed a smile, trying not to look too threatening, then remembered my fangs. Lim cocked his weapon, and then his hand froze over with ice.

Tester materialized between us. She was much taller than I was, and in her current form, far more demonic than I'd ever seen her. In short, she was really ticked off. I could feel waves of heat rising off her skin. Her voice was cold, angry, but controlled.

"I make hard arrangements to save your sorry hide and this is how you repay me? Stop trying to kill my daughter and put that thing away. We have a contract. I agreed to save your life, and you repay me by serving my needs. As for the boy, he saved your life twice now, killing him would be real bad karma, if you know what I mean."

The ice melted, and Lim holstered his pistol, and started rubbing the blood back into his pasty colored hand.

Tester vanished as quickly as she had come, speaking to neither of us. Lim quickly adjusted his position, staring at us. I let my wings drop and cover my body, protecting me from his prying eyes.

"I signed a contract with the Devil," Lim paused in his thought, "and now I have to work with a demon."

"I'm a member of the Angelic Host. I'm not an embodiment of evil, which is how I believe you are defining the term 'demon'." I feigned the proper level of indignation. "And mama isn't evil, no how."

Fluff removed his hand from the hilt of his sword. "So you signed a contract with Mother Tester. Must be why I went in your place to Earth and died there."

"You died for me?" Lim seemed taken aback.

"I'm a guardian after all. I took half a dozen arrows in your name. We had to work really hard to change Jodiah's memories so he'd think you had survived long enough to reach the Otherspace boundary. You have, after all, worked for him in the years since that day."

Fluff adjusted the ship's course. The pirate ship resonated and twisted. In Otherspace, gravity wasn't a constant force rising from the center of a mass, but a vector based on one's position relative to any given surface. He stood on the wall of the ship as we both stood on the floor.

"I wonder why your parents haven't tried to contact us?" He said, studying the receiver antennas through a thick glass port. They seemed intact to me. I leaned back against a wall, and gravity pulled me from two sides at once. "Well, my guess would be that they're trying to decide if we're friends or enemies."

Fluff thought about it. "We'd better wait to hail them when we've set down in Idaho."

I never imagined going to Idaho. "Why Idaho?" I wondered absently.

"It's far away, relatively unpopulated, and it's a good place to give this ship a thorough overhaul before going on with our mission."

It took very little gray matter to realize that Fluff was right. I looked at Lim. "Are you going to be part of our crew, or do you want us to dump you into Otherspace so your body and soul can drift back to whatever world it calls home."

Lim closed his eyes for a moment, as if making a major decision. "Unfortunately, I'm still under the statute of limitations for several minor offenses that would put me in jail for up to ten years. I've no choice but to stay here."

I wondered how Lim got to be a cop with a criminal record on his home world.

"Bit." Fluff said. "I think you should be Captain of this vessel."

I looked shocked. "Why me?"

"Why not?" Fluff said. "I'm a good navigator. Lim's good with support systems and weaponry. Truth is, you aren't much good at anything. That makes you perfectly qualified to be Captain. We'll follow your orders. Just play the part, and you'll do fine by it."

"All right. I'm now Captain of the Pirate Ship *Persimmon.* Our duty is to see to the safety of my parents and to steal whatever it takes to keep alive."

Lim scratched his cheek. "Isn't stealing a bad thing?"

"We stole a pirate ship, so we're going to play pirates for awhile." I said.

"Do you think that if we try to hail anybody with this ship, we'll be received courteously?" Fluff added.

"This is going to ruin my civil service career. I'll have to change my name and move to a whole new planet when this is over."

"I'm sure you will." I said. "Get yourself to the weapons console. Get us to Idaho. As for me, I'm going to open contact with our newly found treasure." I opened a frequency before Fluff could complain. "Civilian craft, you've been captured by the Pirate Ship *Persimmon.* Prepare to be boarded and to surrender all your valuables and even your lives to Captain Bit, a.k.a. Gracie."

"Gracie?" Tiffany's voice sounded relieved. "We looked for you for so long, only to have you find us."

The tether tightened, and the civilian ship was drawn into the hold.

Tiffany's timid face looked out at me, and she lit up with delight. "We thought we'd lost you forever." I humored her, allowing her to hug me and worry over me for a few moments. Just when I thought I was safe from further harassment, it was father's turn.

He gave me a stiff hug and a hard stare. "Captain Bit, as if Gracie wasn't a good enough name for a pirate?"

Lim whispered something to Fluff who shrugged. "People often see only what they want to. Maybe they don't want to see Bit for what she is, only what they want her to be." I could hear them clearly. My parents shouldn't have been able to hear Fluff's whisper at all.

"Well, I can say one thing for this ship." Tiffany said, "It needs a thorough cleaning."

"Well, get to work then. Swab the deck and clean out the pre-thrusters." I said.

Koti stared at me, surprised. "You have some serious explaining to do."

I tried not to blush. "You're embarrassing me in front of my crew. I really don't want to have to throw my own parents in the brig on charges of mutiny. Lim's little attempt was bad enough."

Kotian smiled, saluting playfully. "Very Well, Captain Bit. What're your orders?"

I could see he thought it a good game. "Lieutenant Fluff will take the time to give you a tour of the *Persimmon*. If you and father would please be kind enough to fix the janitorial drones, this ship might just be in good shape by the time we leave Otherspace."

Fluff saluted me, trying to be as much like a Lieutenant as possible. While he and mother were away, I sat on the bridge, trying to do Captain things.

"Captain Bit." The words were respectful.

I turned, looking at the source. Lim Sevenson stood there, very relaxed. "Yes, Private?" I asked.

"You're not the girl I knew for so many years, are you?"

"I'm an angel, and the mask I wear is that of a pirate. Our life will be one of violent high adventure."

"Yes, Captain." Much to my surprise, Lim bowed slightly. "I signed a contract saying that I would serve the needs of your mother when she calls on me until my death. To serve you best I need to know what's going on."

"It's simple, really. If the universe were a machine, it would have a broken part. We have to find that broken part, and repair it. Because of that tiny piece, the Scandivats and Humanity are now at war. If we don't fix things, the Human Race will be destroyed, and probably the Scandivats as well."

Lim looked shocked. "I never believed in spirits until I met Tester, and even then I thought she was just some shape-changing alien. Now I'm expected to believe in angels, and God and all things like that?"

"Believe in what you want. You're in my service, and because we're on a pirate ship, Lieutenant Fluff and myself are playing the part of pirates."

"What do you know about being a pirate?"

To be honest, I didn't know much.

"What's there to know? You raid a ship, strip it and its occupants for all they're worth, and get out quick. They collect their insurance, and nothing comes of it."

"Well, you need to know how to swing a sword, and how to shoot a pistol." Fluff said from over his shoulder. "I mean, we have to make a profit, after all. Can't do that by being courteous."

"Very well. Mum and Pop taught me all about pistols, and I'm good with a knife. So those will be my weapons."

Tiffany had followed Fluff onto the bridge. "Honey, did I just hear you say you intend to use a pistol as your main weapon?"

"Yes, mum, I do." I said.

Kotian coughed, trying to hide chuckle.

"Dear, you couldn't hit the ground between your feet. Might I recommend that you leave the fighting to your crew?" She giggled and I pouted.

"Some pirate I'll make if I don't take my share of the bruises." I was sorely frustrated now, because I remembered how Fluff had saved me from the men on the beach. In another life I would've been able to splay them both. Of course, being able to do something physically, and being able to do something mentally were two different things. I don't think that in any life I could have done what Fluff did to those guys in defense of myself.

"I don't know about the rest of you, but I'm tired. I and Fluff will be retiring to our quarters now."

Tiffany coughed. "Dear, humor your mother and try to at least pretend that you're still a virgin, and not some bed-hopping tramp."

"For an ex-concubine, you're quite prude." I said.

I didn't mention the fact that I was still a virgin, it would only cause her to think me a liar, and my dear father would tease me endlessly.

Chapter 6

I lay in bed, a sticky sweat covering most of my body. The ship's life support systems were temporarily off-line, and Idaho was making its hot, humid way into my quarters. Staring at the ceiling, I wondered how Fluff slept through such sickening heat. I could barely stand the feeling of sweat slipping off my chest, making the places under my arms and between my legs slick and uncomfortable.

"There's nothing so exciting as Idaho in the summer." I said sarcastically.

The place was flat, terribly flat. And hot, the humidity around ninety percent. Fluff had recommended Idaho because of its relatively low population density. I wondered why anybody would want to live there. A mosquito buzzed my ear, seeking blood.

We'd set down the night before, and Fluff and I hadn't bothered to get out of bed yet. Last night we had gone to bed, and he did to me what I felt at the time was the ultimate insult. He'd kept his hands to himself. Shortly after life support came back online, restoring a comfortable atmosphere to our room, Fluff sat up, stretching, then let his legs slide out over the edge of the bed.

As I waited for something romantic to happen, he got up and took a shower. Having been so completely ignored, I got up and searched the *Persimmon*'s outdated memory files for anything that might resemble the data crystal that we were supposed to be looking for. I did this from my private console. When Fluff came out of the shower, I was still undressed, and still working at the computer console, only now I was trying to look seductive.

Fluff set his bottom at the edge of my bed, stared at me for the longest time, and I thought he was going to make a move. When he didn't, I took action, walking over to him and sitting on his lap. He looked away from me. I thought to myself. He's just avoiding me because the last thing either of us need right now is a kid.

Of course, I wasn't too fond of father and mother holding a shotgun wedding in a cornfield in Idaho. Not only would Tiffany and Kotian be upset with the thought of being grandparents. Fluff had expressed this as a particular concern of his on many occasions.

"Isn't it romantic?" I said. "I'm the Captain of a pirate ship."

"Yeah." Fluff admitted. "Real romantic." I would've done anything to turn him on, but he didn't seem to love me like I love him.

He changed the subject as quickly as possible. "I was wondering if you would do me the honor of giving me some lessons in sword fighting." Fluff said. I was surprised; my parents always teased me because I wasn't very good with a sword. As we fought, Fluff got me pinned up against a barricade, and I had to think fast to escape defeat.

"I love you." I said.

It caught Fluff off guard. Fluff let his sword drop and I put a mock stab through his chest, doing a little victory dance on the cargo hold floor. Lim, Kotian, and Tiffany gave the ship a once over while we talked and kissed. Fluff would push away when I got too serious, and I was beginning to wonder if I would ever win his heart. My crew reported to me at the most inopportune times. Over all it was a most wonderful day.

Lim showed me his results. "We have full weapons, but one of the shielding coils is damaged. We'll lose twenty percent of our shield power when it finally burns out."

"Make a list of the parts we'll need to steal to ensure that our ship keeps flying." I said. I kissed Fluff on the neck, but it felt cold. Okay, so maybe I couldn't win his heart. But what happened to change his mind so quickly? I looked across the room in the mirror.

Am I ugly? I asked myself, not for the first time.

Kotian and Tiffany step forward together. "I've got the repair drones on line, and Tiffany got the service drones working. The ship had a crack in the left forward impact strut. The problem is already repaired. Otherwise the *Persimmon* is fit for flight. Captain Bit, can I speak to you as your father."

"Sure Papa." I answered respectfully. "What is it?"

"I really do hope you two are using protection." Kotian said, obviously uncomfortable.

"I'm a virgin." Fluff blurted out, embarrassed.

I flushed red, and slapped him. A welt rose up where I hit him, I tried to apologize, then thought better of it. "You have just ruined my reputation."

I began to think, perhaps Fluff's physical age was less than his true chronological age. I was only about thirteen angel years old. I had only been an angel for thirteen human lifetimes. Fluff might be thousands of angel years old. The age difference and experience difference might very well play a part in his behavior. As an angel, it would be very easy to remain a virgin for thousands of human lifetimes.

Kotian looked relieved, and Tiffany stared at Fluff in disbelief. Tiffany would doubt anybody our ages could be virgins. Knowing Tiffany's past, I understood her disbelief. I looked nervously at Kotian, who seemed to tell me with his eyes that I had his permission. I wondered at this, because even with his permission, I still had to get Fluff to like me enough to make love to me.

With the ship ready for battle, we left Earth for deep space. We would then link into GWIN, the galaxy wide information net, and would try to find information on data crystals. I looked back over my shoulder, through the rear portal. The cornfield had some mild damage. Burned in its surface was a series of symmetrical patterns: Patterns that the farmers might eventually find. With any luck they wouldn't place any religious significance to them. Perhaps they would blame insect damage for the circles burned into the field. More likely they'd be baffled completely.

"Where to now?" I adjusted my new pirate's garb.

Fluff looked at me, "Well, the governor of the Forever Children is dead, perhaps we can find this precious memory crystal and claim it for its rightful owner." I hadn't told Tiffany my plans yet, I didn't want to worry her.

"How current is the database on this ship?" Fluff wondered, trying to find an update record.

"It was sitting dormant for nearly five years before you two stole it." Lim said.

"We could drop our grid maker into the ship's computer, and update the historical records." Tiffany suggested.

"I hadn't thought of that." Kotian ran back to his ship, still sitting in the cargo bay. "Here you go, Captain Bit, our data files."

I took the small mechanical device from Kotian and plugged it into the computer port. Within seconds, our ship's memory banks were completely updated. I ordered the computer to scan for any recent thefts of neurocrystal technology. "Tiffany, we're looking for a memory crystal, one so old it might even be considered a museum relic, if it wasn't still capable of storing about five times the data of all the data crystals in existence today."

I wondered how Tiffany, with her rose pale complexion could have had such a dark skinned girl like me as a daughter, even with Kotian's help.

"No thefts, but a discovery. Lysatoma Enterprises has acquired the crystal, and has it stored in a safe zone."

"Does it say where?" Tiffany asked. "Does the data tell us which company is in charge of security."

"Manapou Industrial Security. Manapou is owned by Lysatoma."

"We need to sneak into Manapou." She said.

Fluff looked at me as if I'd left my brain in another room. He didn't have a chance to say anything insulting.

"We can't." Kotian said. "Manapou uses an entire solar system for its headquarters and storage facilities. The entire system is heavily secured. There simply is no getting to the core."

I smiled. "The data files say that the crystal is stored in a pocket of Otherspace, and if that's the case, we can probably go right to it, as soon as we know its coordinates in Otherspace."

"You mean they would keep it in an Otherspace well?" Kotian liked the idea, "Of course, Otherspace is the safest place to keep anything. Weapons don't kill in Otherspace."

"I bet once we get to that crystal it'll pop to its original coordinates in Realspace, and an entire task force will be waiting for us." Fluff said.

I looked at Fluff, delighted at the prospect. “This’ll be our first pirate raid. Let’s go get ‘em.”

“With that crystal.” Kotian said, “We could buy ten of these ships.” He always had a mind for money.

“It’d be suicide to attack.” Lim said.

Fluff quick to point out complexity of the feat. “It’s going to be tricky. Maybe we should try the direct approach. If we ask for contact with the crystal, they might grant it to us. After all, just looking at something isn’t a crime – is it?”

I reluctantly agreed. “We’ll do it, but you people sure know how to take the fun out of being a pirate.”

The *Persimmon* entered Otherspace with a click and a pop, its Otherspace engines wining. The complaint ended with a sharp ping. Tiffany and Kotian seemed ignorant of our angelic metamorphosis, and again Lim was baffled by it. I knew better – Tiffany may have mothered me, but she was no idiot. She probably knew I was an angel all along, and was waiting for the most prudent time to point it out.

Chapter 7

I should've been sitting across from one of a thousand lackeys in the corporation, but after our initial radio contact, I was treated like royalty. A secretary led my crew and I to the head of the company. Mr. Lysatoma greeted me as if I were the most important person he'd ever had in his office. He was nearly three times my current age, at least in appearance, but boy was he a hunk.

His body was chiseled by hard workouts in a gym, but still had enough fat to suggest that the man by no means had to work hard for a living. His attractiveness made me think of Fluff, who had been giving me the cold shoulder lately. I'd done just about everything right, as far as seduction goes, but still Fluff didn't seem to be interested in me. I was beginning to get the feeling he didn't like me. Mr. Lysatoma started to talk, and I barely heard him, my mind lost in his muscles and tanned skin.

"I'm Erik Lysatoma, and yes, I'm the head of the company. You're Gracie Alderman. We scanned your DNA twice now, just to be sure. I'm actually quite surprised it took you as long as it did to retrieve your property."

I looked at him, trying not to show my surprise. "Yes, well, things have been hectic, with the recent attack on my home world."

Fluff spoke up, not blinded by obvious lust. "How much do we owe you in storage fees?" He said.

Mr. Lysatoma waved a hand. "As was agreed by your business contact, we'd get to study the crystal until your arrival. We do wish that you'd come later. Our scientists have only started to glean the most basic secrets of its storage techniques. A few more years and we might actually have been able to produce another crystal with one-tenth the storage capacity."

"Perhaps we'll return in the future, and allow you to study it further." I said, standing as he did. The crystal was brought in from wherever it had been stored, and placed in my palm. It looked like a sphere of pure diamond, the size of a tennis ball, with four black disks equidistant in its highly polished surface. It tingled in response to my touch. I quickly tucked it into my mother's purse, and shook Mr. Lysatoma's hand.

"Thank you for your time."

We left Mr. Lysatoma and returned to our ship. As we walked, we talked about the ease of our transaction.

"That was easy," Fluff said. "Maybe we're just getting paranoid."

I doubted it. I knew paranoia. It crept up one's back, seemingly intent on murder, then left you in a sweat, unharmed. This was too much like luck, and I never questioned good luck. I also wasn't one to question the mechanics set into motion by the previous governor.

"I wonder if I should give it to Tiffany right away?"

"That depends, how long do you want her to think of you as a daughter?" Fluff said.

"What do you mean?" I said, confused.

"As soon as she touches that crystal, she'll be imbued with thousands of lifetimes of knowledge and understanding. She'll remember not only the past lives of the governors, but also most of her own. She'll also see you for what you are, me for what I am, and then her opinion of you might change." Fluff didn't seem to mind. "At any rate, she'll be Governor, and her sense of duty will change focus."

"I hadn't thought about that." I said, flabbergasted.

I felt like a total airhead at times, but this went beyond even my normal level of blissful ignorance. We boarded ship and were in Otherspace before I thought about the crystal again. I stared at it, letting it roll around in my palm. Fluff looked over my shoulder at it, studying it with his dark, curious eyes. Mama was on my left, Koti at her right. My little girl and Fluff's little boy, both grown up to have me as their child.

"Well," Fluff began, his voice husky with fear. "I guess we both know that it's time, don't we?"

"Time for what?" Tiffany said.

"We were willing to fight all of Lysatoma's security forces to get this for you. As luck would have it, arrangements were made for a more peaceful acquisition." Fluff said, motioning for me to give her the crystal.

"Think of it as a present bigger than any before." I said, putting it in the palm of her hand. "And always remember that I love you."

At first nothing happened. Tiffany stared at me, her pale features uncomprehending. When Kotian touched her shoulder, leaning over to see the prize, it glowed from within, spinning in her hand. Kotian and Tiffany would share the title of Governor of the Forever Children. I stepped back, Fluff stumbling over my toes in his retreat. Lim watched in surprise, wondering what to do. I ignored him, more worried about the outcome of the transference. What if mama didn't like me anymore?

Minutes past, our ship tucked safely in Otherspace, as Tiffany and Kotian stood enveloped in the light of the crystal. When it stopped spinning, its glow died down to a mere glimmer. Their expressions of both my mother and father were almost sublime. They looked at Lim, smiled slightly, and then looked at us. Kotian made no efforts to conceal his emotions.

He took Fluff in a great hug, kissing the boy on his forehead. He said nothing more, just smiled and left us. I had no idea why he did this, and I never got an explanation. I stammered something incomprehensible. Tiffany still thought of me as Gracie, even after the knowledge exchange. She handed me the crystal.

"If you could please integrate this crystal with the ship's design while we're here in Otherspace, Kotian and I have work to do. When we're done, we'll set coordinates for a Realspace position." She paused on the way out the door. "By the way, I've never met a more beautiful creature than you, Bit, and I'm happy to be your mother."

I stood in shock for several moments, watching her and Kotian leave Fluff and me on our own. Fluff took me in his arms, tears on his cheeks.

"He apologized to me."

"Maybe he knows more than we do. That crystal's got tons of data we aren't privy to. Is she still my mother?"

Tester's voice clicked harshly. "Yes, and she knows all that you did for her to make her life bearable when she was a child. And Kotian knows your suffering for him, Fluff. I put that knowledge in them, so they'd love you both for all of your actions, and not just the ones they remember. They know your duty, your need to protect them, and understand their own duties."

Tester twitched her tail, thinking. "I've just one question for both of you – have you devoted any of your time to finding out what might have gone wrong with the universe? Something is broken, chaos has overstepped its bounds, and the result is a sentient race out of control."

I looked at her, dumbfounded. "My goodness, mother, we've just awakened. Tiffany and Kotian are working with Lim right now. They know more than us anyway."

"What? How could that be?" Tester took the crystal up, studying it closely. "Oh great, there's a two soul limit on the design. It can't exchange knowledge to anybody else until Tiffany and Kotian are dead and their knowledge returns to the sphere."

Tester tossed the crystal between her hands. "I wonder why the angel that invented this crystal designed it with this limitation? I can't redesign it, because of the divine contract, so you'll have to find a way to acccss that knowledge on your own."

Fluff stammered, "I hope that you aren't seriously considering killing Tiffany and Kotian."

"Of course not." Tester said. "Only they can make that choice."

Wisdom materialized, forever the clown, in place of Tester. "It may happen. Not that it's something I want to see happen, mind you. I think it would be a real kick if a concubine saved the universe. Be quite a snap in the girdle of all the class codes back on her home world."

Tester stepped out of Wisdom's form. "My goodness there's nothing like expanding into two personalities to make one wish she was alone again."

I giggled, I couldn't help myself. "You and Wisdom are the same. Why is it you always feel you should come in one form or the other, or a mix of the two, but not in your truest form?"

Tester twitched her tail. "Divergence was necessary for sentient life to exist." She clicked her tongue, as if thinking. "I don't know if you could see my truest form, or even understand its commands."

Fluff sounded respectful. "Tiffany said we should use the crystal as a data bank for our ship's computer."

"You'll have to figure that part out for yourself. I just used the crystal as an excuse to visit my two favorite angels." Tester said.

I looked at my angelic father. "You look like you've got a better idea."

"I've no idea what you're talking about." Tester said.

Wisdom chuckled. "You know exactly what I'm thinking of, you always do."

"Of course I do. But I can't believe you're suggesting it. If you do it, it could damage the crystal, the ship, or both. We said we wouldn't intervene. We agreed not to get involved in sentient issues eons ago."

Wisdom giggled, juggling balls of light in his hands. "Oh, I've no intention of bending the rules. I intend to break them. She's our daughter, after all, and the universe has suffered enough."

As I listened to them talk, I knew that it was one entity making a final and powerful decision. As they shifted to a form that could break the rules, I got a glimpse of the face of God, and was envious. Not just a galaxy, but also all galaxies and all the stars of a hundred universes, glowed in her eyes. In Wisdom's was all the space around the stars.

She raised her hand, merging with Wisdom, and I felt an infinite number of universes snap open around me. With a mere shift of thought, a few of this universe's rules were temporarily rewritten, and the effects woven into the ship. Hanging in the air on a pillar of light,

the crystal exploded into a thousand shards of light.

The shards struck things and bounced around, shattering until nothing remained but a dusty afterglow. The entire inside of the ship was covered in it. The powder was so refined that it tickled my nose and made Fluff sneeze. The ship hummed and resonated for a brief second, then snapped out of Otherspace into Realspace.

The ship's computer voice came on line, slightly feminine, and with a hint of emotion. "Unexpected shift from Otherspace caused by damage to the transition motors. Beginning immediate repair of engines. Left shield conduit needs repaired as well, beginning reclamation cycle, replacement coil is still necessary. Estimated repair time, thirty minutes."

Lim ran down the access hall. "The ship is repairing itself. It's possessed, I tell you. Evil is afoot." His eyes landed on Tester's still glowing body, "Not her again. Oh God, I am truly doomed."

I laughed at him without consideration for his emotions. "Silly man."

Lim ran back down the hall to hide in his room.

"Ship, what is your name?" I asked.

"My name's logged as *Persimmon.* I've begun an initiate scan of my subsequent defensive and offensive systems, and the previous Captain's log, and I've determined that this is a pirate ship. Am I to be a pirate ship, then?"

"Yes, why is it you ask?"

"My records indicate that the Lenitians have a heavy class system and are singularly responsible for the galactic slave market. My previous Commander abhorred them for it. Slavery is an unacceptable behavior in an advanced society. A Lenitian pleasure ship is within our attack range. We could use a teselar beam, pull them out of Otherspace and perform an act of piracy against them."

"Perhaps we should." I said.

Fluff let out a savage whoop. "Arming the beam."

"Teselar beams are illegal." Lim exclaimed, having come back from his room when his courage returned. "Only law enforcement agents can use them."

"Shut up. You're a pirate now, so act like one." I said. "Brief my parents on the attack."

"All right. Finally, some action." Fluff yelled, taking a sword and a pistol from the weapons cabinet.

When I turned to say good-bye, Tester had disappeared. The crystal we had just seen blown to pieces was in her place. I took the crystal up and put it in a safe place, not intending to use it any time soon.

Chapter 8

The ship, much like any other of its design, was meant to carry rich people in relative luxury. It was nothing to feel threatened by. The teselar beam had originally been stolen from a Friol law enforcement vessel. The beam disturbed the pocket of energy that a ship needed to remain in Otherspace, causing it to come into Realspace. Once in Realspace, we could trap it near us with a tether line. The beam discharged for only a second and the ship materialized before us. Its engines lost their glow, and it was unable to escape the beam. The tether launched itself deep into the ship's rear bulkhead.

"We've got them Captain." Fluff said.

I let out a yelp of satisfaction.

"A lot like kicking kittens." Lim exclaimed.

I found myself wondering if Lim were the sort to spend his spare time picking on helpless animals.

"Can you take over your own ship's functions?" I asked *Persimmon*.

"Of course." *Persimmon* said indignantly.

I walked down the hall, leading my mother, father, Lim and Fluff to the exit hatch. Lim was giving us advice all the way down the hall.

"Remember, we have twenty minutes before our pressure shields disperse and we end up suffocating in space. They won't come back on line until we get back across and charge them. Get aboard their ship as quickly as possible and secure a breathable environment. We need trainable people willing to work with us, so if you steal the slaves along with all the money, we'll have an actual crew in no time. We have forty-five minutes until the teselar field disperses and the Lenitian ship slips back into Otherspace."

"We're not taking money." I said. "No jewelry either. We're here for two things. Parts to repair our ship and slaves. And we're not going to take on extra crew."

Lim nodded. "So we strike hard, get in, get out, and try not to hurt anybody, right?"

I looked sternly at Lim. "We aren't doing anything, Lim. You're staying behind and guarding the hatch. Tiffany's in charge of battle tactics."

Tiffany giggled, locking her weapons to her belt so she wouldn't have them in her way when she jumped across space.

"Let's go." She said.

One by one we jumped into a strange parody of normal space – the environment around us was twisted and distorted by the teselar radiation. The ship hung half in and out of Otherspace, and was fighting to break loose. Using our foot thrusters, we pushed ourselves to the hull of the enemy ship, right next to the airlock. Kotian shoved an armor-piercing spike straight into the computerized lock, twisting it open with brute force.

"Great key, isn't it?" He said, his voice sizzling over the radio.

I couldn't help but laugh. Once inside, he forced the doors closed with the same stab and turn technique, then we readied our weapons while he and Fluff worked the next door open, filling the lock with air and exposing all of us to enemy fire. Our atmospheric shields discharging, I fired round after round at our enemy guards, until finally one of the tranquilizer darts hit flesh. One guard fell, paralyzed. My pistol was empty, and I had to reload.

"Good shot." Tiffany said, dispatching the other three guards with three clean shots. We carefully advanced forward, and Tiffany checked for pulses. "They'll be out for hours. Let's get moving."

Tiffany's tranquilizer pistol and sword were both drawn, and she pointed first with one and then the other, warning us of two hatches on the left and right. Just as she had suspected, two slow, heavily armed guards were waiting. The drug darts had much the same effect on them as anybody else. They fell to the floor with sickening thuds, weapons clattering from their hands.

We broke into the main hatch, where a disgusting exposition of fear and weakness was being portrayed. The slaves were the only ones dressed – children mostly, further separated from the masses by a tattoo on their left cheek. I ordered their capture. There were six of them in all. Tiffany pointed to the slaves, and Kotian quickly separated them from the crowd. A woman tried to stop him, grabbing the slave by the arm.

"I paid a year's salary for that one." Kotian smacked her hand away, taking the slave with him.

"I'm Captain Bit, protector of slaves and a really mean pirate. Surrender peacefully, and nobody gets hurt. Resist us, and we'll blow a hole in the side of your ship, leaving you to die in space." I said, angered by so many weak minds and bodies in one place.

Unfortunately, I wasn't a very threatening image, and I had to make an example of one person who thought she could laugh at me. I snapped a dart off, leaving a massive bruise on her chest, just under her left breast. She lay there; her eyes open despite her unconsciousness. I closed them for her and turned my attention to the Commander, who wore something similar to the service uniform of his slaves.

"Are you a slave too?" I wondered.

The Commander paused to consider. "I'm happy to serve." He said.

"That's deep." I giggled girlishly, and Fluff couldn't help but groan. "Get over here, I want a word with you."

"Whatever." The Captain walked slowly towards me.

Tiffany stepped between us. She patted her pistol holster, her voice quiet. "This is a nasty weapon. It's got copper bullets, designed to kill by crushing bone, tearing flesh, and grinding innards." She paused, drawing a nine-mill. An American model, apparently, from the markings on its holster. "Nobody's been killed yet, and if you listen to Captain Bit, nobody will have to be."

"We notified the authorities of your actions. You are in Lenitian space, and can't expect to escape in one piece."

"The authorities are not our concern right now." Kotian said.

"What're your demands?" He asked.

"We're here for some very simple things, really. First, order all remaining guards to stand down."

"There were only six guards aboard, and you shot them all."

Tiffany let a thin, stressed looking smile cross her lips. "To waste all your reserves at the front door is too stupid, even for a Lenitian. Give the order."

The Commander clicked a button on a small pencil-like transmitter, "All Guards and messengers, clear the halls and put up no resistance. Await further instructions."

"We need a gourmet food processor, six bottles of wine, and your aft shielding coil." Tiffany said. "You got a problem with that, Commander?"

"No problem at all." He pulled a communicator from his front pocket. "Beta servants, bring them what they want. These pirates mean business."

I studied the man closely. He was as much of a wimp as his passengers. Fluff intimidated him, and Fluff looked a lot like me – wet behind the ears. Once they brought us our supplies, we strapped them to our backs and made a quick exit to the airlock. Before I left, I turned and gave the Commander a nasty glare.

"Remember my name, and the name of my ship. Captain Bit of the *Persimmon*. Just because I've captured you once doesn't mean that our paths won't cross again."

We were off ship with our stolen goods in just under ten minutes. The slaves had to survive a few seconds in space, but with a little medical attention, all recovered quickly. Once we were aboard the *Persimmon*, we jumped into Otherspace, leaving the damaged Lenitian vessel in need of repair. For days we traveled, back to Earth, a place where nobody would bother to look.

This time we set down on the ocean floor, just off the coast of one of Earth's many continents. We must have seemed like bad guys to the slaves. They all cowered in their rooms, afraid to come out without permission.

"How is the status of repairs?" I said, once the ship was safely hidden under thousands of feet of water.

The *Persimmon* issued a status report. "The food processor has been installed, and in two hours time, the shielding system will be fully operational again."

"Thank you." Fluff said courteously.

I turned my attention to Fluff. "What are we going to do with the slaves?"

"I talked to each one, and asked them what they wanted. Every one of them wanted to go home to their mothers and fathers. They're only children after all." He said.

"Well, that's a big task." I said. "We'll probably never be able to find out just what planets the Lenitians kidnapped them from."

"We shouldn't need to. I tossed them into Otherspace just before we landed. You know what happens when you leave a ship in Otherspace – you go home."

"But – oh, never mind." My mind drifted.

I hadn't ordered him to dump them into Otherspace. I hadn't thought of it either. Otherspace, for all its peculiarities, was a perfect way to ensure somebody got safe passage to their place of origin. I hoped that all children had a happy reunion with their families. My mind drifted back to our next mission.

Kotian studied the database. "The Scandivats have attacked two worlds since Friol."

Tiffany looked at the data monitor; her eyes level with Kotian's shoulders.

"You know what we'll have to do, my governors, if you can't stop them before they reach Earth."

I turned, surprised by the unfamiliar voice. A boy with blue skin and purple eyes had somehow popped aboard my ship. He was absolutely beautiful. He was looking straight at Tiffany and Kotian.

"Three years is all we have left to spare you. Then it'll be beyond our control." I looked away for a moment, and when I looked back, he was gone.

"Who was that? What's he talking about?" His words worried me.

"Genocide." Tiffany said, as if it explained everything. "Three years it is, then. I see an avenue, one that our pirate renegade children should love intensely. Look at the survivor ratios from the three fallen worlds. A lot of refugees – and most of them old enough to fight."

Tiffany brought up a map, on a side screen. "We could put up some resistance between Earth and the Scandivats if we could unite the masses against the cause."

"Hey, all of you are going way over my head here." I said, totally confused. "I mean, are we talking war?"

"Yes, dear." Kotian said. "It may be the only way left to save both races."

"Can't we find a less violent way to handle things?" I said, stammering nervously.

Persimmon sounded annoyed. "Some Pirate Captain you are. I've flown with some of the best, and let me tell you, none of them were backing down from any fights."

Fluff came to my defense. "Are any of your old Captains still alive?"

Silence was the only answer.

"If we start a war, a lot of people could die."

Fluff smiled wickedly, "People die every day. Even in the seemingly immortal societies, death is an unavoidable result of birth."

A strange occurrence ended our conversation.

"We're in Otherspace." I said, astonished. We shifted back within seconds. "What the hell just happened?"

"An anomaly just passed close to Earth. The field being emitted by the anomaly pulled a good portion of the Earth, and us along with it, partially into Otherspace. It is currently heading straight for the sun."

"We need to go after that anomaly. If it's a ship, it's in serious danger." Tiffany said, her blonde hair flowing behind her as she headed for the bridge.

I followed her, shouting orders. "Get us into Otherspace on a matching trajectory with the anomaly."

"Aye Captain." *Persimmon* entered Otherspace, then drifted into orbit. The effects on the planet were minimal, the effects on me maximal. Lim sat at the weapons console, ready to fire tethers or blasters, whichever were needed. The blasters would be nothing more than a light show in Otherspace, but the tethers might come in handy.

What I saw in Otherspace surprised me. It was a ship all right, a

Scandivat craft, and it had been blown to pieces and left adrift, its engines sputtering out of control. I got ready for a flight.

"Tether the craft and pull it off course."

"It's too damaged. If we try to tether it we'll tear it to pieces. Sensors show the survivors huddled on the bridge at the front of the ship. All but one of them is Scandivat. If we tether the bridge, we might be able to tear it loose from the rest of the ship, keeping it relatively intact."

I thought quickly. I didn't do any calculations, just went on intuition. "Get us as close to the ship as you can, and then launch the tether. I'm going out. Fluff, you're in charge."

Though it was both my home and the place of my first birth, Otherspace always felt strange to me. One need not eat, sleep, breathe, or perform any other bodily functions, because time wasn't actually passing. Most people preferred to continue with life as normal – it reminded them that they were alive. I took advantage of the not breathing thing. With a length of rope hanging from my hand, I jumped into the vacuum, spreading my leathery wings to the Otherspace wind, wind that should not have existed.

Persimmon fired her tether deep into the bridge of the crippled ship. The tether sunk soundly into the metal, and proceeded to tear the bridge in two as my ship slowed the other ship's progress. All but the Scandivat managed to get to the tethered part of the ship. I flew hard and fast toward the Scandivat, my wings aching with the strain.

"I'm definitely out of shape." I said, panting.

The Scandivat reached out for help as I drew closer, its claws snagging my wings. It must not have done it on purpose, because it let go instantly. It was a creature of great size and almost reptilian appearance – a cross between an iguana and a wasp. Though I was angry that my wings might scar, I tossed the Hunter an end of the rope, and the alien grabbed the rope tightly with both hands. I pulled with all my might, flapping my wings until the minor cuts became small tears.

"Come on Bit." I said to myself, dragging the creature back toward the others. "You really should've exercised more while growing up as a human."

Just when I thought my wings were going to tear to shreds from the stress, the ship's gravitational vector gave way and we were launched at the hull of the *Persimmon.* My back slammed into the hull of the *Persimmon.* The Scandivat struck nearby, much more gracefully than I did.

"This hero stuff is really starting to suck." I groaned, trying to get a full breath back into my lungs.

The Scandivat gave me its equivalent of an apologetic wincing stare. It crawled through the *Persimmon*'s access hatch, pitting the ship's metal skin with its claws. The holes sealed shut behind it as it moved, as if they were skin, healing super fast.

"Sorry." It hissed as the others helped me into the portal. "I'm Captain Reed. My ship's vanquished. My life is yours."

Five humans huddled in the bay. Some had the look of primitives – of people who had never traveled the stars. Two, who looked a little out of place with their primitive counterparts, acted more at home on a star ship. They were both conversing with Tiffany, and I was astonished at how smart my mother was. Still, you could tell that she was in some ways the little concubine I had been sworn to protect some time before, and not all that ashamed of it.

Her attitude shifted violently when she saw Rusty's eyes drift to my chest. Tiffany smacked Rusty on the back of his head, as only a scolding mother can do to any man younger than herself.

"You aren't used to seeing an angel, are you?"

"Pardon me ma'am, I don't mean to stare, but I never saw a woman with wings before."

The man was attractive without being overly handsome. He wasn't exactly weak, but he was pudgy in a cute, well-pampered sort of way. A man of means was always attractive. Tiffany gave him a look of vehement death, letting him know that I was completely off limits. He quickly looked away, and I felt a strange sensation overcome me. I flushed, letting my wings cover my body, as if the bodysuit weren't enough.

"I think my colleague is trying to say you're beautiful. I'm Jonathan Holstein, a Professor of Biology. Who, pray tell, are you?"

"I'm the Pirate Captain Bit, and you're on my ship, the *Persimmon.* We can send you home, if you'd like."

"Like that, ma'am, but I haven't got a home – it's why we didn't bale ship – no safe place to return to and no guarantee we'd go anywhere. The not so human Captain here saved our lives just before our star went nova. His ship got caught in the after-blast, and we've been drifting in Otherspace since."

"Well, it's a good thing you passed by us." Tiffany said. "If you'd drifted much longer, you would have ended up in the gravity well caused by the local sun. We might not have been able to get you out of there."

I flexed my wings, stretching sore muscles. Tiffany noticed my injuries and grabbed a first aid kid. She dabbed my wounds with antiseptic, worrying unnecessarily over me. "Oh, Gracie, you've gotten yourself hurt again."

"My fault. I forgot to retract my claws." Captain Reed said, touching me with the back of his scaly hand.

He looked part wolf, part reptile, and mostly insect. The combination wasn't a mismatch, but rather my best interpretation of the fluid work of the artist, evolution.

"This body isn't always merciful – even to my friends. I'm a Hunter of the Scandivat Race."

"It would seem your mind wasn't designed for the body it was put in." Fluff said.

"My body was designed to protect the collective from attack and to hunt for it. Hunting takes cunning, and defense takes sentience, the Hunter body is result of these two merging evolutionary necessities."

"You're with friends now." Tiffany said. "Maybe I'm misunderstanding your emotional state, but I think you're feeling out of place."

Captain Reed let his massive arms droop, and his tongue flicked. "To feel truly one like the others, instead of forever alone. Such is my fate."

"I don't understand." Tiffany said.

"I'm separated from my people, exiled and alone. I've only had these two humans as company. Our people refer to humans as the others who are alone."

"What about the three in the corner? Who are they and why do they cower from all of this. You all are from the same planet, right?"

"You'd better field that one, Jonathan." Rusty said, leaning back against a bulkhead.

Jonathan explained quickly. "Just before the nova, time and space got terribly distorted. I think they're from a primitive backwater world like Earth, and their language is unlike any I've ever heard before. They seem to think that we are all minions of evil, sent to carry them to their own personal Hell."

Chapter 9

I grimaced when I heard that our temporary guests spoke a primitive language. As I'd mentioned before, I'm no telepath. Still, as Captain, it was my job to make my guests feel at home. I tried to reach into the youngest mind and draw from it his knowledge of language. It is possible for any human, with enough training, to do this.

All human bodies are basically bioelectrical, and the signals being processed by the brain will follow certain patterns, regardless of what language is being spoken. By tapping into his mind, I could, with some effort, translate it into my own mind's language. For me this was only theory, I had never actually succeeded at it.

Sensing my attempt, the boy replied in Galactic Standard with a mild accent. "Hello. My time in transcendence has been close to a century. A long, boring century where I had nothing to do but listen to everybody talk and learn how they speak. I was on my way to meet you anyway. You're helping the Governor, and that makes us friends. The two behind me had a chance to merge with their Great Spirit. Their time here has been but seconds, and soon they will embrace the Truth and move on."

That made sense to me. Time in Otherspace could be influenced by human consciousness. The more intelligent a person is, the longer the time is that they spend in Otherspace. To spend a century when others only spent months or days implied a sort of brilliance. To speak the pidgin language that evolved into the Galactic standard was something akin to genius.

The boy waved his hands, and the two who were with him vanished. "Wow, I wish I could do that." I said, awed.

The boy grunted, teasing. "Some angel you must be."

I snapped my wings tightly shut, "I do the best I can."

"I'm sure that you do. The Scandivat, whose hands sliced your wings, is a strange one of his kind. Has no link with his people, but knows of the war they're fighting. He wants peace, though he looks hideous. Have to go now, got a planet to look after. But I'm supposed to give you something."

He pulled a copper bell from his pocket. "You can use it to protect your girl. All things that make sound affect space and time. This bell is well tuned to spirit energy. If you strike it, the dead can talk to you. But you have to know them first. It won't call just any dead person in for a casual conversation."

The bell was a flat affair, made of pounded copper, small enough to fit in my palm, hanging on a silver chain. He hung it around my neck, and vanished into countless dots of light that spread rapidly into Otherspace, like a million fireflies freed from a jar.

"Who was he?" Fluff said.

"A Forever Child, I think. He gave me this bell, said it would help us."

Fluff studied the bell, and noticed its intricate symbols. "This bell is charged with old magic. Are you Sure you should wear it around your neck like this?"

We shifted out of Otherspace, I took my human form, and the copper bell took on the appearance of a delicate glass rose. It glistened like a jewel. I took the rose up by its tiny stem and smelled it in my imagination. It had no scent of course, but that didn't matter. Tiffany was busy speaking with Captain Reed in the quick words of his native language. I couldn't understand even one syllable. It sounded like whistles and chirps.

Captain Reed responded, his Scandivat hands swirling in a language of their own. I figured that of all the languages, I would never master Scandivat tongue. Tiffany said a phrase, perfectly imitated a Scandivat laugh. She seemed to be whistling through her nose. The Captain paused, and walked off the bridge, past Lim, and into one of the chambers. Tiffany was wearing tense smile.

"What's going on?" Lim demanded. "If I didn't know better, I'd think you took that ugly beast in as a member of the crew."

"She wouldn't do that without asking me first. He's my guest, and you'll show him some respect." I said, puffing out my wings. Lim looked down his nose at me.

"Or what?" Lim said, his hand sliding to his blaster.

Fluff's sword shot out, landing squarely against Lim's throat. "You're in no position to threaten her."

"You have a Rogue as a first mate, Captain Bit. Perhaps he'll turn on you someday." Lim disarmed Fluff with a simple snap of his wrist, but before either of them could go for their blasters, Father took action.

He'd been speaking with the professor as if oblivious to the entire affair. But his fluid reflexes betrayed his seeming lack of concern. His blaster was drawn and he armed it with a quick flip of his thumb. The blaster slowly charged to full, emitting a sound that got higher in pitch until it passed out of the range of human hearing. The barrel was pointed at Lim's temple.

"She's the Captain and you'll do as she says." Kotian said, his voice a barely controlled whisper of anger.

"Yes Sir." Lim said. He hadn't even unclasped his holster yet.

Kotian drew Lim aside for a moment, his words quiet. But not so quiet that my keen ears would have missed it. "If you ever threaten my daughter again –"

"You'll kill me." Lim finished for him.

"I'll turn you over to her Fairy God Mother, and let her decide your fate."

Lim's face lost a lot of blood. "You owe our guest an apology. He can hear every word we're speaking now, and you're making a fool of yourself – even in his absence. Do us all a favor and respect the Captain's wishes. She's in the position for a damn good reason."

I wondered just what that reason could be, I never felt like a Captain. It all felt like a game, a dangerous game I was desperately trying to learn the rules to. Lim hurried to his quarters.

I hugged my Papa close, "Thank you Papa."

"Thank Fluff, not me. His life was actually in danger." I had every intention of thanking Fluff in a different way, if he'd let me. I took Tiffany's hand.

"Where to now?" I asked her.

"We need to raise an army, to try to slow the pace of the Scandivats. The Professor has a few very good ideas."

"I'll let you handle this then." I hugged mama and then spun around, taking Fluff by the hand. I half dragged him toward our private quarters.

Tiffany smacked me on the butt, her eyes playfully teasing. "All right if I take the bridge?"

"Yes, it's all right." I said, "Just fill me in on our coordinates in the morning."

I closed the door behind Fluff just as the ship turned on its axis. He looked at me, uncomprehending. What did I have to do to the guy, pound him unconscious? I lovingly laid my head against his chest, and wrapped my legs around his hips. He held me for a moment, as if I was something terribly fragile.

"Let's talk." He said.

I sat down on the bed with him, and I didn't want to talk. "Your body isn't in the mood for words." I said, toying with his wings.

I found myself wondering when he'd earned his wings. His wings made him even more pretty to me. He was quivering with nervous fear, as if his words took courage.

"I had lived a hundred lifetimes centuries before your conception. I'm sorry. I just don't love you Bit."

"You're not ready, is that it? Well I am." I kissed his neck. He jumped up, putting his back to the wall.

Tester flickered onto the wall behind me. When I looked back, she looked like a really bad video recording. "There's no need to rape the boy."

I turned away from Fluff. "I've tried everything. I thought men were supposed to be easy."

"That's Tiffany's influence. I should've never let you be conceived again. Sharing parental responsibility can be so chancy. Fluff, do what you know in your heart is right." Tester faded from view, leaving us alone. Fluff lay down on the bed with his belly to the mattress. I lay next to him, and he rolled on his side and held me close.

"Being human has changed me a little." He said.

My eyes snapped open. I had expected a kiss. "What do you mean?"

"I don't know if I love you. I've said it about ten times now, but

you haven't been listening."

The copper bell fell against the bed, and it rang out in Otherspace, making a strange, wailing sound. "Help me." I said carelessly.

The bell hummed like a creature trapped in a glass box. It wasn't designed to help with this kind of hurt.

I looked fearfully at Fluff. "You really aren't ready, are you?"

Fluff held me close. "It's more than that, and I think we both know it."

I forced myself to standing, trying not to look as upset as I felt. "I'll wait for you."

"Don't do that. I'll just let you down."

I left him alone, kissing his neck as a way of good-bye. I went back to my private quarters, to get some sleep. The first clue that the ship was out of Otherspace woke me up with a pounding heart and put me in a cold sweat. I had to remember to breathe. This in itself can be a terrifying experience, especially for a body just about to expire from lack of oxygen.

I could smell Fluff's body next to mine, a perfect sweet scent, but when my eyes opened I was alone.

"Get a grip on yourself." I rubbed my temples, trying to force the heat flashes out of my body. "Must be genetic."

When I checked on him, Fluff was still asleep, and I left him to his dreams. I had other matters of concern. After removing my white bodysuit, I stepped into a bath. I dumped a bucket of water over my head to wash the sleep away, then pulled my pirate's uniform on. I never did understand the Otherspace law that says that angels who shift bodies in Otherspace will instantly become naked, then find their human clothes hanging in the closet as if they had never been worn. I hate cleaning and ironing, so it's quite an advantage.

I walked down the steel hall, the rose that had once been a flat bell glistening in the ship's light. "So, mama, where did you take us?" Stretching, I made note of a few peculiarities.

"We're at an Elfin festival, by invitation of the King of Elves himself. I need to speak with a friend of a friend about the Scandivats." Tiffany spun around in her evening dress. "How do I look?"

She looked beautiful. Kotian and Professor Holstein were in

tuxedos, and they clapped and cheered like a couple of schoolboys. Mother blushed.

"Can't you tell by our fashionable duds," Rusty said, his rodeo hat making a statement all its own, "I even polished my boots."

I looked down at my bare feet and frowned, "Mama, where'd you get those wonderful clothes?"

Kotian smiled at me, patting me on the head. "We had them replicated, dear. Even a Pirate Captain has a mess dress. We left yours hanging in the replicator, and put Fluff's by his door, though I'm not surprised you didn't see it when you walked past."

I was stunned and disappointed at what I found with my name on it. It was a formal outfit that fit my rank in society, if not my desires.

"Why can't I wear a formal gown? Shouldn't a Captain turn more heads."

"Not more heads than her aging mother." Tiffany scolded. "Besides, you are playing the part of a pirate Captain, and you should at least try to look the part."

I quickly put the Captain's uniform on, and was thoroughly impressed. Not only did it bring out my limited feminine attributes without exposing any of them; it made me look suave in a definitely female sort of way. I looked quite militant, and yet I felt like a Princess. A woman of the world, I looked ready for anything. The boots, made from black polished leather, were a perfect accent to the silver buttons that kept my white cotton shirt closed. The black pants were good for a fight, and were fashionable. The sword, now hanging at my side, had a blade with undulating curves. It looked like a snake slithering, like a single dancing flame.

Tiffany tossed me a pistol – this time with lead in it. "Be ready for anything, Captain."

Unhitching the safety on the pistol, I made sure I was.

Chapter 10

It may be a prejudice, but I found my Papa far more attractive in his tux than the Professor. Fluff walked down the center hall, looking proper in his first mate's uniform. Lim and Rusty were both opposite ends of the same hue. Lim was dressed in a gentleman's garb, the likes of which hadn't been worn in centuries. Rusty was dressed in a cowboy outfit from Earth. Papa and Mama were like two dolls crafted for each other.

I looked at myself in the mirror, the glass rose on my silver necklace glistened in the cool white light, and I couldn't help but feel sorry for it. It seemed so lonely, because it was the only piece of jewelry I owned.

"Don't worry, little flower." I said, "Someday I'll get my ears pierced like Mama's. When I do, you'll have company." Fluff looked at the rose, entranced.

"It draws attention to your breasts." He said, squeezing my hand for a moment. Something in that touch made my heart feel empty.

Tiffany adjusted the collar of my tunic. "Try to remember what I taught you about social graces. We can't afford to seem uncouth."

"Who are we meeting?" I rubbed my nose against hers.

She smiled, "King Lotus."

"Who's he?"

"King of the Elves." Kotian said.

With Elves everything was either totally formal or totally a game. "Maybe Rusty and Lim should stay behind so they can keep me company."

"I'd think you'd want to meet a King." Tiffany said, surprised and

disappointed.

"As a Princess maybe, or a Duchess . . ." I said daydreaming, "But never as a pirate. I mean, pirates are the sworn enemies of kings, at least in fairy tales."

"You do have a point there. But since these are Elves, and not fairies, I think it should be safe." Tiffany giggled, adjusting my hat.

Her extended knowledge hadn't changed her at all. As a Governor she was just as fashion sensible as before. Only now Mama was a person with a clue. A portal popped open within the ship, and I could just make out a blur of movement beyond. Kotian and Tiffany interlocked their arms and smiled.

"Shall we join the festivities?" Tiffany said.

Kotian smiled, "Why certainly."

The two stepped through the portal, followed, my crew, my guests, and myself. Hunter Reed stayed behind. The first thing I noticed was the food table – stacked high with exotic dishes from all over the galaxy. People who looked twice my age and were for the most part taller and more sophisticated than myself, roamed around the room.

They all danced and talked and drank generous glasses of wine. As we walked by a servant, we were stopped and Fluff was administered a small flower. A servant placed it in the lapel of his shirt. I'd never seen anything like it. It was pure white except for green and gold spots that glowed eerily. It was an exotic, probably incredibly rare, orchid.

As we walked toward the center of the room, my eyes were brought to focus on a woman, her dark skin accented by an alexandrine pendant. She wore a sword at her side, with an inch-long diamond on the hilt. These two things, and her stunning beauty, were all that seemed of value, until I drew closer. With Fluff at my side, I took up a glass of wine and worked through the crowd to get a better look.

"Who is she?" I said, awed by her ideal traits.

Fluff, as always, seemed to have an answer. "Princess Lotus, I'd guess."

There was nothing gentle about this woman, except her eyes. There was something soft about her eyes. The Princess, dressed in a loincloth, had a crystal stein; half of its wine had already passed her blood red lips. I stepped in even closer, to get more detail. The loincloth she was wearing was studded with silver topaz.

Her bodice, which was all she wore over her skin, was covered in similar beads, a little darker than the topaz around her waist. She was definitely an Elf, and much prettier than me. My jealousy, a typically human emotion, was so hard to overcome – I focused instead on her features. Elfin to a fault, with high cheeks and structured lines that would put a sculptor to the test, she seemed the center of attention.

Fluff explained to me the history of the Elves. "The humans and Elves once shared Earth, but the Elves were forced to leave rather quickly – along with their fairy cousins – due to interracial tensions."

"Fascinating history," I said, stifling a yawn. "Never did ask, what is the purpose of this festive occasion?"

"I must assume that both of you are party crashers." A young Elf that stood an inch taller than myself had overheard our conversation. He stared at me in a way that only Elves can. His beryl eyes, tinted gold, were slit more like a cat's rather than a primate's, and his expression was a mix of stoic philosopher and predator.

"Actually we're here with my parents. They didn't tell me much, just that we were required to attend." I said.

Fluff and the Elf next to him were now staring at each other, neither willing to look away. The two were quite proud, the staring contest could get out of hand.

"Come on gentlemen, no time for chivalrous riots." Fluff broke his gaze returning it to the Princess.

I could practically smell the testosterone rise in the room, and I had to resist the urge to gag. The Elf continued talking, toying with his pitch-black hair. His skin looked more like milk than flesh.

"This is the Princess's Grand Ball, to put it in simple terms. She's seeking a husband, by order of the King."

Rusty sauntered up next to us, "Hey, this is really quite a shindig."

"Well, yes it is," I had to admit.

A drum beat nine times. Somebody took my hand and drew me away from the Princess – and away from Fluff. I looked up and saw that it was Tiffany, and she smiled at me, her teeth covered, her eyes soft, as if she were about to cry. For each beat of the drum, another male walked from the crowd until nine men stood around the Princess. A large circle of men surrounded her.

Fluff had to be shoved into the circle on the ninth beat, but there he stood, with all the others. The Princess had long brown hair, her sideburns grown into battle braids, an Elfin tradition that I never quite understood. It made her look like a creature with reigns, and only her sword would keep anybody from suggesting it.

Tiffany walked up next to me. "The festivities are at their climax now. Fluff's a handsome young man, isn't he? He'd look nice in an Elfin wedding."

"What do you mean?" I asked, suddenly worried. My mother had a strange tone in her voice.

"There were nine men chosen by the King himself as suitable mates for the Princess. They were all given Portuca flowers to put in their lapels. Apparently your first mate is one of the nine suitors." Tiffany giggled. "Don't worry, I think she'll chose another. Fluff's a scrawny waif, and human at that."

"She'd better choose another." Fluff had grown distant from me since he'd been born a human. If he fell out of love with me and in love with her, I knew he'd be gone from my life forever. Princess Lotus looked like a military inspector as she walked around each of the nine men. She was obviously as disgusted by the tradition as I was. The men, all in a circle, answered her questions cordially and with nervous haste.

She started each spat of questions with the same word. "You." She grunted in Elfin, a harsher language than the singsong fairy tongue that I'd grown accustomed to in my angelic life. She stepped in front of Fluff, her eyes becoming slits, as if she recognized him. My hearing became suddenly acute. Instead of the usual gruff ritual, she paused.

"A first mate, from what service do you hail, Sir?" My eyes were too clouded with jealousy to judge her tone mocking or respectful.

Fluff answered admirably. "I am First Mate aboard the *Persimmon*, a pirate ship with an honorable Captain. I don't want to be here."

"You're honest, if not admirable."

Without waiting for Fluff to defend himself, she put a single finger under Fluff's chin, and pulled his lips to meet hers. My hand went instinctively for my sword – I'd never felt such a desire to give another woman a more thorough pounding than I did right at that moment. Then I saw Fluff's face, and hers, and my hand dropped back to my side. I groaned, the battle had been lost without so much as a swing of steel or a blast of gunpowder.

I bit my lip as the woman who stood a good head taller than my little Fluff, walked on. Her voice returned to its usual gruff courtesies.

Tiffany looked at me, her eyes glistening with excitement. "Seems that the young Princess has a fondness for our first mate."

"Maybe she was just trying to humor him because of his incredible youth." I said hopefully.

Fathers can be such a drag. Even when they try to help they tend to blow it considerably. "Stop teasing Gracie, dear. I'm sure that the Princess has no reason to be interested in our weak and inexperienced first mate."

"He's not weak, nor is he inexperienced. He's a good man, and she knows it. She's chosen him." I said, nearly choking. My head began to throb.

Princess Lotus paused as if to think, then returned to the center of the square. She looked straight at her father, whom I had not noticed before because he was mingling with the crowd as if he were one of them. He was now separate from the crowd, several paces beyond the circle of suitors, seated in an amber throne.

"My choice," She began, "is made."

My bones grew cold as she reached out and took Fluff's hand, drawing him into her arms. Out of seven Elfin warriors, one fairy scholar, and a human first mate she had chosen my angel. My heart missed a beat, then raced violently as I realized that Fluff wasn't protesting.

The King's voice filled the ballroom with its loud, bass vibrato. "Is there a person present who can give good reason to protest this union?"

I started to bawl out a protest, but mama's hand, placed gently over my lips, stopped me.

"If he doesn't want her, he'll protest it himself, then you'll know the truth of it."

But Fluff didn't protest. He just stood there while the festivities drew onward. My love for him destroyed me when he started to dance with her. My beloved, soon to be a Prince, had chosen that older, taller, more beautiful woman in place of me. The music had already started again, and Fluff was dancing with her, dancing on air, it seemed, his face aglow with what I had felt for him.

I ran from the dance floor, trailing tears. I was headed back toward the portal to my ship, but stopped, seeing the food trays. Tiffany had followed me for a short walk, but Papa kept her near him with harsh toned words. Mother and Father danced together around the ballroom while the Professor and Rusty danced with respective female courtesans. I stood alone, a wallflower, dumped by the man I had chosen to love.

The Elf who had been next to us before, his catlike eyes glistening with a pride that matched my own, was the only one not dancing. I looked at him and he at me.

"It appears that your lover has been chosen by the woman I love, and he has made a choice to keep her." He said, his voice a parody of control.

"You're very obtuse." I said, trying not to cry, I grabbed the leg of some unknown animal and chewed on it half-heartedly. "But so was I, to think anybody could want little old Bit when they could have a goddess like her."

He took my hand, squeezed it once, and then walked quickly into the crowd. In moments his body was lost, mixed in with hundreds of others, and I felt utterly alone. At that point I stationed myself behind a table stacked high with food and proceeded to eat myself into oblivion. At some point, after I'd consumed six platters of alien cuisine, Fluff managed to disengage from the dance to come back to talk to me. I wasn't the most courteous person to him.

"What the hell do you want?"

Fluff bowed his head. "I don't know how this happened, but I have to be with her now." He said. "She needs me."

"That amazon doesn't need anybody." I said savagely.

"Yes, she does. And this is a part of the thing called destiny, my duty to protect her. I don't know why I fell in love with her, but I did. I don't know how, but I am, and that's all that matters."

I let my heart stop beating for a moment, wishing that I could die right in front of him – just to spite him.

"You are hereby relinquished of your duties as first mate, and decommissioned from all officer's privileges aboard the *Persimmon*. Should you wish to travel on my ship, it will be as a guest, and at a price." I looked past him, into the crowd.

"I wish we'd never come here. Then maybe you wouldn't be crying right now." Fluff said, turning away.

Leaving me in my solitude, leaving me in my despair. Leaving me to eat four more platters of food. I sat there for what seemed an eternity, eating everything that wasn't moving. A massive thunderclap announced an unwanted visitor. I could tell right off that this visitor, for all of his power, was no super good Prince here to take my heart and make me the envy of that battle-ax that'd stolen my man.

I looked over a pile of empty plates, knowing I was responsible for about half of them. I saw the looks of fear on the face of the King and Princess Lotus as the Elf walked defiantly into the room, his black armor shining in the lights. He pushed his way through the crowd, drawing as much attention to himself as possible. His voice was like a cracked bell, harsh, loud, and discordant.

"I, Prince Wastik, do now and forever contest this unholy coupling."

"Oh brother, it's a bad man with a really bad opening line. Are we in for it now." I grumbled, taking one last bite of sweet, fattening meat.

For once I wish I hadn't been so right.

Chapter 11

As with any situation where a band of well-armed men entered a room of unarmed diplomats, the crowd spread back. Wastik enjoyed this powerful influence, accurately thinking himself the source of the problem. He signaled to his companions, who herded the crowd back further with arrogant shouts.

Princess Lotus spoke loudly, her voice seething with rage. “You were not invited, Uncle.”

“Shut up, Niece.” Prince Wastik smacked the Princess down, his armed soldiers keeping even her father from acting with anything akin to haste.

Tiffany and Kotian were helpless as well, watching, waiting. They weren’t dressed for a fight, and wouldn’t stand a chance without weapons. Fluff had no sword, and he was also helpless, though obviously enraged.

“I came because I chose to come. I will stop this wedding and your consummation. I will stop the birth of a child that your pure and perfect form and this flawed mutant will inevitably produce.” He drew his sword, raising it to slash Fluff down.

Before I even knew what I was doing, I drew my own sword and jumped between them, keeping the young Prince Wastik at bay with the sharp tip of my blade.

"I am the infamous Pirate Captain Bit, of the *Persimmon*, and if you want to kill my First Mate or beat up his future wife, you'll have to get through me." My sword drawn and at the ready, the sweat of fear ran down my brow. My stomach felt about to rupture from my overindulgence.

"Bit, that man will cut you to pieces." Fluff warned. "Why are you doing this?"

I ignored Fluff's whispered question, and focused on the dark Prince. I could see in my peripheral Fluff and Princess Lotus. She lay on the ground, that perfect face already starting to bruise. She had been bested in just one hit. Wastik was as strong as he was savage. He smiled at me, a sickening hatred seeming to ooze out through his words. I almost recoiled from him.

"Very well, it'll be one less human woman to spawn more of her kind when this fight's done."

His sword flashed three times, and I guarded my body instinctively. We fought harshly, and furiously, and I had to admit that I was being bested, when a reserve of youthful strength and practiced skill gave me the power to force Prince Wastik back, and knock him to the ground.

"I can't believe that a mere human could possibly be so good." He rolled back far enough to give a small speech, already on guard for my next attack. "Unfortunately for you, I've made a few unholy allies of my own. Meet Hunter Force Alpha, at my disposal. I've allied with the Scandivats, and this is how they're going to help me rid the galaxy of impurities such as yourself."

The Hunters spoke in their strange language of chirps and hums, and hustled into the crowd, forcing Elf, fairy, and human aside with heartless swings of sharp edged limbs. King Lotus used powers I had no idea he had, shifting the ballroom into Otherspace.

"In a place of peace and love, you have brought only hatred and war. Otherspace will make things even, Wastik."

I was impressed. I could never have drawn so much mass out of Realspace. King Lotus had made a wise decision in staging a battle in a place where people can't die. In Otherspace the battle would be safe.

If I killed Wastik, he'd be sent home. There was no way I was going to let him kill me. We drifted in open space, and I was cautious. As I looked at Otherspace, trying to see the gravity vectors, letting my wings fill with wind, something didn't feel quite right. Otherspace had changed, and so did its rules.

The sky, normally golden with wind from the direction you most need it, became gray, and the wind unpredictable. The Hunters attacked Fluff, and I was helpless to stop them. They sliced his angel's form to pieces, and the human Fluff emerged, snatching Uruza's sword, eyes flashing, and mind seeming blank of angelic memory. I know that had he been killed in the ball, he would be an angel, but he had made a choice, and by letting the angel in him die, he was fully resigning himself to a purely human existence.

I had read about it happening, an angel resigning his position of service to become a human. I'd never imagined Fluff doing it. A sword slash at my face brought me back to my senses, and I blocked it, then slashed back. I stabbed, blocked and kicked, sending Wastik spinning backwards. He fell on his butt, the grin on his face one of surprise and confidence. The Otherspace ground was beginning to break away, we were rapidly losing a sense of ground – and the gravity that came with it.

"Oh, a dangerous enemy is this, an angel who's barely a child. I'm surprised you can even swing a sword, knowing your kind and their weakness where bloodshed is concerned."

He jumped over me and tried to get a stab in from behind. I spun, knocking his blade back, then flew out of sword reach. He swung forward, as if propelling himself from a cliff-side on a rope, hitting extra hard with his first strike. Then we were fighting again, like animals.

"You stood a better chance against me as a human, angel of deception." He said with smooth, charismatic tones.

If he weren't so bent on killing me, Wastik might have been attractive. Our swords flashing, we fought on, I oblivious to the battle around me, unable to fight everybody at once, the Prince focused intently on killing me. He cast a spell that twisted the local Otherspace, turned its light dark, and left me feeling woozy and disoriented. I knew the shift was one that made Otherspace a dangerous place – no longer safe haven for anybody.

The ground had disappeared, pieces of it drifting away. The absence of solid ground hardly seemed to bother Wastik. The *Persimmon* flew into Otherspace, toward the center of battle, affecting local gravitational vectors with its approach. Captain Reed jumped free of the airlock, howled in rage, and met the Hunters head-on. He was bigger than the other Hunters were, and his scales and claws sharper and tougher, but there were six of them – and they were intent on killing him.

I focused solely on staying alive. Then a scream broke my attention, and I was ill rewarded for my lack of concentration. Wastik slashed my arm open, and I yelped before backing away from his next attack. The wound was minor, and I countered with a harsh stab at the Prince, cutting his hand and forcing him to rethink his attack. His sword drifted free and he sputtered profanities at me.

"I will have my revenge." He fell back toward his sword, taking it in his good hand. I looked back toward the scream I'd heard before, and saw Tiffany and Kotian dead, adrift in Otherspace. Blood sprayed into the ethereal plane, their life force drained and gone.

She wasn't supposed to be lying lifeless with her husband at her side – Otherspace normally wouldn't allow anybody to die. The Prince had done something terrible to Otherspace, and I had to find out what that was. Mama was supposed to end up back in Realspace should she start to die, back in her home, with maybe a few bruises to remind her that she'd lost.

King Lotus and Captain Reed held the Hunter Force at bay, kept them from killing Uruza. Prince Wastik kept me from getting close enough to help them. I knew that to end the fight I would have to force Wastik to retreat from Otherspace.

"You've corrupted my home." I said, and sliced him on the arm. "I don't know what you've done to Otherspace, but I'll use your own laws against you." I slashed out in rage, and he fell back, fear in his eyes. "Live in fear of me, of what you've brought on yourself. I'll avenge my mother's death. I'll see that my father knows peace."

I swung again, slashing his cheek open and very nearly killing him.

Time froze, and I was sitting in Otherspace, with nothing moving around me. Tester and Wisdom were there, separated into their dual forms. I had never seen Tester looking so sad.

"We have to go now. And you need to calm down."

"What do you mean?" I asked.

"The problem is out of hand. People with shallow minds are gaining too much power. I have to return to the First Magnitude, to my origin. We are going to rewrite the laws. You're on your own, kiddo." Wisdom said.

"I need you." I said. "I don't have a clue what to do next." I started to cry. "I've already failed my parents. Otherspace is corrupted by Wastik."

"It is as it is. Your friends will help you."

"You knew Fluff would leave me, didn't you?" I said, sobbing openly.

Wisdom and Tester both hugged me close. "If he met the Princess, we knew he would rekindle his love for her."

"He loved her before? It's not fair. We were in love." I stamped a foot on a nonexistent ground that felt real despite its absence.

"No, you were in love. It works that way sometimes. He's chosen. He's a thousand years older than you are anyway. Realspace and Otherspace are merging, a dimension is dying, and we have to disperse ourselves to another plane, called Zerospace, to keep that from happening." Tester kissed my forehead. She faded from my sight, "Remember that we will always love you. You are the last of the angels, do us proud."

Time asserted itself, and I was instantly back into the fight against Wastik.

"You'll suffer tenfold." I said.

A Hunter broke past Captain Reed, its claws and scales slashing violently against anything it could reach. King Lotus was slammed in the chest by one of the Hunters, his ribs splayed open over his heart. The King was dead, and my hope dwindled. Then my eyes locked with Wastik's and I knew that I couldn't lose hope. My mind focused intently on one thing – survival. I felt no mercy in my heart.

Prince Wastik bled from a dozen wounds before I was finished with him, his blood hanging around him in globules and drops. He faded from view: His spell had obviously not worked against him. I might have to face him again, and now that he knew how powerful I could be, he would come back stronger. Hot tears streamed down my face as the Hunters vanished one by one, returning to their home.

Fluff helped me with the bodies, pausing over the angel he had once been.

"He was a pretty boy, this angel." He said, in retrospect. "He was your friend, wasn't he?"

I choked out an answer. "He was everything to me."

I looked around me. The Professor, Rusty, and Lim lay in blobs of floating blood – killed in the attack. Captain Reed had survived, cleaning his wounds, and so did Princess Lotus and the human side of Fluff, and me. The rest of my friends and family were dead.

"I will have answers." I yelled into the void, "I will have answers."

The bell around my neck hummed quietly as I drew nearer to the bodies. I took all the bodies into the ship, brought them into Realspace, and hoped it would revive them. It was strange, seeing Fluff's angelic form in front of me, and Fluff with his wife. Part of me knew that Fluff had made a choice: He had chosen love with the Princess over his divine service.

Prince Wastik had played a dirty trick, changing Otherspace the way he did. I ignored my missing clothes to see to the needs of the dead. I touched the rose around my neck, and for a moment it hummed like the bell. A light erupted from the bodies, and tiny dots of energy spiraled up from my dead parents and Lim, spreading into Otherspace like so many cinder-sparks spreading from a fire. One dot lingered for a moment, forming a human face in front of me.

"The universe is really coming apart." Tiffany said, her eyes saddened. "It's up to you, honey. You have a lot of secrets to learn, and so little time."

I tried not to cry. "How could he kill you? How could he kill such a beautiful woman?"

"He didn't kill me – the Hunters did, and they're not self thinking like we are. They're part of a race to which the whole is one. Use the data crystal, learn all you can from it – find out how the Prince twisted

Otherspace to his needs. Then accept your duty as Governor of the Forever Children. I pass the lineage onto you."

"You knew Fluff would fall in love with her."

"Yes, it was in his eyes the second he saw her. He never loved you like that, but he tried. Give the angel within him that peace. He tried." A single tear fell down Tiffany's ghost face. "I wish it had been different."

Kotian's form hovered near her, "I never imagined dying this way. I'd at least hoped you'd give me a grandchild first." He paused. "In another life, I'll pay you back for all you have done for me. I love you."

The rose stopped glowing, and the spirits faded away, leaving me with Princess Lotus, Fluff, and the eminent Captain Reed. His bug eyes didn't focus on anything, but somehow I felt like he might be looking at me.

"So what do we do now?" Fluff asked me, holding Princess Lotus' hand in his. I stood for the longest time, looking at my mother's face, the only part of her body that wasn't covered in clotting puddles of blood. The features of that face were what she had given my human form. Kotian had given me my skin color.

I choked when I tried to talk. I had to try twice before words came out. "*Persimmon*, Begin a ceremonial orbit around the local star. We will dump these bodies into its light before we do anything else."

"Yes ma'am."

Shifting into Otherspace one more time, *Persimmon* flew quickly to the center of the system. The blood that had been a part of Otherspace was gone; it was the same ethereal plane of transition yet again. As an angel I was ignored, probably because the only person who had nobody to mourn was Captain Reed, and being from a different species, he couldn't fathom my sorrow. At least I hoped as much.

Once out of Otherspace and into Realspace, I worked alone at my task of dispatching the bodies. I launched them through the airlock and wiped the blood off the cargo bay floor. I turned my attentions to Fluff and Lotus. "Will you help me get this ship around, Fluff?"

"He'll help." Lotus said, "And I'll be your most loyal crew, if you need one."

I bit my tongue, because I wanted to tell her that I didn't need anything from her. Had we not gone to that dance, Fluff would still be mine, my parents would still be alive, and she'd be with another suitor.

I slowly undid my fists. "That's acceptable." I looked at Captain Reed. "Will you be crew?"

"I would be honored. I'm a weapon's tactical specialist, it is a genetic advantage of mine." Captain Reed said, his voice raspy.

"Very well, I won't demote you to first mate. Instead I'll make you Captain in charge of Navigation. Though you're probably older physically, I'm Senior Captain aboard the *Persimmon*." I turned my attention to my new crew. "If at any time any of you losers feels the urge to mutiny, talk to me first. I'm not an unfair or cruel leader." I said. "You're all dismissed. The *Persimmon* will train you at Navigation, Captain Reed. You'll pull double duty as weapons master, Fluff will assist you while he's aboard."

When Fluff and Lotus left the cargo bay for their quarters, and Reed left for the bridge, I started to cry. My eyes burned with tears big and bitter, more so than any I had ever felt in my short life. I fell to my knees, only to be caught up by powerful limbs. I couldn't see through my tears at first, but soft warm hands held me, hands big enough to hold my head in one of their palms.

When I finally cleared my eyes, Captain Reed's voice filled my ears. "Hush child." He whispered rhythmically, rocking me, "Tears from a pirate are no tears at all."

He rocked me like a mother rocks her child, and I was probably about the size of one of his children. I cried a while longer, and pushed my head close to his chest, which felt nothing like a human chest. Its warm, unyielding scales seemed softer for Reed's concern. His faceted, unblinking eyes seemed to peer straight through me.

"Why are you crying, little pirate," He asked.

"I am truly alone, my family is dead."

"I know the pain of being alone, and the power. I'm Hunter Reed, I'm Captain Reed. The stars that shine brightly and I are one – I know loneliness and yet I embrace it, because it is what the universe sometimes feels, alone. One of many, but still one of a kind."

"Are you one of the great 108?" I wondered, awed at his

equanimity.

"I don't know. Shaman McKechni called me something like that. He called me the Alien Glass Buddha."

"Shaman McKechni. Who's that?" I said.

"Someone I met while drifting in Otherspace. He was a strange man with many bodies, and he was very nice to me. He spoke to you and gave you that necklace. He lives there, most of the time, in Otherspace, because his planet was destroyed when its star went supernova. I don't know if he is a vision, or if I was his vision, but he wasn't a body in Otherspace, he was a spirit." He said.

He retracted and extended his claws, and it made me wonder why he didn't do this when he reached for me in Otherspace. Probably fear. "What are we going to do now?"

"We're going to save the universe, of course." I said, wiping the last of my tears away.

Deep inside I felt my mind and heart switch modes. I walked to the bridge, pulled the crystal out of its data case and studied it closely. This data crystal held a thousand lives in its memory, and could store a thousand more. It reached into me, sending its data stream without my request. I felt invaded, as if my very soul was being torn apart, and I rebelled, forcing the knowledge into a blank part of my mind. I don't know how I did it, but I did. Then the crystal started to pull my memories from me, and tried to rearrange them, and some part of my mind went on the offensive.

The data crystal shattered violently, and my own blood trickled through my fingers. My mind had taken all the knowledge and carefully dumped it in some unused part of my brain. I was now the governor of the Forever Children, and I knew I had to protect them at all costs – because I would be the last governor. Captain Bit, pirate, governor of the Forever Children, last of the angels. Too many masks as far as I was concerned.

I looked up at Captain Reed, who was at the battle stations, awaiting my commands. "What have I done?" I said, staring at my bleeding hands.

"You've cut yourself." Captain Reed pulled the shards of the crystal from my hands. He took a first aid kit from the wall, and opened the antiseptic, daubing my wounds with quick, thorough movements, and wrapped my hands in clean white bandages.

I didn't wonder for long at the fate of the crystal. As the *Persimmon* lay adrift in Realspace, I studied the recent news files. I knew there was a link between Prince Wastik and the plight of the Scandivats, and I had to think of a reason. While I wracked my limited mental reserves, Captain Reed whistled to himself. He sung in three note sequences, and they sounded too structured. As I listened, I realized that he was speaking to himself in his language. Noting this, but not knowing how to use it, I went back to studying recent events.

Chapter 12

Realspace shifted violently, and two ships came into stable view through the forward port. I'd taken the *Persimmon* out of Otherspace to give the engines a rest and allow my temporary crew a chance to calibrate its pulse centers. If the *Persimmon*'s sensors hadn't triggered an alarm, I might not have noticed them at all, as deep as I was into my research. My crew rushed onto the bridge, and my annoyance turned to concern.

"We're being hailed," Captain Reed said.

The ships looked formidable, a sensor sweep confirmed their battle ready modifications. *Persimmon* called Fluff and Lotus to the bridge, because the ships were in a standard attack formation, something I would not have recognized on my own. I reached over to the communications console, and flipped the transmit switch.

I cleared my throat. "This is Captain Bit, I send a greeting to whoever is hailing me. How are you doing?" I tried to sound casual, as if I wasn't worried about them.

"We're doing just dandy. This is Captain Jonas." The man sounded like a sarcastic pig. I'd just met him and I already disliked him intensely.

"Fact is, I heard that there was this new hot pilot of the *Persimmon*. I wanted to see just how tough you really were. We thought maybe you could join our bandit's party and fight at our side. Fight for us, or fight us now."

"Listen boys. I've had a real bad day. My whole family's dead, my boyfriend not only got killed, but he left me for another woman at the same time, and because he's dead he can't even remember dumping me. To top things off, I'm in the middle of trying to save the Human Race right now, so unless you have the same goals in mind, I highly recommend you get out of my way."

The bandit laughed and cut communications.

I looked back over my shoulder at the Scandivat. "Get us battle ready Captain Reed. Hurt them."

"I need to do a sensor swipe." Captain Reed said.

The *Persimmon* shifted out of firing range, turning on a strategic path; the enemy had already started firing their weapons. Three-dimensional images shot into view, so my crew could evaluate the enemy clearly. One of these images was noting calculated trajectories and possible escape routes. There are two types of weapons commonly used by star ships. The first are matter based and very high velocity, the rest are plasma and laser weapons.

Unlike us, the pirates had both at their disposal. Fluff sat at the weapons console, Captain Reed issuing orders in calm, passive tones.

"Two ships, six person crews, heavily armored. Scanning for target points. Weaknesses found. Bring me astern, I need to lock weapons on their belly sensors, there's a gap in the armor there. If we blind them they'll have to surrender."

"You're so calm, Captain Reed."

"I am working well within my abilities." Captain Reed said. His large claws clicked across his keyboard, and I wondered how he kept from leaving holes in it.

The ship lurched around, having taken a hit to a rear armor plate. The minor damage was worth the resultant counter strike. The heads-up display betrayed Captain Reed's brilliance. A spread of perhaps eight blasts was split between both ships. The ships came around like wolves, and we took serious damage as we passed through the middle of them a second time.

"Hard astern, Fluff, give them chase until they split course, then come to a full halt." In that moment of pause, he looked at me.

"Our damage is significant. We've lost port and belly shields, and our aft armor plates are all heat stressed. I'd like permission to use lethal force, if necessary."

"Do what you have to. First the Prince and now this. Why me?" I wondered, upset that my precious *Persimmon* had taken damage.

The *Persimmon* moaned as Fluff brought the ship hard to port. The ships split in two directions, both so close that their engines blocked out our forward view. The void lit up with plasma; our sensors showed that *Persimmon* had fired four shots directly into both ship's engine cores. Sensor swipes showed both ships adrift, their engines melted to sludge. The fight was out of them.

"We're being hailed on auxiliary channels." Princess Lotus informed me. "Opening audio only."

I smiled at the static coming over the line. "Why, Captain Jonas, are you all right? Need assistance?"

I ignored the fact that my own bridge was waist high in blue-green clouds of engine coolant.

"We surrender already – by whatever terms you set."

I thought about it. "*Persimmon*, how are you doing – will you need any spare parts?" I asked.

The *Persimmon* threw the information onto a text screen. "The audio emulation system was damaged by a power surge, but is self repairing. The shields are merely overheated and will be back on line promptly. The engine core coolant systems are already resealed and pressurized. No other damage to report."

"Do either of your ships have injured crew?" I asked.

"None that need serious attention." Captain Jonas said. "And our ships can crawl back to the nearest dry dock for repairs."

I was happy that nobody had been hurt. "My terms are simple. I'm going to enter Otherspace and go far away. You are going to enter Otherspace and go the other way, as far from me as you can. And if we cross again, it will be on peaceful terms. I don't have anything to sell you now, but in the future, if my ship's hull is full, maybe we can negotiate a trade."

The defeated Captain Jonas didn't seem too happy with the

outcome, though I had spared him his life. "Aren't you going to raid our ship and rip us apart?"

"We have what we need to make repairs. We only take what we need." I said.

"Why, that's bloody communism. That's no way for a pirate to act."

I tried to fathom communism for a moment too long. He added quickly, worried I'd changed my mind. "Not that we don't mind the courtesy, of course."

"Of course." I smiled. "One more question," I said as I input coordinates into the ship's navigational computers.

"Yeah, what is it?" Captain Jonas said.

"Are there any slaves aboard your ship?"

Jonas was quick to respond. I could practically hear him spitting in disgust. "Slaves? What a horrid thought." The man cut communications abruptly.

"Take us into Otherspace, keep your weapons on track, your shields up, and be ready for anything. I'm feeding you homing coordinates now." The ship lurched into Otherspace and I felt my body shift to its angelic form. "Captain Reed, you have the Bridge."

I paused, looking at Princess Lotus. "Girl," I said, abruptly, "What's your first name?" I'd heard it before and forgotten it.

"Uruza." The woman answered, not a hint of emotion in her voice. Her eyes sparkled for a moment, and I had to try to interpret that glimmer. Elfin people had a strange set of emotions to work with – angels and humans often have a hard time understanding Elfin psychology.

"Uruza." I looked away, holding back my tears. "I'll be in the cargo bay. Practicing my sword skills."

Having dumped Tiffany and the others into Isastan's sun, the cargo bay was empty. Being roughly the size of a couple of tennis courts, the bay was a good place to do some hard practice. I stood straight, wings forced tight against my naked back, striking, slicing, and practicing every nuance of the primitive art that had become such a critical part of my life. I flapped my wings, swinging out with my saber, then drew my pistol for a mock shot. I continued my imaginative practice for a while

longer, then began working on technique, creating a little dance, practicing and repeating it as I went.

"Captain." The voice disturbed my practice, and I flipped twice, landing in front of Fluff, my saber at his bare throat.

His sheep eyes were fixed on mine, and I wanted to kiss him, so I looked away, studying the gleam of my pistol. My sword went to its scabbard, my hand on the pommel.

"Yes?" I wiped the sweat from my brow, and Fluff returned the motion as if it were a salute.

"I've hurt you, in some way." The angel within him dead, his memories of us died as well.

"It was another life. It's not important now. When we get you and Uruza home, you'll be permanently dismissed from duty aboard the *Persimmon*."

"Yes ma'am." Fluff saluted me again and left me alone.

I was about to restart my practice when Uruza disturbed me. I realized that height must be an Elfin trait. She made me feel like a dwarf. Though two and a half feet taller than myself, she was still cautious. She kept her sword in its scabbard. She spoke quietly, in an aristocratic tone that rattled my nerves.

"You love my man, don't you?"

I felt a little defensive anger from her, and started to feel some myself. If her father hadn't just died, I might have been more cutting.

"Do you even remember the ball, where you took him from me?" I sheathed my sword, practiced my blocks, punches, and kicks, waiting for her to talk.

"I remember, but Fluff doesn't. Not like you and me, anyway. When his angel half died, he lost a big chunk of his memory, didn't he?"

"What do you want anyway?" I snapped at her in anger, trying to forget Fluff's fallen form, covered in blood.

"If you want him you have to fight for him. Only a contest of battle will give you the right to reclaim him."

"Is that the way the Elves do things?"

"It's Elfin law. The ball wasn't officially ended, so until Fluff and I get married, there is no official bond holding us together."

"Oh." I thought about it, a simple hope rising just long enough to be snuffed out. "Besides the fact that you'd crush me, there are other considerations."

"I wouldn't underestimate you." Uruza said. "What else is there to consider?"

"The law doesn't change the heart. I could no more regain Fluff's love than I could snuff out a star. And I could never kill you." I paused. "There'll be no competition from me. The one I loved died protecting you."

Uruza looked through me, and in her eyes I could see she was caught off guard. She seemed to be studying my soul with her deep green eyes.

"I was giving you a chance at him, because your love is strong. You've never killed before, have you?"

I snapped my wings tightly around my body. "I never will, if I can avoid it." I said. "*Persimmon* is scanning Realspace and Otherspace for signs of enemy ships. You'd better get with your man. I'm supposed to protect you two, and to do that I need to practice with my weapons. My duty is the only certainty in my life right now."

"So duty is important to you?" Uruza sounded mildly surprised.

I raised an eyebrow, then decided to let it go. "I've work to do if I'm going to succeed. We might be friends, someday, when you tell me why you took him from me."

"His soul called to me. It's an ancient Elfin tradition, to seek out the soul mate. The formal ball is merely a way of bringing two kindred souls together." Uruza bowed slightly and left me to my thoughts.

With what I considered to be a deft draw, I slashed at an invisible enemy. I wondered how the other angels must be faring, what parts they must be playing in defending the universe. I considered visiting them, jumping into Otherspace and transcending long enough to ask, then thought better of it. Without a ship around me I would be easy prey for Prince Wastik and his dangerous powers. I studied the small bell around my neck. It had changed, slightly. The symbols were the same, but the bell seemed shinier, almost golden in appearance. In Otherspace, the more something was used, the better it looked.

A boy materialized in front of me, that blue skinned child I had found so fascinating before. He drew a magnificent blade, and smiled at me, wild cunning in his tiger's eyes. Brown and shiny, with incredible depth, he studied me, talking quietly.

"Still playing pirate, Governor."

"I'm forever a pirate, boy. Why are you here? Did I summon you?"

The Forever Child raised his sword, slashed down twice. Not at me, but at nothing. I blinked, and opened my eyes, seeing a world instead of a ship. Trees reached high into the air, blocking out the sun. The Forever Child no longer held a sword. It had been replaced by a gnarled wooden stick, only a little shorter than the sword had been.

"Forgive me, I love grand entrances and exits."

"No problem. Where are we?" I asked.

"On the world I've been born to protect. There will be sentient life here someday." The boy removed his clothes and walked naked through the woods, every part of his body a deep shade of blue. "Walk carefully so you don't step on the flowers."

I flapped my wings, hovering over the flowers entirely.

"Are we still in Otherspace?" I wondered, because I was still an angel.

"No, we're not, I kept you this way for a reason. It is possible to stay an angel in Realspace, though I am certain you have never imagined doing it."

"What's your name?" I asked. The knowledge pumped into my brain via the data crystal wasn't complete, and seemed to be fading with time.

"You ask a lot of questions." The boy paused, turning to face me. He seemed carved from a chunk of finest turquoise, and I couldn't help but wonder why. "My name's Falcon, Satrap Falcon Lotus."

"Lotus?" I paused. "Is it a coincidence that you have the same name as the Elf King?"

"He was my son." Falcon said.

My mouth gaped. "Your skin doesn't match his."

"The King of the Elves was my boy. Genetics are sometimes tricky. Blue skin is recessive."

"You ever thought of having more?"

"Is this a proposal?" Falcon said as he ran forward. His head bobbed left, then right, searching.

"No, just curious." I blushed at the thought.

The young Satrap paused, his sinuous body poised on a rock. I caught up with him, looking down at a chasm, most of which was filled with a lake of freezing fresh water. Cold wind was forced off its surface; it must have been icy. Angelic senses being what they are, I knew the lake would kill me.

"Why have you brought me here?"

"Always curious." He chuckled. "I've brought you here to give you a gift from Level Ringbreaker. I'll have to find it though, it's at the bottom of this lake and I may be gone a long time."

"How did it end up at the bottom of the lake?"

"It's a simple warding stone. I got bored and tried skipping it – you know, like a regular rock. It bounced three times, which was a severe disappointment. Usually I can skip a stone a good twenty times." The Satrap put his arms around my neck. "Take care of the planet for me, in case something happens while I'm gone." He kissed me on the nose; a serene and loving gesture. It felt nice, like rose petals being rubbed against my skin.

My pain was lifted for a moment. Before I could ask him why he kissed me, he ran away from me, caught the edge of the stone with his toes and jumped into the abyss. He was fifty feet above the lake's surface, without wings, and yet he feared nothing of the fall. He arched into a dive, breaking the surface and disappearing deep below. His blue skin camouflaged him within seconds.

I flew nervously around the lake, wondering if the poor boy had drowned. Two more nights passed while I waited, worrying. At daylight on the third morning, the water broke and Falcon was propelled on a fountain of water back out of the chasm. He stepped onto solid ground with the sluggish grace of a sloth. Shivering violently, he clutched something in his tiny hand. He was nearly too frozen to talk, and I carried him to a patch of sunlight.

The morning was chill, making him shake even worse. The water began to freeze on his skin, forming a white cake of ice crystals. I put my wings around him, warming him. Within an hour his shivering stopped. The chill past from his body to mine, my teeth were clattering, despite the sun's brightness. He forced open his palsied hand, cramped into a tight fist, and pulled a small, gold loop from an Otherspace pocket.

He looped whatever it was that he had gotten from the bottom of the lake onto it, and held it up for me to see. It was something of a fascination, really, about half the size of Earth's moon as seen from the Earth. Small, flat, and pitch black, the stone was worn through the center by years of exposure to the elements, so that a hole peeked through it. Lightweight and smooth as satin to the touch, it stole the sun's light as it hung on the gold loop.

"Now stand still." He said.

I couldn't have moved, I was caught in the beauty of his eyes. His hand slid deftly across the side of my face, and I felt a slight stinging sensation on the lobe of my ear. With a touch of his finger, the pain was gone and my ear was pierced and healed. Though I hadn't recognized, the loop was actually an earring, and now the stone hung from my ear. I flew down to the still lake surface, and saw my reflection, then flew up to Satrap Lotus.

"Do I look pretty?"

The Satrap giggled. "Yes, you look pretty. I needed you here in angel form, so I could give your angel body the stone in Realspace."

"But, why?" I asked.

"The stone is a guardian. It uses your will to create a psychic shield. Like the bell, it's old magic." He paused. "I hope you like your jewelry."

He moved his finger down twice, and I was whisked away, back to my ship. When I opened my eyes, Uruza was staring at me, as if stunned.

"You're truly a creature of great power, to teleport like that." Her eyes widened with momentary fear. "That stone is dangerous. Who gave it to you?"

"Your Grandfather did." I looked at myself in the mirror. The bell on its thin leather thong and the stone were both very complimentary of each other, but I couldn't tell if they were all that pretty on me. "Tell me, does the jewelry make me more attractive?"

Uruza studied me closely. "That would be impossible, Captain Bit."

I smiled, then frowned. "What the hell is that supposed to mean?"

"Forgive me." Uruza paused. "Elfin culture isn't very emotional, and we always assume a positive tone. I've been jealous of your beauty ever since I first met you. Both your angel and human forms put my Elfin body to shame."

"It appears we have a lot in common. I've often felt the same about you. Let's practice together, shall we?"

"Only if you take that stone off your ear."

"I can't. What could it possibly do to you?"

"Legend says that Elves and fairies should beware all sacred stones. That stone is sacred, I can feel it in my bones." Uruza said, taking an involuntary step back.

I could remember no such legend. "Touch it."

Hesitantly she did. The stone didn't even issue a warning sparkle.

"See, nothing happened. It only hurts those who try to hurt me. Uruza, you never tried to hurt me, so it won't hurt you."

Uruza smiled. "If the legends are true about that stone, I wouldn't want to be your enemy." She drew her sword, and snarled savagely. "It's time to play."

We thrust slowly and carefully, our swords moving at quarter pace. Uruza was a warrior, and had probably spent many hours practicing with live steel. When I bested her for the first match, I heard an Elf giggle for the first time. It was an impressive, beautiful tone. Pretty soon she was laughing so hard that she had to sit down, her sword cast aside, her hands raised in surrender.

"Don't hit me, please. I was just remembering the way you beat that little prick uncle of mine around. Here he is, twice your size, and he's being pounded like a twelve year old."

"Sure, a twelve year old. Did you say that both of you were related?"

She stopped laughing and wiped a tear off her cheek. "I'm sorry to say that we are. My uncle has fallen in with bad company. He wants the Elves to segregate from all other tribes of Humanity, and enslave the fairies. He wants Elf kind to be the only intelligent life in this galaxy."

"Why is it he would want that?"

"It's really very silly. All the races of man come from Earth. The differences aren't so much of species but of culture. Elves, fairies, and angels went to war for Earth, against the Human Race. In the end, we left Earth for other worlds, and the angels for Otherspace. It's in the Elfin lore – related from the eldest and long dead King Exodus and his recordings of a conversation with the mighty Avatar, Wisdom."

"Never knew where angels came from, I never thought to ask." I flapped my wings out, then let them snap down violently, a sign that I was thinking.

Uruza misinterpreted it. "Have I offended you?"

"No, tell me about this discourse with Wisdom," I said. "My father's done so much I don't know about."

"Even though the Human Race is the current holder of the Jewel of Earth, five great races have been spawned from it in the past. Because only one sentient race can hold a biological niche at a time on any one planet, many races have left Earth behind so that new races could grow and shed their home world as well." Uruza paused. "Don't you angels have anything akin to a history lesson?"

I frowned. "I'm only a Guardian Angel, I always fell asleep in my classes."

"The angels were the first Human Race, and after the great angelic wars, angelic law was established and the angels moved into Otherspace. The next three races evolved simultaneously, only a few thousand years after the angels, and within a few thousand years of each other. The fairies, the Elves, and the humans all went to war."

"But what about the Forever Children?"

"The Forever Children are called the mother race, because they carry no individual genetic codes. If they mate with an Elf, an Elf will be born. If they mate with a human, a human will be born. I don't know if this holds true for other sentient species that aren't human, or even if they can mate with non-humanoid species, but I suspect that it does. They left Earth shortly after the angels, and we Elves still don't know how or why they left. There's said to be at least one on every planet that harbors life.

"There are also the fairies. The Elves call the fairies the Grandfather race, because they came before us, and are very wild and generous souls. You'll know if you ever meet a fairy. Although they have wings, they look like smaller versions of us. Even the smallest is large enough to mate with other Homo Sapiens.

"If you aren't careful around one, you'll probably end up pregnant – the creatures are masters of seduction. They left Earth for the planet Isastan, and after a few thousand years, my people joined them. Since then our races have successfully merged as one.

"I'm hoping that the advanced humans who've left Earth will also join us on Isastan. It's my belief that the reunification of the human tribes can only strengthen genetics and culture. Wastik and I are very polarized on this issue."

"Your uncle voiced a lot of opposition to your marriage with Fluff. He even put me down for being an angel."

"He wants power. I don't know that he really believes the racist nonsense he's spouting, but his followers do, and he is using them as a level to gain the Elfin throne of Isastan. Since he's got the Scandivats on his side, we've got a problem. He has a strong following among the Elves. We're fighters by nature, so when Elves go to war, it's not a pretty thing." Uruza adjusted her loincloth, rising to lean against the wall.

"Mother Tester thought that something had been damaged in the machinery of the universe, and that as soon as the part was fixed or removed and replaced, everything would return to normal. Do you think it might be Wastik?"

"You're asking me if Wastik has the power to break the universal machinery. I don't know. I do know that if there was some event or condition he came across that he could use to his advantage, he would. It would be better for everybody if that man was dead."

"If I have to kill, then things must really be bad."

"I've heard that angels who kill become demonic in appearance – have you killed before?"

"I think I'm an exception to the rule. I look a lot like my mother is all."

"Just like her. And just like her, you have two bodies at the same time. Except her other body is Wisdom."

"Not exactly. I can't split into two separate entities at the same time. I can't be human and angel, or male and female. I'm Bit no matter what body I'm in, a woman soul in kindred bodies." I leaned against the wall, next to Uruza. "I've tried very hard to be strong, but strength is useless against loneliness."

For a moment Uruza's eyes softened, as if she understood. The blare of the service horn ended our conversation. As we came out of Otherspace, I shifted human again with nothing but a bodysuit to cover me. It wasn't unattractive, it just wasn't what a Captain of a pirate vessel was supposed to be wearing. I had to walk to my quarters to change before going to the bridge.

Uruza said one last thing to me as I left the cargo bay for my room. "I'll kill for you, if I have to." The tone in her voice turned my blood cold.

Chapter 13

I had to walk to three separate rooms to find my uniform. They ended up in Fluff's room, and he was still sleeping. I tried to sneak in without waking him as I got my clothes, but my movement startled him, nonetheless. Fluff looked up at me as I dressed, blushed slightly, and still groggy, closed his eyes and put his back to me.

"Sorry." He said, confused. "How did your clothes get in my closet?"

I pulled my sword belt tight over my pants. "I left them in here. I'll make sure it doesn't happen again."

I left him to sleep a little more, and went to the bridge. He followed me instead.

"We're on our way to the surface of Isastan." Uruza said. "Will you be staying for the wedding, then?"

"No ma'am." I said. "This is Prince Wastik's home, and I'll only be here long enough to have words with him."

"Entering Isastan atmosphere, Administrator Cupan will meet you at the dock." *Persimmon* said.

I looked out the forward port, onto a world with forests reaching half a mile into the air, and fairies fluttering and playing in the breezes. The pressure locks broke seal, and the ship settled onto the dry dock. The dock was well hidden beneath a forest canopy, and I led my friends into the docking bay, where a tight-lipped young Administrator waited for us. Though he seemed impatient, his smile looked genuine enough.

He wasn't particularly handsome, more feminine than most men, thin skin with a slight frame adding to his gentle nature. His eyes scanned his notepad, and his fingers jittering nervously as he scribbled his notes. His uniform was well starched and ironed, made of dark gray wool, and looked terribly uncomfortable. The clothes were tailored, and he seemed almost cozy in his attire.

His thin tongue snaked out, only its tip wetting his lips, "Captain Bit," He began, formally, "It is so good to meet you in person. And you brought the Princess back in one piece. That was a concern, I must admit, considering your chosen profession."

"I didn't want them to miss their wedding." I said, ignoring his question of my integrity.

"Then you understand that once the young man has married Princess Uruza, he will be King."

"Such are the dangers of being a Prince."

"Prince Wastik is still disgusted with the marriage. He was bragging about killing the King all the way to his prison cell."

"I want words with Wastik. Can that be arranged?"

"I'm afraid not, ma'am. You're a human, after all. This is an Elfin affair." The Administrator's pencil clicked across his notepad one more time, and I was dying to know what he was writing.

"Give the woman a break, my uncle killed her parents. She just wants a few words with him." Uruza said.

Cupan looked nervously from his pad to the Princess. "Yes, your Highness. But how will we ensure the Prince's safety? I'll simply have to appoint someone to take her."

I wanted to say that the Prince was a murdering psychopath that deserved whatever he got, but that would have cost me access.

“I’ll go with her, and ensure the safety of all.” The sky brightened for a moment, the voice coming from above.

A fairy landed on the deck, as graceful as a hawk. His skin was a shade of orange like no human I’d ever seen. He had bright red eyes; his canines were tiny white spikes. His thin muscled form sent waves of passion through my body. He had a wingspan of a little over six feet when he extended them fully in flight. His wings were the colors of a peacock, shaped like a butterfly’s, their combined width was twice his physical height.

“Genesis, I’m honored by your presence.” The Administrator bowed reverently.

Uruza did the same, and I wondered what importance Genesis could possibly hold to the Elves. Genesis took my hand and led me away. We walked for twenty minutes through an Elfin version of a city. Stone buildings that descended deep into the soil were built with the forest in mind. There were only entrances at the surface, with stone markers set in the ground, describing the building that had been built below.

“Why did they treat you with such respect? I mean, who are you?”

“They respect me because I’m the Eldest Forever Child, and they think I’ve limitless knowledge.” He giggled, sounding like a schoolboy. “All really quite silly – there are countless smarter than I am, though only a few older. There are stars younger than me, but only a few dozen in the entire universe. Of course, I could be lying about the star thing, I’m getting a little senile in my old age. You’re starting to gain quite a reputation, among pirate Captains.”

“Really?” It surprised me; I’d only attacked one ship and defended myself from one group of bandits.

“Yes. Word has it you only attack ships carrying slaves. Is there anything I can do for such an honorable pirate while she’s on my world?”

“Children would be asking too much, wouldn’t it?” I thought aloud.

“Do you have a crush on me? I’m older than dirt, you know. Oh yeah, we’ve already established that.”

His wing wrapped lovingly around me, and I looked up into his eyes. On the center of his forehead were three horizontal blue lines, the color of Satrap Lotus' skin.

"Don't toy with me." I said.

"I'm sorry, I often forget how fragile a young lady's emotions are."

We walked into the depths of a building, stepping into a fairy shaft. I wouldn't have known it was a fairy shaft if it wasn't marked in three languages: "Warning, this is a fairy shaft, if you don't have wings you'll fall and hurt yourself."

Genesis was forced to flutter down with me in his grip. "You're quite heavy."

"Hey, I'm not a pound over one hundred and twenty. Besides, If I could just figure out how to turn into an angel in Realspace, I'd fly down under my own power."

"Well maybe I can help you with that, before you leave." Genesis caught a steel beam in passing with one hand and swung out into the open.

The landing would have been perfect if not for my clumsy feet. I tripped and we landed in a heap.

Genesis laughed, picking me up off the ground. "Don't quit being a pirate for ballet. The cell's this way. I've visited him twice, trying to figure out why he hates me."

I followed Genesis into a cubicle that made my quarters on the *Persimmon* look like hell's worst dungeon. "So this is how you treat a mass murderer," I said, anger trickling out from within.

Genesis ignored me, touching an interface console, its screen lighting up under his fingertips. Wastik sat in a chair, surrounded by Elfin women eating and dancing, playing and drinking, talking about him, calling to him, telling him how nice it would be for him to be part of their world.

"This is all an illusion, isn't it?" Nubile women danced around him, eating and playing, but none of them let him eat. I touched one of them in passing. She felt real enough, though some part of my senses told me otherwise.

"Yes, an illusion of the greatest complexity," Genesis said, sounding distracted. He made a few more keystrokes, then stepped away from the interface.

"And why doesn't Wastik partake of the illusion?" I asked, curious as to why Wastik wasn't trying to escape.

"Because Wastik can't move." Wastik answered sarcastically. "I'm bound to this chair, you idiot. I can only get up at certain times – and at those times the room is empty."

I sat down in a chair next to him. "Sounds fitting for a man whose actions cost my mother and father their lives."

"Sometimes things have to be done to ensure one's success, and most of those things can be rather nasty."

I wondered how a man who would try to kill his own brother could live with himself. "I didn't come here to talk ethics. Why'd you kill my parents?"

"They were in the way, nothing more. The Hunters were supposed to kill only my brother and my niece. With them dead, I'd be the rightful keeper of the Elfin clans, and I could issue the proclamation that would continue the traditions that Uruza and father are set on ending. But your parents got in the way, and being only human, I saw no need in worrying about sparing their lives."

"Do you have any more questions Bit?" Genesis said.

"Yes." I was beginning to hate this man, not a particularly good emotion. "How did you get the Scandivats to side with you?"

"Wouldn't you like to know?"

"I'll find out, eventually. You'll just be saving me some time."

Wastik remained silent, his eyes glowing defiantly. He didn't seem the man that torture would force words from. I wasn't the kind of person to torture somebody. "I'll find out your part in this, and then I'll see to your justice."

I got up to leave, disgusted that I couldn't learn more. Genesis raised a finger, motioning for me to wait, then turned back to the trapped Wastik.

"I've something to tell you, and you'll know it's true, because I never lie. To help remind you of your little lesson, I've already started making changes to your prison illusion, so that you learn your lesson well."

Genesis bent over and whispered something into Wastik's ear.

Wastik looked straight ahead, his eyes widening with terror. Genesis smiled as he finished his little secret. Wastik started to babble profanity, and then his words became more coherent. He bent his head until his chin touched his chest, and he began to moan.

"I'll never let it happen. I'll kill you. You hear me, I'll kill you."

Genesis laughed. "Let's go dear. Wastik has thinking to do."

I followed Genesis from the chamber.

"I'm afraid," Genesis said, walking back to the shaft, "that the truth has driven the young Prince insane."

"What truth is that?"

"I told him the truth of evolution on Earth, in a voice he couldn't ignore. He knows now what you and I both openly accept: That all human life originating from Earth, regardless of magnitude number, are members of the species Homo Sapiens."

"Wow, and that drove him crazy?"

"Yes, at least for now. I created a new illusion, an illusion of the future I am working toward on Isastan. It was a union of all Human Races, and eventually a place where all sentient species can meet in peace. He's terribly upset because he knows that with my guidance, it'll come to pass. He won't have the power he craves on such a world."

"Does Isastan's future include angels?" I wondered.

"Especially angels. Otherspace is deteriorating, and the angels have already started coming here." He turned to me, his wings flipping gentle puffs of air toward my face. "You're going to have to use the ladder and climb back out of the cell. It'd tear my wings trying to carry such a big girl back up the shaft."

"You said you were going to show me how to shift my body in Realspace. Now would be a good time, I think." I really didn't want to climb all the way back up to the surface.

"It might be."

"And maybe while you're at it you can tell me how to keep my clothes on – or at least quickly accessible."

"Actually, I was going to suggest that you take your clothes off for this first try, until you learn how to put them in a bubble while you're shifting forms."

I blushed at the thought of undressing in front of Genesis.

"How is it an angel used to gallivanting around as you do with nothing more than a bodysuit is suddenly shy?"

"This body doesn't have wings." I said, as if it made all the sense in the world. It really didn't make any sense to me, so I could understand the confused look on my benefactor's face.

"Well, perhaps now is the time to fix that. Do you know how to make a pocket of Otherspace?"

"Not really. It was always something angels did."

"Anybody can make an Otherspace pocket – even a seemingly normal human. It just takes a little know-how. I don't have another form, so I can't honestly teach you how to draw your other body into Realspace. I can tell you how to make a pocket around yourself and draw yourself into and out of Otherspace."

"When I was an angel I could take on illusory human forms, but I don't know how to become my angel self as a human."

Genesis fluttered around me, studying me from all angles. "Have you used the data crystal?" He asked.

"Yes, and I broke it."

"That shows a strong will." He clicked his tongue in surprise. "Then you probably don't have very much new information at all. Yes, I think you can make a pocket. Take your clothes off."

"Are you sure this is a good place to do this?" I blushed again.

"Nobody on Isastan gives a damn about clothes." Genesis said, growing testy. Reluctantly, I removed my clothes, and waited for his instruction.

"Now close your eyes."

His fingers touched my temples, and I felt as if his mind touched mine. His thoughts and mine became one. He opened my mind, and studied it, trying to find out how to make things happen. Within a few seconds he showed me how to form an Otherspace bubble around my body, which shifted me almost instantly and automatically, into my angelic form. I looked at the dark skin of my wings, flapped them, and felt myself rise slightly off the ground.

The Otherspace bubble vanished, leaving me an angel in Realspace. I struggled to shift back and forth a few times, just to make sure I had the feel of it. It proved easier than I thought it would be. Genesis, growing bored, started for the surface.

"Hey, wait for me." I yelled, flying after him.

I followed Genesis up the flight shaft to the surface. "You're leaving your clothes behind."

I sighed, drifted back down, and picked up the reminders of my Humanity.

Genesis was kind enough to wait for me. "Maybe I can find a uniform that'll work for both bodies."

Genesis laughed. "You'd look quite sluttish as a human, and it would be very strange indeed for an angel to wear clothes."

"My mother kept me in a bodysuit."

"Your mother was a good woman. Did she die bravely?"

"She died unarmed and without hope. Wastik changed Otherspace, making it dark. But he couldn't use it on me, because I was too close to him. He escaped death because he was in a pocket of Otherspace. I was an angel because I was fighting him directly. I was in no danger, though I thought I was. He knew he'd be safe – so he kept me focused on him while his Hunter allies did their dirty work. My parents never stood a chance."

"What happened to the bodies?" Genesis asked.

"We shot them into Isastan's sun."

"Well then, everything isn't lost. Follow me home, and I'll give you one more present. Oh, and go ahead and dump your clothes. I'm sure you have more on your ship."

Tossing my clothes aside, I followed Genesis high into the clouds. We shifted into Otherspace, and materialized in a forest. We flew to a tree as ancient as the forest itself. The tree was higher than a skyscraper, its trunk nearly as thick as one. Genesis flew close to the bark, fairy folk flying around him, greeting him with kisses. The fairies were around me too, asking a million questions in a language I could barely understand.

"You and Captain Reed are all that stands between the universe as it should be and total chaos." Genesis put a wand into my hand, and I could feel power stored within it. "I've charged this wand with one special talent. This wand will bring one person back to life.

"But you have to focus wholly on that one person, because it isn't strong enough to grant you more than that. If you want your mother back, this wand will do it." He materialized two more wands and handed them to me. "Use these wisely, these are the only three wands of their type in the galaxy."

"All these wands restore life to the dead?" I asked.

"Just be warned, I can't make more." Genesis kissed me on both cheeks, and hugged me close. "Don't be selfish, Governor. Use your bell first and talk to those you wish to bring back." He gave me a sash to hold the wands in, and I wrapped it around my waist. "If you can do one thing for me in return. There is a Forever Child on Earth who wishes to see you, she'd be very happy if you would go to Earth and have words with her."

He waved his hand and I was back on my ship. I decided that teleportation would be the next skill I learned.

I took human form and looked at Captain Reed. He sat at the navigation table, seemingly oblivious to my nudity.

"Where shall we go next?"

"Into Otherspace. Don't set coordinates yet, I've some research to do." I said, "Follow me back to the cargo bay." The *Persimmon* drifted away from Isastan, then shifted into Otherspace. From the information the computer had, I discovered that the Scandivats' home world had been hit by a meteor some time back, and I tried to figure out a connection between Wastik, the murdered Forever Child, and the Scandivats going on the war path.

It seemed to me that they should all be related. Wastik was allied with the Scandivats, the Scandivats had gone to war only after the meteor strike, and the death of the Forever Child coincided with the meteor strike on the Scandivat home world. By the time I got done reading about teselar fields, I knew how Wastik had damaged Otherspace. He'd used a pulsed source of teselar energy. Space was shifting back and forth between Otherspace and Realspace at thousands of times a second.

All he had to do to protect himself was to create a reverse phase pulse to neutralize the original teselar emission source. Though why he would do such a thing made little sense to me. Such technology had to be dangerous, and exposure to it potentially harmful to him. The risk of using it just to kill two people and take power of a throne hardly seemed the risk of cancer and brain damage.

Not to mention the incredible amount of power it would take to maintain such a field. Wastik didn't strike me as the kind of person who'd waste such a massive amount of energy for a mere assassination. The Prince had bigger plans, and I had to find out what they were.

Chapter 14

Clearing my mind of the unsolved mysteries, I walked back to the cargo bay. I sat there, holding my bell out before me. It was now pure silver, with bright gold symbols etched into its surface, and I could see myself in its reflection. Thinking it would be polite to ask first, I tapped the bell and called forth my mother's soul.

Tiffany's body formed from nothingness into a lightly glowing specter. "Tiffany, Mother." I said quietly.

"Hey pretty girl."

My eyes started to tear over. "I wish I could see you and daddy at the same time." The bell continued to hum, each second it grew weaker. "I found a way to bring you back. If you want to live again, you can."

Tiffany thought about it. "Is the universe fixed?"

"No, mama. But I'm close. I think I've found the broken part."

Tiffany put her hand on my cheek. I couldn't feel it. As the bell grew quieter, so did her voice. "I may not be much good to you, I'm no longer Governor, and therefor no longer privy to the knowledge of the data crystal."

"I need you, mama, not what you know."

"I'll come back only if my Sparrow comes back. Will you be bringing Fluff back as well?"

I sputtered a little. "Fluff isn't dead, mother, but his memories of us are gone forever."

"I'm sorry. I know how much he meant to you."

"You've always meant more."

I rang the bell again. Tiffany faded with a smile on her face. Father appeared before me.

I quickly explained my conversation with mother.

My father was a man of few words. "You need me. Make it so."

I touched his spirit with the first wand, and he fell forward, naked and uninjured. The wand vanished without a trace. With his claws retracted, Captain Reed caught Papa and helped him sit against the wall. Tiffany's face reappeared, and I touched her with the second wand. I rang the bell again, a thousand notes merging into a single beautiful tone. This time I asked the universe to send one person who was needed most. King Lotus appeared, and I touched him with the wand.

King Lotus shrugged off help from Captain Reed, forcing himself to stand on wobbly legs.

"You must have met Genesis." He said, his voice raspy.

"He gave me three wands." I said.

"Three? He must have really liked you." King Lotus coughed, trying to clear his throat. "Genesis can only produce three of those wands in a millennium. Has my brother been put in prison?"

"Yes. Genesis had words with him, and those words have driven him completely mad." I turned to Captain Reed. "I'll tend to my parents. If you could please take us back to Isastan so the King might do the same for his daughter and her future husband."

"Should you ever be in space with one of my loyal Elfin vessels, you will have their alliance, I assure you." King Lotus said. The *Persimmon* was only about halfway into atmosphere when we were greeted by another ship and escorted to the surface.

The King was taken on board, and I left Isastan without so much as a good-bye to any of my friends. "Mama, Papa, if the two of you would help me fly this ship again, I'd be very happy."

"I'll take life support and Sparrow will sit at Navigation." Tiffany took a chair. I wondered if she remembered that I was a person with two bodies.

The view screen illuminated Kotian's soft eyes. "We may be in Otherspace, but we're not going anywhere. Where would you like us to set course to?"

"Genesis has requested that we go to Earth and have words with a young Forever Child."

We were about seven hours into Otherspace when the ship lurched and shuffled, and we were drawn violently into Realspace.

"What is it?" I got up from the ground, trying not to look embarrassed. Nobody else had fallen from their seats. I quickly unruffled my clothes, acting casual as I sat back in my chair.

Captain Reed studied his sensor readings closely. "We've been hooked by a teselar field."

"Who did it? Are they hailing us?" I focused and tried to keep my angelic form as the field distorted and rippled Realspace and Otherspace.

"Aye, Captain, sending transmission to main screen." Kotian said. The image wasn't a pretty one. "This is Commander Barrot, Law Enforcement for Kottanna Local Space. Prepare to be boarded."

I snarled at him, "We've committed no crimes against the Kottanna government." I said. "By what authority do you feel you can drag us away from our duties?" I signaled Captain Reed to lock all exterior hatches and activated the ship's exterior defenses.

Commander Barrot was calm, and apparently aware of my tactics. "By my own authority. We only want information, we need to talk in person. If you could lower your defenses."

"I don't take orders from you." I tried to look threatening.

"This isn't an order, it's a request. An unofficial and personal request of services, nothing more."

"Oh really? Then why'd you strong arm me?" I said, frozen with indecision. "You wouldn't lie to a woman with wings would you?"

"I don't lie. It would be very inconsiderate of me to lie to a woman with horns." Commander Barrot said, waiting for my answer.

I put a hand my head, and wondered how he'd seen my stubby horns through the hair. My fingers touched the tips, and I was mildly surprised. They'd grown a good half-inch since the last time I'd thought to check on them. "Give me ten minutes, turn off the teselar reactor, and you've got yourself a deal."

After contact was broken, I gave the ship an order. "*Persimmon*, assist Captain Reed in a safe shutdown of your Otherspace drive system and localized defenses."

True to his word, the Commander cut the teselar field as soon as we powered down our engines. I ran through the ship straight to my quarters, pulled my uniform from its hanging rack, and pulled it on over my human form. I tightened my boots into its holster, strapped my sword to my side, and locked my pistol into place. Then, with a flick of my hand, tossed my hair out of my eyes. I set up a bottle of wine and a couple of glasses at the ship's mess hall table.

I got a scolding look from my mother. "You know, this isn't a date."

I tried not to blush as I set a cold platter of sliced cheese and bread on the center of the table. "Come on Mother, it isn't like I've anything to worry about with you here. Besides, I'm just trying to make him feel at home."

"Getting him into bed may be trying too hard. Just because you're an angel doesn't mean you're invincible, after all."

"You know I'm an angel?" I said, surprised.

"Of course I've known. I always have – and so has your father. It was pretty hard not to notice that Bit and Fluff both disappeared when I got pregnant. Even harder not to notice that you turned into an angel every time you got exposed to Otherspace. Why do you think we had you wear that bodysuit under your clothes? One Otherspace shift in a public park, and you'd be running around naked."

The airlock between ships unsealed, and Kotian led Commander Barrot into the mess hall, disturbing our conversation. I leaned against the wall for a moment, smiling coquettishly at Barrot. Tiffany quickly and courteously seated him, then left us alone. His eyebrows were definite lines of black marking his face. He couldn't be more than 25, but already he was the Commander of a police flagship. His black hair and brown eyes contrasted his pale skin, and his entire posture was one of utter confidence.

"Have some wine, Commander. It's nothing special – just something we picked up while touring a Lenitian pleasure ship." I said, taking a sip of my own.

He took a glass and sipped it carefully. Then he finished the glass in one gulp and set it down gently. For some reason he was looking around, as if curious about his surroundings. His uniform gave him a stiff, symmetrical outline.

"It is awful trusting of your crew to leave us here alone, isn't it?" He asked.

I completely missed the intention of his question. "Are you kidding? They're probably watching right now, making bets on whether or not you'll make the first move." I paused, embarrassed at my own forwardness. "What's your business, Commander?"

"Rumor has it that you set slaves free as a hobby." Commander Barrot finished his glass quickly.

"Yes." I said. "Whenever the opportunity arises. I've another mission right now, however, so if this is a matter of me hunting down a slave ship for your amateur forces –"

"I'm asking for you to help me, Captain Bit." He wasn't speaking to me, but around me, as if he thought someone more important was listening.

I humored him as best I could. "Tell me what I need to know, and I'll see what I can do."

"I'd rather speak with your boss." The Commander said. "This is a personal matter, after all."

I rose slowly, almost gracefully, and poured the Commander another glass of wine. When he sipped from his glass, I started to take off my clothes.

"I'm trying to help you, like a good Captain should, and all you can do is question both my intentions and my position on this ship." My voice was soothing. "If this is personal, then we really need to be friends. And if we need to be friends, I need to know that you trust me."

Once I was down to my bodysuit, I could see it took all his effort to put his wineglass back on the table without shattering it. His nervousness kept me from changing right away – the original intent behind my removing my clothes. I got right in his face, rubbed his nose with the tip of mine.

"Well, Commander, can we be friends – or not?"

"Though I must say that Captain Bit has wonderful taste in women, I really need to speak with her personally, and not with her servitor." Commander Barrot said, trying to be polite and failing miserably.

My emotions flashed from seductive to angry, and I shifted to my angelic form, my puppy fangs bared. It took every ounce of will to keep from winging him upside the head.

"I'm the Captain, you moron. Can't you get that through your thick skull? What do you want?" I tightened my wings around my shoulders and chest.

"Oh." He answered, stunned to see me in my angelic form. "Oh."

I laughed at him. "You're beginning to annoy me, Commander."

"It appears I've made a fool of myself. Rumor had it you were a shape-shifter, I should have known it was you all along." He swallowed another glass of wine and set it down. After three glasses, he was beginning to loosen up. "A Lenitian trader took my son to sell as a slave, and I want you to get him back."

"If this is a kidnapping –"

"No it's not a kidnapping, it's a misunderstanding between the mother and myself that caused this."

"Explain this misunderstanding."

"The situation is one of diplomatic severity." He said, trying to whisper.

"Don't bother whispering, I'm not recording this conversation, but my crew is. They like to play it back as training material for future encounters." I wondered what could possibly matter when one's own son is in jeopardy.

"I don't care what you do, but I can't have my superiors hearing about this conversation."

I smiled, shifting back to my human form. "*Persimmon*, seal all exterior hatches, and activate the secure perimeter defences. Focus the Otherspace drive on this room and ensure our privacy."

"Your necklace changed." He said, a curiously superstitious look crossing his face.

I diverted his attention from my chest. "Yes, well normally I look like an angel in Otherspace and in Realspace I look more like my human mother. It's a strange side effect of being an angel born into a human body. Now, what's this deep dark secret that you can't tell anybody but a cutthroat pirate? And be careful, you might damage my innocent ears."

"You seem anything but innocent."

"I'm a virgin, you jerk, and I'll stay one until the end of all time with idiots like you flitting around the galaxy. Get to the point."

"Five years ago, when I was new to Kottanna, I found a woman and got married. Things didn't work out so well between us, and we promptly filed for a divorce. We had a child during the marriage, and after it was determined that the child in question was a boy, she asked me what I, as the father of the boy, wanted to do about it.

"The child was mine, and I wanted custody – which should've been no problem – she didn't want to raise the boy alone. We agreed verbally that I would raise the child and she could visit it any time she wanted. The woman in question, however, had other plans. After I paid for all the medical expenses and raised it to a somewhat decent age, she sought to spite me by selling the child to a Lenitian trader and leaving me without my son."

"And why didn't you go public and ask friends and family for help?"

"Because nothing illegal has occurred. I never officially accepted full custody of the boy. Slavery isn't legal on Kottanna, but selling slaves is acceptable business – we deal with our criminals that way, and with unwanted children. So my hands as a legal official are tied. If I do anything overtly, I'll lose my job – and probably end up on a slaver ship myself."

"So you're attempting to do something covertly. It's people like you who keep us pirates in business. Give me the name and description of this baby boy – and I'll see what I can do."

"Well, for starters he has my hair, my eyes, his mother's nose, and he's five years old."

"Five years. It took you five years to take your son into custody?" I wondered at the oddity of this situation.

"I can't nurse him, after all."

"Yes, well, continue." Something didn't feel right about the Commander's story.

"Here's his picture. He was taken aboard a slaver ship bound for Earth, for sale on the local market. That was three days ago – they should arrive on Earth a couple of days ahead of you."

Commander Barrot gave me a hologram of his son, and I set it on the table, studying it closely. "As it so happens," I said, wondering how such an odd coincidence could come to pass, "I'm in route to Earth now. If I should see your son, I'll do what I can to ensure his best interests. Good day."

Captain Reed escorted the man back to the airlock, and sealed him in his own ship. The *Persimmon* shifted us back to Realspace without warning me, and I put my clothes back on before heading for the bridge. I buttoned my last button and belted my sword and pistol to my side.

"I don't trust him." Tiffany said.

"Neither do I. He's hiding something."

"Did he promise you a reward?" She asked.

"No. He asked me for a favor."

"And of course he didn't sleep with you. So I really don't trust him." Tiffany said.

"I didn't want to sleep with that man. I just wanted to be out of my clothes so I could change into an angel in Realspace. I like a little melodrama once in awhile."

"Very cunning, daughter, and very dangerous." She clicked her tongue. "I think he'll have a hang over, that's for sure. What if he was a mean drunk?"

"I knew you would take care of me." I put *Persimmon* back on course. "We'll send a closed frequency broadcast when we get there, and try to make contact with any Lenitian traders."

Kotian hissed a surprised warning. "The Lenitians are not our friends, Gracie. Things could get ugly."

"We're going to Earth to meet a Forever Child, and it is strange luck that Commander Barrot stopped us and asked for help. I may not trust the Commander's intentions – but the least I can do is check and see to the safety of the children." I closed my eyes and let my mind drift. "How long until we're in Earth orbit?"

"A few days in Otherspace at most Captain Bit." The *Persimmon* answered cordially. I spent a few hours studying the limited information on the Scandivats, and afterwards took a long, discontented nap. The ship's engines hummed me to sleep, and in that slumber I dreamed about Fluff, dreamed of losing him, and dreamed of starting over. I woke up shaking.

When I woke up, I started thinking about my mission on Earth. I tried to piece together Commander Barrot's story – but none of it made sense. I had only stopped one ship and freed a half dozen slaves, hardly enough of an act for me to have the kind of reputation that'd have legal officials pounding on my door.

One thing I was certain was true, the future life of a child hung in the balance, and it would be impossible for me to let a boy go through what Tiffany went through growing up. It had been hard on me then – when I could only make life easier for her by making everything seem all right. Now, as an active participant, I would actually be able to change the future of whatever slaves I freed.

Chapter 15

We caught the Lenitian slave cruiser at the edge of the Earth's solar system. They turned on us in a cloud of debris, attacking before we even had a chance to hail them. The battle was an ugly one, and I ordered an intensive scan to make sure we weren't risking our lives over nothing. A sensor sweep of the ship confirmed the presence of slaves. The human cargo was too young to be crew, and their quarters were too cramped for them to be passengers.

We were forced out of battle by a solid hit to our engines, its plasma coupler melted to slag on the engine room's floor. Reed's skills saved us from further attack, the slave ship chose to run rather than risk another of Reed's impressive counter strikes. If Jupiter weren't in our flight path, we might have made it to Earth. In our current condition, we simply didn't have the strength to escape Jupiter's substantial gravitational field.

"How long before our engines come on line and we can catch those bastards." I asked.

My language was rewarded by a prompt smack on the back of the head. "They're not bastards, dear, the title's too good for them." Tiffany frowned, studying the screen. "Two hours. They won't reach Earth for four hours yet, so we have time."

Kotian and Captain Reed worked together on the engines; I studied the cloudbursts buffeting my ship's front portal. It would be difficult to affect repairs without getting out of Jupiter's upper atmosphere. We had to bring auxiliary engines on line to get into a low-level orbit, and that took us too long. Kotian used the intercom to update the status.

"Auxiliary Engines are at one hundred percent. We're in orbit now, and will be ready to leave Jupiter's orbit in a little over an hour."

"Can you use auxiliary systems to give chase while repairing the main systems?" I said.

"We could, but if we got attacked before the engines could be sufficiently repaired, we might end up crippled."

"Let's go for it. Set a course, half speed, for the enemy. Where they go, we'll go."

Tiffany studied the sensors. "When we dropped into Jupiter's upper atmosphere, they must have thought we went down for good. They've shut down to half speed for repairs and are making straight for Earth."

"Well then, full speed ahead. We'll catch them at Mars and bring them to ground."

"Uh, dear, I know you mean well, but maybe we should force them to ground on Earth." Tiffany said.

"And why not on Mars?"

"Because Mars doesn't support human life, love." Tiffany explained.

"All right, Earth it is then."

By the time we reached the Martian orbit, our engines were repaired. They had set down on the far side of the moon, and taken their cargo to the Earth's surface by shuttle. We raided the war ship, using stun darts to disable the crew. We stole their power cores and shielding coils, raided their data banks for the landing coordinates, erased their navigational data, and trashed their bridge. After that we destroyed their slave cages, then made quick tracks back to the *Persimmon.*

When we determined the shuttle's trajectory, Mama looked nervous. "What's wrong?" I asked.

"Those coordinates put us near my old home." Tiffany said, her fingers jittering on the console's edge.

I looked at the map. Of the seven countries the Lenitians were traveling to, the first purchase point on the map brought them within twenty miles of Tiffany's first home – Roan's domain. I wondered if the times had changed, if her Drug Lord was just as corrupt. Mama and I went to the weapon's locker and suited up, expecting trouble.

"What if we meet him again?" She said, perhaps still afraid of the man.

"I'll protect you. You're my girl after all."

I switched to my wingless body and pulled my battle armor tight. Since learning to transform, it became necessary to shed my clothes quickly. I had the ship's computer redesign my suit with quick snap clasps, so that should I need to, I could shed the armor with a simple – and impossible to imitate – voice command. I strapped a pistol at my side, along with my dart gun, and my sword.

We set down a half-mile from the checkpoint and moved in for the strike. Captain Reed and Kotian remained behind to guard the ship, and mother and I moved in together. We hid in the shrubbery at the edge of the clearing, and I could make out the boy amongst all the others. We were looking at an older Roan, but he hadn't changed much. Tiffany inhaled sharply.

"Don't worry, mother, he's no match for me. Let's listen before we act."

The conversation between the two had just begun. "So what do you need, Roan? I don't have any women on this trip, only a few boys."

"I prefer women." Roan said.

"Ah yes, a lady's man. You do have a taste for the young ones." The Lenitian trader said.

Roan, a man in his late fifties, took the trader by the skin of his chest and hefted him off the ground. No easy task, the trader was a portly man weighted down with armor, weapons, and tools. His yellow skin looked sickly to me, though perhaps only because the specimen in question seemed so sallow.

"I need a tester on sight to show my clients that the product they're buying is pure. A girl makes a perfect product test." Roan looked at the sorry group of slaves, tossing the trader to the dirt.

He took the youngest boy from the crowd, and set him aside. Guards were posted on both sides of the boy. By some strange coincidence, the boy was the one Barrot had asked us to reclaim.

"A drug tester." Tiffany whispered. "He didn't have one of those when I worked for him."

I hissed, unable to contain myself. "We need to strike now, while the trader is on the ground and vulnerable, and while Roan has his hands full."

I moved into the clearing, looking at both men with calm regard. I was ready to kill them; I could feel the evil Jodiah had unintentionally created so many years ago. I could feel something else, a whisper of Tester in my soul, calling for justice without mercy. Tiffany had risen with me, hands at her weapons. She spoke before I could, ruining my usual opening phrase.

"You've gotten old and wrinkled."

He recognized Tiffany almost instantly. "It's you, isn't it?"

Tiffany smiled that innocent smile she had been trained so well to use with men like Roan. "It's been a long time."

"A long time, indeed." Roan said.

"The woman with Tiffany is Captain Bit, a pirate who despises slave trade." The Trader said.

"What brings you here now, and with such poor company?" Roan asked, his entire personality shifting.

"It'd be wise if you spoke of my daughter with more respect. I must ask a favor of you. Fulfill your promise to me."

"Promise?" Roan scowled, then smiled. "I can't believe you're serious."

"What promise?" I asked, curious.

Roan, all poise and no grace, looked at me with his cunning, lustful eyes. "Years ago – after I had thoroughly pleased myself at your mother's expense, I lay there, talking nonsense. I promised her that someday, when I had enough money, I would leave the business."

"The money you got for me could've bought you a small country." Tiffany said. "I didn't know that then, but I do now. So why don't you keep you're promise?" I wondered how she could talk to him so calmly.

Roan spoke to the trader first. "My guards will finish heckling with you over the price of the boy. My old friend and I have to catch up on some old business." He approached Tiffany, and I knew his intentions. I wanted to claw his eyes out right there.

"So," he asked her, "Did you raise your daughter to be a whore like you?"

Tiffany's teeth flashed a bright smile. "Of course not. It would be futile to raise a pirate to be a whore."

Tiffany backed into the bushes, Keeping just out of reach of Roan. I tried to follow her and protect her, only to be blocked by two guards. Before I knew what was happening, the guards had me pinned to the ground, and both of them were trying to get my armor loose.

"Wisdom." I said under my breath.

My armor broke away, leaving me vulnerable – until I shifted into angel form and tossed their oversized human bodies to the dirt. Like a switch, my body snapped into action, drawing on angelic reserves long untapped. The closest guard suffered most, my fist cracking his head up and back. He fell to his knees. Jumping past him, I snapped my knee into his face, extinguishing what little senses remained in his dense skull. He wouldn't be waking any time soon.

The other guard went for a knife, and lost his hand for the effort. I took my sword from the ground and lunged for him, my sword flashing in two crisscrossing strokes. He fell to the ground, holding his hand and trying desperately to put it back on. I slammed a wing out violently, capping his head and knocking him cold. With a quick touch, I restored his hand to his arm. I didn't let him come back to consciousness, however, he would just be in the way.

My sword flashed again, cutting the trader's pistol hand up the middle before he could safely draw his blaster. The sluggish man tried to run away, but I cut his clothes to ribbons, humiliating him as he fled to his ship. The only reason I didn't chase him down was my concern for Tiffany.

Even a few moments might be too long with such a corrupt man. "Roan." I yelled, "If you hurt her in any way I'll force you to eat your own liver."

I burst through the bushes, sword drawn, ready for anything, only to find Roan on the ground. I looked closer. Tiffany had caught him in the neck with a dart. From the looks of the bruise, she'd pegged him at point blank.

Tiffany smiled wickedly. "It's about time you showed up." Her armor hadn't even been scratched.

"I'll send these slaves into Otherspace, then we level Roan's home." I went back to the clearing; the trader had abandoned his slaves.

I touched each slave, and using what Genesis had taught me, zapped each child into Otherspace – and therefore back home. The child I had been sent to return didn't cross over, and I knew instantly that Commander Barrot must be a corrupt man. It also meant he had no safe place to go to.

What are we going to do with this one?" Tiffany wondered. She smiled at the kid, trying to keep him calm.

"I don't know what to do." I said, stroking his head. The boy acted confused but unafraid.

Tiffany smiled and patted him on the head. "I would say he's too young to be a pirate. He doesn't look a day over five. That's still nursing age on Friol."

"I'll take care of him." A girl said.

I turned around, not having expected somebody behind me. A snake coiled around her left leg, writhing slowly about. A five-pointed star was painted in gold on her forehead. She looked like an ancient goddess. Her eyes were disks of darkened turquoise, her expression wizened far beyond her physical age. Her body, covered by a black sari, seemed young. Her fingers were thin and fragile looking, but she had an aura of authority about her.

"Governor, I ask only to be of service. I'm the Forever Child of Earth."

I bowed slightly, because she was so short, and so cute. "What's your name?"

I snapped the magnetic seals of my armor back into place. Roan and his guards had vanished with the girl's appearance. The girl smiled, seeming to read my mind.

"Call me Lynette. Don't worry. I sent them so far away that they probably wouldn't ever find their way back here." She took the boy's hand in hers, "Would you like food, child? How about a planet all your own? We'll need a Forever Child at about the time you're old enough to be one." The boy was either unwilling or unable to talk.

Tiffany looked anxiously around. "Are you sure Roan's men won't return? He's a dangerous man."

"The dangerous man is currently trapped in a glacier of ice in the Antarctic. I'm the only one who can thaw him out and revive him – and I've little intention of doing so until you and your daughter have safely left the planet. I was asked to give you something, and I want to ask you a favor as well."

She closed her hand, then opened it, and pierced my remaining ear with a silver loop. The loop held a stone much like the one in my left ear. Only this stone was white as bone. Tiffany showed me a picture of myself in a mirror. I smiled because now my necklace had two friends.

"When these stones work together, they'll protect you from any magical attack. We're giving you our most powerful magic. My brother was sent to the Scandivat world, and he never returned. I miss him, I want you to find him."

Lynette took a deep breath, a storm building on the horizon. "I have to go now – that storm is caused by my worry, and I have to curb its ferocity before it hits a city and levels it. Be careful." She vanished with the boy, in a swirl of dust.

"Two earrings and a bell. So far I am getting plenty of gifts." I toyed with the new jewelry.

"The Scandivats are the symptom, maybe we should be looking at their world."

"And give up my life of crime? Never." We laughed together, mother putting her hand around my waist.

Rain pelted our skin as we walked back to the ship, and thunder could be heard every so often in the distance.

"I remember when Roan sold you to Grandpa, and you were taken away. I was kind of jealous. Nobody would ever have given so much to save my life."

"You're worth more than anything to Kotian and me. We don't have it, but if we did, you would be worth an infinite amount of gold." Tiffany said.

"Oh. But if there were an infinite amount of gold, wouldn't it become worthless."

"That wasn't my point."

"I know it wasn't. It just came to mind." I put my arm around Tiffany's shoulders, leaning close as we walked.

We entered the *Persimmon* as heroes, and were on board and drinking hot chocolate within minutes. Captain Reed stripped me and my mother of our armor, and took it to the service room to professionally clean it, and Kotian took a few minutes to dry my hair, which – fortunately for him – was cut shorter these days.

"So your mission was a success."

"Yeah." I said. "We dusted the trader's plans. He fled the planet with his life, but no sense of honor. I slashed his clothes from his body and stole all of his slaves – sending every one of them home."

Tiffany put her hair up in a towel, and draped a towel around her body. "We met Roan." She said. Kotian paled noticeably. "He tried to take my daughter for his private collection – so we've decided to level his house and teach him a lesson."

"He tried to do more than that mother, but you were sneakier than he thought. Even if you weren't I would have clawed out his skull and used it for a cooking pot."

"Let me help with this one." Kotian stood and walked to the bridge leaving his half drunk chocolate on the table.

I sucked it down after finishing mine off, then rushed behind him, wiping chocolate from my lips. "What's wrong?"

"The amount of gold my father paid for Tiffany made Roan even more of a tyrant." Kotian said. "He owns all the local commerce, and has every local official in his pocket."

"It sounds like you've been checking up on him." Tiffany said.

"Yeah. I accessed my data banks. Roan is currently trying to gain enough money to buy a Lenitian war ship and expand his sales into the galaxy. With that kind of power, he could rule the Earth."

The *Persimmon* took us to Roan's temple.

Kotian smirked. "Wouldn't it be better to freeze his assets than to level such a beautiful and sacred place?"

I smiled wickedly. "What do you have in mind?"

"You'll see. You stay here this time."

Kotian armored up and loaded a dart gun. He left the ship for a brief while. When he returned, he had with him a tied up concubine and five unconscious drug testers.

The poor girl, who was being used as a tester on the side, had become addicted to the drugs. She pled in her native language to be killed rather than go on without a fix. She couldn't be older than fourteen. Tiffany locked the children in the cargo bay, then joined her husband for the next assault. They had to tie the girl down for fear she'd commit suicide.

Looking through the forward port, I could see everything my parents were doing. They tranquilized the farm hands and carried them unconscious from the temple grounds. Kotian took out a fist-sized bag of seeds, loaded his dart gun and launched them out over the field. Within a decade the opium field would be covered in fruit trees, the opium poppies would go wild and become useless.

With Tiffany's help, they dragged the guards' bodies beyond the temple walls. The two held a lively discussion as they worked. They were very good at arguing in a loving way. One of the guards who had escaped their initial assault fired a round into Kotian's back, and sent him spinning to the ground. Tiffany shot the man with six darts before he fell, then turned her attention to Kotian.

Kotian forced himself upright, rubbing his back. Tiffany helped him to stand, checking him over. His armor had absorbed the blow.

After dumping the last guard well outside the temple grounds, Kotian and Tiffany disappeared into the temple for several minutes more. They came back onto the ship, Kotian limping and Tiffany laughing. I was quick to help them out of their armor, and tried to treat their wounds. Kotian had a bruise the size of a small pancake on his back, and Tiffany had a smaller version on her leg. Neither of them would let me help them, so I pouted and stared through the port.

A bright purple shield came on line; a shield that would keep humans away for at least twenty years before it malfunctioned. Nobody could get through that shield, even from underground. The locals couldn't see it, and wouldn't bump into it. It was a type of field that made people nervous. Its energy would also keep people from remembering the temple when they weren't looking straight at it.

"Let's get space-bound. I want words with the merchant." I said, heading for the bridge.

I ordered *Persimmon* into lunar orbit, and made contact. The trader's eyes were a fit of anger. When he saw me sitting at the command chair, he scowled and looked away.

"What I am doing is perfectly legal. You're nothing more than a criminal, standing in the way of commerce."

"Why thank you." I smiled, wishing I'd stayed an angel a while longer. "Coming from an obvious pig such as yourself, I'll take that as a compliment."

Kotian interrupted our childish discourse. "I don't want to see you trading slaves on Earth again. If I should happen to catch you with slaves in Earth system, I'll defy my Captain's orders and put a hole straight through your fat little skull." Kotian left the bridge, angry.

"I got the slaves safely back where they belong. I won't do the same for you. Your ship's defenses, weapons, and engines have been crippled. When you've managed make repairs, you'd best crawl back to Lenitian space and stay there. The galaxy's not a safe place for you to play." I cut communications and broke orbit, heading for the edge of Earth system.

We'd be in Otherspace for a few days at least, because the kids we'd collected from Roan's home needed special care. After treating the drug testers and concubine for addiction disorders, we sent them through Otherspace to their proper homes. It took only a few days of my time to heal them in Otherspace, then I was back to my original mission of trying to keep Humanity and the Scandivats from destroying each other. I turned my attention to Captain Reed, who had helped without complaint.

"Is there a way we can make contact with your people so that we might begin peaceful negotiations?"

Captain Reed let a high-pitched whistle emit from his throat before speaking in my language. "No. It would be bad to try. They don't take kindly to outsiders. They don't even take kindly to me."

"Do your people live in a totalitarian state?" Tiffany said, curious.

I listened to Captain Reed's words. I hadn't thought to ask him about his people, and knew that he might be the key to solving the Scandivat part of the puzzle. "We call ourselves the Scandivat, which means collective. The Scandivats exist as one thinking being. I'm one of the few who are born with enough intelligence to be considered separate from the whole.

"For every ten thousand mindless Scandivats, there is at most one of me, a Hunter. All Hunters are different than the others – all of us are alone. In my case, I'm an outcast, which makes me even more alone. The Central is the only entity within the Hive that we must answer to. All the thoughtless ones answer to us.

"I don't know what cataclysm befell the Central who spawned me, I'd been sent away to study your species. I know only that it must have killed her. Perhaps her premature death is responsible for the race war. Perhaps the actions of humans have cost the Central her life. The problem is that the Scandivat consciousness does not comprehend Humanity as being different. If a human did kill the Central, then they would think the whole Human Race responsible, and that could trigger a war."

"That's bad." Tiffany let out a worried little sigh. "So even if the human beings responsible have already paid for their crimes, then the race may continue on its destructive path until the new Central is aware of the difference in human social structure."

"Wow, this is way over my head." I said. "Why haven't you gone back and imparted your knowledge of human individuality to the

Central."

"Because I can't. I'm exiled. The link's broken. I've thought a great deal about this, and can fathom only two reasons. The first reason is that I wasn't present when the old the Central died, and therefore have no link to the new Central. The second is that the current Central has exiled me." Captain Reed clicked his jaws once. "I think the second reason is the most likely one – I could pose a threat to his control of the Scandivat Collective. There may be other possibilities beyond my comprehension."

I shook my head, trying to gain new knowledge from the old. "New mission. Mama, Papa, we're taking Captain Reed home. We're going to the Scandivat home world."

"My people are no longer on their home world." Captain Reed said.

"We need to go to your world and try to find out exactly why they've left." I explained.

Captain Reed set the coordinates into the navigation computer. We jumped unexpectedly into Otherspace, and I had to smile. "I take it we're on our way now."

"Yes." He said. "We'll be there in ten hours. Thank you for your help."

"If you wanted help, Captain Reed, why didn't you ask for it before?" Kotian said.

"I don't know that your human mind will understand, but when one has lived a lifetime in the Hive, one does not learn how to ask for help. Only how to give it."

Using the Otherspace laws of gravity to my advantage, I walked up the wall next to Captain Reed, staring down at him. "If you need help, you really need to ask us."

Captain Reed pulled his claws back into their pads, then touched my cheek. "Why are you doing this?"

My answer was instinctive. "Because it feels right."

"Did it feel right," Captain Reed said. "To leave your mate to another?"

"Sometimes things that feel right hurt like hell. Such things are best not discussed. At least not right now."

It had hurt to find out he didn't love me, it had hurt even more to see him leave me so soon after admitting it. Especially since I still loved him. Using Otherspace gravity laws, I walked up to the ceiling, then out of the room, leaving my parents and the Captain to discuss human emotions. I didn't care; I just didn't want them to see me cry. As it turned out, I didn't shed a tear.

Chapter 16

The *Persimmon* set down two hours early on the deserted world of the Scandivats. The air was bone numbingly cold, so we voted to stay aboard ship. They'd taken their agriculture with them, leaving massive tracts of land to erode from the elements. The Scandivat race had become such an integral part of the planet around me that it was dying without their presence. I said as much to Captain Reed, worried for the planet's future.

He clicked his tongue. "The Scandivat race would never violate a world like this. Something terrible must've happened. Our race genetics and consciousness must've changed drastically." He looked around him. "The heart of the colony is, no, was, thirty clicks magnetic north."

He led us back to the *Persimmon*, watching every shadow. The planet felt all but lifeless. Small bushes, a few herbivores, maybe the occasional predator. Nothing that seemed threatening to humans or our Scandivat friend.

Kotian looked at me, his heart aching. "I've never felt a planet like this one. If it wasn't for the atmosphere, I would think we were on Lotil."

Lotil, the lifeless moon of Friol, was a burned out cinder floating in space.

"This must be what a world becomes when it has no Forever Child guarding it."

We stepped into the *Persimmon* and flew under Captain Reed's direction. I caught my breath when I saw the size of the colony. Massive hexagonal slabs thrust skyward, jutting out of the ground. Like spires or turrets of a castle, they were dull gray, made of stone paste. Much like concrete, only coarser, we had to tune our sensors to its odd chemistry. The spires were connected at various points by irregular, twisting tubules that proved large enough for the *Persimmon* to fly through.

"Oh, my Goddess. Why is it so large?" Kotian asked.

Captain Reed answered from memory. "It was determined by the third Central that we would need to focus our species in one place if we were to survive and protect the resources of our world. One hive, one colony, one relatively small area of ecological destruction. We grew ninety percent of our food within the colony itself. Hunters, who had originally sought out food beyond the hive, were reassigned to structure and order the mindless worker classes."

As we flew closer, we found an entrance to the center of the colony, and the *Persimmon* flew in through it. Bodies lay decomposing at the gates, skeletal remains ripped apart by scavengers from beyond the colony. Captain Reed was neither upset nor surprised.

"The Guardians are the simplest of our race. Being designed for one purpose, they had to rely on Feeders to take care of them. They kept intruders out of the colony, but once assigned to guarding an entry, only death will remove them from their post."

"Sounds like a horrible retirement plan." Kotian said.

"Their brains are simply plotted for the sole purpose of brute force defense from the predators that still roam our planet. Because of the simple structure of their brain, they weren't true sentient thinkers such as myself. They also live less than a decade, making their life span significantly shorter than the centuries I'll live."

"Barbaric yet functional." Kotian said. "I like it."

We flew on for hours, Captain Reed setting the course. We flew deeper into the colony, using artificial light to guide us. There was no light in any of the chambers or halls, and sonar and radar weren't entirely reliable.

"My goodness, how did your people see in here?"

"Fire moss were kept healthy and in abundance. Though not true members of the Scandivat race, they were valuable assets to the hive. We fed them nectar and they emitted light for us to see by. They were undoubtedly harvested and taken with the colony when it left."

The colony ended abruptly, opening into something none of us expected. We were at the edge of a crater that extended a half-mile deep into the rock of the planet and two miles in every direction. "Was this here last time you visited, Captain Reed?" Tiffany said.

"Of course not, the Hive was complete then."

"Does anybody have a clue as to how we determine the age of this crater?"

The *Persimmon* answered. "I've studied the sensor readings closely, and by accessing the database, I've concluded that this can be the result of only one type of incident. This crater is the result of a natural thermonuclear detonation."

"What do you mean, natural?"

"The fission that occurred here was the result of a series of asteroid strikes – all happening within nanoseconds of each other. Trace remains of fissionable materials suggest that the asteroids were composed of unstable elements in crystalline form – uranium among them. The asteroids compressed and went fission upon impact, resulting in a thermonuclear detonation."

A map of the colony came up on screen, the area of damage highlighted in red. "This information is based on the colony outline as gathered from space." Tiffany said, a sickening overtone to her voice.

Captain Reed bowed his head. "The Central Complex and the northwest hub have been completely obliterated."

"This happened approximately three years before the Scandivat upsurge, or roughly forty years ago." I said. "It was recorded by Level Ringbreaker. He had sent a Forever Child to study the Scandivat culture, and to protect the new intelligence. It was generally assumed that the child had died in the blast. The Forever Child was never seen or heard from again."

Captain Reed made a sound somewhat like a sigh. "The damage would have destroyed the Central and the sentient Hunters. Our whole colony must have been in danger of extinction. The egg chamber was destroyed. Without a Hunter to go through transition and replace the

Central, the colony should have perished within a decade. If I'd only come home sooner, I would have been that Central."

"But something kept that from happening – a surviving Hunter, perhaps."

"Perhaps." Captain Reed said. "I felt no urge to come home, I had assumed that a new Central had risen to power. Then, when my contact was cut off for a second time, I felt exiled, and was afraid to return home."

"I've seen enough here." I said, turning my back on the screen. "Take us into space. We have to find the Scandivats' colony and stop them before they're destroyed. Plot a course for Friol, *Persimmon*. We'll follow their trail and try to gain more information."

The *Persimmon* broke away from the planet and escaped into space. The Scandivat were acting like a hive of wasps, aggravated by a child's well aimed stone, I had a sneaking suspicion that Wastik was the child in question. Captain Reed had said that the Scandivat did not understand human individuality. If Wastik had been responsible, then the entire Human Race would be blamed. Of course, that didn't explain how Wastik had united with the Scandivats, and for the moment I didn't care. Earth was the target of the Scandivats, and if they succeeded in taking Earth, Humanity might perish. If Wastik was responsible, then he was even more brutal a creature than I suspected.

I woke up on Friol, now rebuilding after the initial Scandivat attack. We settled in at my old home. Many of the cities would never recover. Alora, the Capital city, had been leveled, and so had Lute, the Center for Artistic Education. Jodiah greeted father and me, and was surprisingly cheery for a 150-year-old man who had just recently helped force back an alien invasion. Having somehow survived the attack, Jodiah smoked his smelly pipe as he explained to us what we had missed.

We thought it best to keep Captain Reed on ship. There would be little love for him on Friol, so soon after the Scandivat attack. Tiffany was still on ship making some minor repairs, but I couldn't wait to see

Grandpa, and ask him about his adventures. I'd missed most of the fight, getting mama and papa away.

Grandpa's leathery voice was filled with awe and confusion. "The ships came down from their mother ship like hornets seeking flesh. The sky turned dark, there were so many of them. The mother ship was as big as the sun, at least in perspective. And the damnedest thing about the entire attack was that after the Scandivats conquered us, stripped us of supplies, and killed the resistors, they took whatever they wanted and left. I'm living proof that they were only after raw materials. They took every person they captured and dumped them – still alive – in the remains of whatever city they assaulted. Same ilk as my Granddaughter, through and through."

"I don't have the foggiest what you're talking about." I said, trying to look surprised.

"Your reputation as a pirate precedes you. There's even a reward out for you. The Lenitians want you dead, of course. If they wanted you alive, I'd turn you in, collect the reward, and bust you out."

"You're so ornery." I said, pouting. Tiffany smacked Grandpa on the arm.

"What? I'd split the reward with her." He said, then mumbled, "60/40," under his breath.

"Papa, stop teasing her." Tiffany said, finishing her work on the ship. "How are you doing? Do you need anything?"

Jodiah gave her a loving hug, and set her down next to him on the bench. "Business is booming. Every insurance company on Friol is bankrupt, though, so I don't expect to show a profit for at least another two years."

"Hope you show a profit much sooner," Kotian said, "but we can spare some resources, if you need any help."

Grandpa, as always, ignored the offer.

"Where's the colony headed toward now?" Tiffany said.

"Using sub-teselar modulation drives, it's currently pushing its massive self on a course straight for Earth." Jodiah inhaled deeply on his pipe, and I started to succumb to the flavor of the tobacco.

"It'll take years to reach Earth at that rate." Kotian exclaimed.

"I don't think time's a concern for them. The colony will pass three worlds rich in the same materials they took from us. My guess is they'll take what they need to get to Earth. They won't get there for at least seven years."

"What planets do you think they'll go after?" I said.

"We've been watching them closely. The flight path is all over the news. But we aren't sure if they're really headed for Earth, or if they intend to change course for another world. My guess is that the colony can't support itself in space, and needs to attack worlds to stay alive until it reaches its final destination."

"Thus the rather long flight path. I'm going after them." I hugged Grandpa and left with a speedy good-bye.

"Why the rush?" Grandpa said.

"The fate of the Human Race is at stake. Even Seven years may not be enough time."

Captain Reed had already brought up the path of the colony on screen when we entered the bridge and set out to find Captain Reed's people. "I listened carefully to your father, and it appears our Central is using our original Harvesting technique on a galactic scale. It's strange that this Central showed mercy, however. It implies that the colony sees humans as equals, and not as prey."

"Is this a good thing?" I said, studying the incomprehensible data that Captain Reed used for navigation.

"Yes," Tiffany said. "If we were prey, Grandpa would be food."

"Oh." I thought about it for a moment.

I was about to issue an order when a small boy materialized between the command seat and me. He was dressed in a loincloth, his skin covered in painted red dots, each forming designs that made a mask of his face and a pattern across his chest and back. Adding to my confusion, he sat down in my command chair. His tiny teeth, strung like pearls behind his lips, were the most distracting part of his smile. His face was that of a pixy, and his hair had been combed by the wind.

"Hi, pretty Governor. It's a good thing you've finally gotten around to the mission you're on."

Tiffany was quick to scold the boy, taking him by the ear and dragging him out of my seat. "If you want to sit in the Captain's seat, you really should ask her first."

I sat down, and he crawled in my lap, smelling like honey and dirt. "I've never had an angel for a Governor before." He said.

"Why are you here?" Tiffany said.

"How do you pop in and out of reality like that?"

"You can do it – angels can do it any way – and humans, though I've only seen a few who've actually tried." He looked at my confused face. "Don't you remember?"

"I remember doing it – I just don't remember how." I admitted. "Why are you here? What's your name?"

"I'm Squire Lucas. I was supposed to give you something a long time ago, Level Ringbreaker wanted you to have it. I forgot." He pulled something out of mid air and handed it to me, his green eyes flashed in the sunlight, two green gems of uncertain clarity. "It's a clue, I think."

"Looks more like a flute to me." It was a piece of bamboo with a bunch of holes in it, the tube in question but a foot shorter than the boy who had given it to me was.

"It's a bamboo flute – from an Earth country called Asia, where Jupe was first found. You blow across this cut point at the top, and use your fingers to make music. The clue is that it belonged to Jupe. It should still work, but it's changed, and that means that Jupe's changed."

"I've never seen bamboo with such a glossy metal sheen to it. Who's Jupe?"

"Jupe was sent from Earth by Governor Ringbreaker to save the Scandivats from extinction. Only we think he was killed. But his flute's in one piece, so maybe he is too. It was abandoned near the colony. He'd never leave his flute behind. Jupe loved his flute. He believed it had magic powers."

"Maybe Jupe replaced it with another instrument."

"If he did then he's no longer the Jupe I knew. This was a gift from his best friend." Squire Lucas said.

"Great, one more thing to help me on my way."

The boy was excited now, and he snuggled close to me. "Yes, it will help you. I'm sure of it. Level was a smart man. Are you pleased with me?"

"Yes, I'm pleased."

The boy's face split into an incredible smile, and I fluffed his already unruly hair. Without saying good-bye, Squire Lucas vanished from the ship. I instantly missed his presence.

"It just doesn't make sense. If Jupe died in the impact, this flute shouldn't have survived. It looks pretty fragile. But it's changed somehow."

Kotian looked at the flute. "It's been through a lot. But if Jupe is alive, why would he leave the flute behind?"

Unable to answer, I tested it, and with a little practice I was actually playing a simple tune. It was a strange flute, with one hole on the back and four up front. The four up front were spread out so far that I had to play them with my first fingers and pinkies, and I had to stretch my hands to reach them all. Sure enough, the flute worked at my prompting. We breached Otherspace and continued on our course, and I stretched my wings, before letting them settle around me.

"Maybe the flute reflects Jupe's condition." I said, after some consideration. "If so then Jupe has changed a great deal. From the wear on the holes, he must have played this flute all day almost every day."

"A most fascinating linguistic device," Captain Reed said. "The problem is, you don't know what you're playing, and so your attempt at speaking in the tonal language has created a beautiful babble song for Hunter babies."

"You mean, if I played this just right, I could talk to you." I said.

"The scale is the one used in Scandivat communication. I'm certain I could teach you to talk to us."

"Where's Fluff when you need him most?" I said, old fears rising.

"Pounding his Elfin Princess, I imagine." Tiffany giggled.

I scowled at her, and she put a slim hand over her smiling lips.

I returned my attention to Captain Reed. "It's just that I'm not very smart. I mean, I barely passed Angelic. I couldn't express multilinear verbs to save my life – and that was in my native language. Fluff is the language authority. He can learn anything that has to do with words."

"Fluff isn't here – and you're the only student I have. I'm no Teacher, either. I'm a Hunter. We'll both grow stronger from this experience."

I looked at Captain Reed and he at me. His eyes were unblinking, and his voice unyielding.

"All right," I said. "Just don't eat me if I blow a note wrong."

In response Captain Reed laughed. At the time it sounded nothing like a laugh – only later would I learn the mirth behind the tones.

For a year I practiced, and struggled, and was constantly being spoken to only in Scandivat by everybody. There was no reprieve from the Scandivat Language during my lesson hours. *Persimmon*, the little traitor ship of mine, used her universal translator to trap everybody's words and convert them to the fluid language of the Scandivat race. I couldn't even answer in my native tongue; I had to use the flute. It turned my Galactic Standard into Yiddish – nobody on board could understand me without the flute.

I practiced every day until my fingers were numb, perfecting tone and overture. Depth and constancy became clearer in surges, giving me little pieces of confidence that were often badly needed. I learned about the structure and tonal qualities of the language of the Scandivats' colony, and with slow mastery gained the ability to relay emotion and abstraction through my song.

Each word was comprised of three notes, played in strange combinations that sounded nothing like music to the human ear. Sentences rarely exceeded twelve words, and the words were arranged all wrong. I felt like I barely learned the basic language when my patient teacher declared me "precocious," and started trying to teach me how to relay emotions through my song.

The year past, with much to do and too much to learn. I didn't engage myself in the battle between the Human Race and the Scandivats' colony, as that would have been fruitless. First, the Scandivats were simply too powerful for my ship and its crew to turn the tide. Second, I was very certain that as an angel I wasn't supposed to be at war, but seeking a peaceful alternative. I spent nearly three years increasing my reputation as a slave chaser, trying to find out as much as I could about Jupe from the Forever Children that crossed my path, and learning the nuances of the Scandivat language from Captain Reed.

On my fifteenth Birthday, I was given a duplicate of the flute I had grown so accustomed to carrying. My new flute sounded better to my ears, probably because it was mine, and after a few weeks I felt comfortable playing it. Father made me a hip harness for it, so I could wear the new flute opposite my sword. I put the old flute in a safe place, so I could keep my new flute with me.

The third year of study was the one of greatest turmoil. Two planets had been ravaged by the passing Scandivats' colony, and a third was preparing another futile defense initiative. And then things got terribly worse. The Lenitians were making slave runs in groups of three and four, so my duty as a pirate became more difficult.

The Scandivats' colony somehow managed to increase the speed of their encroachment on Earth. What should have taken four more years would now require only eighteen months. Earth was now target number one, and Isastan was the only planet where they could restock their supplies on the way. We jumped into Otherspace as soon as we learned of the acceleration, so that we could properly warn the Elves of their plight. We set down on Isastan three months ahead of the Colony.

King Lotus pulled me immediately into counsel. "Your reputation is growing, and we honor your courage."

I smiled, didn't know what to say, so I changed the subject. "How are my retired first mate and his wife?"

"The infamous Prince Fluff is currently with the Glory Elves in the Riley System, performing some nonviolent political protest." He paused. "The Princess, Goddess bless her, is pregnant, and should bear child soon."

Having heard enough, I cut to the chase. "I'm afraid I'm the bearer of bad news."

"Tell me your news." King Lotus said, his eyebrows wrinkling into a scowl of concern.

"My crew's been tracking the flight of the Scandivats' colony, and they've shifted their trajectory slightly. They've shifted course and adjusted speed. They'll reach Earth in a little under eighteen months standard."

"I was worried about this. Wastik managed to get a transmission to them, at about the time they picked up pace. We have made some preparations." King Lotus clicked his tongue.

"It's time to consider evacuating the surface."

"Elves never retreat." King Lotus said.

"I hate to say it, but your Elfin troops will be slaughtered if you choose to engage the Scandivat Hunter Class. They're a tough breed, and getting tougher as they draw closer to Earth."

"Where would we shelter? We can't escape into Otherspace, the colony has damaged the space for anything but space ship travel. We have angels arriving every day as more of Otherspace is corrupted. Sure, our ships can make it through, and your slaves get bopped home, but the entire library of angelic history is gone. The home of angels, it would appear, is more fragile than they imagined."

I thought for a moment. "Why not go to Earth?"

"What? Are you kidding? Earth society as it stands now won't make it into space for another century. We'll be slaughtered by the superstitious locals, long before the Scandivats' colony gets us."

Genesis flew through a window, settling down next to me. He put a hand on my shoulder, squeezing me. "There's another alternative I think both of you are overlooking."

"And what alternative is that?" I said.

"We could put enough supplies just outside the solar system to get them to Earth. Then they would move on and leave us alone."

"It's a selfish option, Genesis. What of Earth's safety?" King Lotus said.

"Let's solve the problems as they rise."

"I think Genesis has a good idea." I said.

"The Elves and all the fallen angels are going to defend Earth. We'll protect our world by setting the appointed supplies at the edge of the solar system, and defend Earth with our war forces."

King Lotus left me with Genesis, issuing orders and making preparations.

"So how goes the pirate biz?" He said.

"The slave runners are getting smart. But I'll figure out a way to put them down, just as soon as I get done with this little Scandivat problem."

Genesis laughed. "You're ready to try to infiltrate the colony aren't you?"

"Yes. I've learned the language. I just don't know enough about the colony, and none of the probes mother has sent out have gotten close enough to the main cluster to determine a safe way in. Captain Reed is worried that his presence might endanger us."

"Like a nest of bees adrift in space, there are countless stings for every exit and entrance." Genesis said. "If Earth falls to the Scandivat, so do we all. It may take a few centuries, but we human beings will all be extinct. Every Elf, every fairy, every human, and every angel is ultimately bound to Earth. When the Scandivats' colony settles on Earth, it'll destroy the ecology, and Earth will become the Scandivat's domain."

"And when that happens, Humanity will die." I inhaled deeply, not knowing what to say.

Before we could say any more, the temple shook from an exterior attack. I stood up and looked angrily at Genesis. "They shouldn't be here yet," I said.

Genesis flew out the window, and then flew back in. "The Colony isn't, but two assault cruisers are. I wonder what they're after?"

Our question was answered as we watched an Alpha Hunter Force leave their ships and descend into the castle prison, batting the Elves aside in their rush.

"They must be after Prince Wastik," I said angrily, rushing to stop the Hunters. By the time I got to the prison entrance, the Hunters had already gotten Wastik and were heading to their ships. They broke into Otherspace without even bothering to leave atmosphere. "He knew this was going to happen all along, didn't he?"

Genesis dropped to his knees, pounding his tiny fists against the pavement. "It's not fair. If he gets inside the colony, we'll never get you in."

I laughed. "I'll get in, if it takes every last bit of cunning I've learned as a pirate." I pulled Genesis up by his hands and drew him close, letting him put his head on my shoulder. My cotton blouse swallowed his hot tears.

"Hush child. I've some Elves to protect, and your tears aren't helping any."

"And how do you intend to do that?" He said. "With Prince Wastik free, the Scandivats might return to their psychotic attacks."

I looked at Genesis, my eyes serious. "Wastik's obviously allied to the Scandivats. When I find out how, I'll crush his alliance and set things right. You have to keep King Lotus focused on protecting his people. I'm going into space and asking that anybody who owes anything to the *Persimmon* call on their resources and defend Mother Earth." I said. "I know that it's a weak objective, but it's the best I can think of."

I returned to the *Persimmon*, and sent out a long-range transmission, using Isastan's main transmitter as a power base. Every planet in the galaxy with an Otherspace transmitter would resonate my message. I could only hope that people would listen.

"This is Captain Bit of the *Persimmon*. Anybody who cares anything for their lives must think of Earth. For centuries we have been away from the planet that spawned us, but we must remember that she is our mother. The Scandivats' colony ships have left their home world because of a terrible misunderstanding – one I am working to correct even as we speak. To save the Earth will take a united alliance of the entire human galactic community. We must show the Scandivats that we can unite as one against an outside force, and that we're willing to act as one when our future as a race is on the line.

"I know I've made enemies in this galaxy, and I'll not lie and say I'm sorry for my actions. I only hope we can stop the Scandivats before they destroy our ancestral home." I broke my communications link, then turned to my mother and father. "I'm going to the Scandivats' colony now. I can't ask either of you to go with me. I'd rather you stay here and work with King Lotus, where you'll be safe."

"How would you and Captain Reed fly the ship alone? You need us dear." Tiffany said. She didn't have to answer for both of them, I could see in Kotian's eyes that I'd have to fight him to get them off my ship.

I looked up at the screens. "*Persimmon*, take us to the colony."

"How come nobody ever asks me if I want to go on these crazy missions?" *Persimmon* complained.

"Well, do you? I could arrange another ship for this mission."

"Nonsense, my duty is with my Captain. I just wanted to be asked." *Persimmon*'s voice sounded contented, almost like a cat's purr.

I smiled as we slipped into Otherspace, heading straight for the colony. With my earrings, necklace, flute, and my knowledge, I felt ready to face anything. Anything, that is, except an army of Captain Reeds.

Chapter 17

The *Persimmon* was forced into Realspace by sub-teselar disturbances. Because of the colony's extensive defenses, we were forced to finish our trip without sensors – following one of the Scandivat's automated drones. I was awed by the efficiency of the Space Colony. Hexagonal crystals spread out into space in every imaginable direction.

The size of a small moon, and made of a clear version of the concrete used on the original Scandivat home, the ship glowed sublimely from within. Ships flew around it, and as we drew closer, Guardians guarded every sealed air hatch. I took up my flute, hopeful that I might gain an audience with the Central. We opened communications, and I played quickly, knowing our lives depended on it.

"This is Captain Bit of the *Persimmon*, returning a stranded member of your race to the colony. Hunter Reed is ready to be reintegrated."

"Why is it that Hunter Reed travels with humans?" The all-voice asked over an audio only linkage.

"We found him in Otherspace, adrift after an accident. We saved him and brought him here. This is his home, he belongs with his kind. He deserves to integrate." I played my response carefully, not wanting to sound like I was telling the Central what to do.

I'm certain I had an accent, though for the life of me I couldn't hear it. I knew I was a little more emotional than the Scandivat Collective

was.

Again, I had to wait. Tiffany twiddled her thumbs nervously, and Kotian had escape coordinates already plugged just in case our first attempt at peace fell through. Without Otherspace capabilities, we'd have to fight our way out of the range of their sub-teselar field.

"Well spoken – for a human. We will allow peaceful interaction for this purpose. Prepare for ship/colony integration." The audio connection terminated.

I smiled at my cunning. Once inside I had no intention of leaving, even if my ship did. I had to get to the Central and convince the sentience to take his people home. Tiffany and Kotian waited at the bridge while I escorted Captain Reed to the exit hatch. He clearly dwarfed the Hunters sent to wait for him, and they were in other ways built physically different from my friend. They had sharper edges and larger eyes. There were other, more subtle differences, in posture and motion that suggested something about Reed wasn't quite the same as his younger siblings.

"The human may now leavc the colony." The Hunter on the left whistled.

"The human would like to speak with the Central." I answered with as little emotion as possible.

Captain Reed spoke in my defense. "The Central will want to hear her words. Peace with the humans is necessary to continued survival. War will destroy the colony."

"The Hunter Reed has been corrupted." The Central determined. "Integration may be impossible."

Captain Reed was led away by one of the Hunter Guards.

I played my request. "Please let me to talk with the Central."

"Human relations have already been established. Negotiations have been made. Earth is to be the Colonial Home." The voice of the Hunter sounded somewhat guarded.

"Without Earth, the Human Race will die." I said.

There was a momentary pause, and the Hunter waited, frozen, as the Central consciousness came to a decision. "The Central will speak with you now."

The second I stepped beyond the air lock, the door sealed behind

me, and I felt completely vulnerable. Thousands of Harvesters shuffled around me, their hard, mindless bodies doing the routine work that our machines did for us. I don't know how many hours we walked. I found myself wishing for my wings.

The drone of chirps and communication overwhelmed me, and I kept my flute handy, just in case some comment was directed at me. When silence did come, so many hours later, it was the result of a hatch sealing shut. And leaving the workaday world of the colony. I was inspected thoroughly. Weapons were removed from me.

"Why do you carry two vocal interpreters?"

"It isn't a weapon, so it shouldn't concern you." I played, not wanting to part with the flute.

That sedated the Hunter, who left me with both flutes. After an hour, I was allowed to pass through the next door, but only with three Hunters escorting me. I found the treatment silly, because even one Hunter could have slashed me to ribbons a thousand times even if I had tried to break for the door or attack the Central.

When I stepped into the Central's chamber, I was thoroughly surprised. The Central was only about three feet tall, sitting in a human type throne. He looked almost like a human in insect's armor. He had a third eye, right in the center of his forehead. Two were dull red and one bright purple. Only a woman's sense suggested to me that he was male at all. The egg bearing females around me confirmed my sense.

One spat an egg from its ovary tract, seemingly content at its purpose. They were different than the Scandivats, their sole purpose was to lay more eggs, and their limbs were little more than fat covered stubs. The chamber was warm and moist, to help the process along, and I felt sticky sweat crawl down my back.

Feeders carried a sugary substance to the females, and occasionally one of the older feeders, after having expired all of its fluids, became part of the meal. Had the central been female, the breeder structure would have been different. Captain Reed had explained it all to me, to prepare me for these inhuman events. No amount of discourse can prepare one for such base cannibalism. Oddly, the feeder did not struggle as its body was crunched on and devoured. I looked away, waiting to be addressed.

He looked at me through his three eyes. “Human, you’ve been granted entrance. Why are you here?”

I felt it important that he know my name. “I’m Captain Bit, pirate and Governor of the Forever Children. I’ve come on a mission of mercy, in the name of Humanity.” I said with the notes of my flute. “Earth is the human home. Why are you taking your colony there?”

The Central chirped a few commands to the worker drones, then returned his attention to me. “Our race can no longer survive on our home world. A localized apocalypse has destroyed many of our resources and poisoned our fields. The atmosphere and surface has been severely damaged.”

“We went to your home world. It is true that it is dying, but it can be healed.”

“We have already had negotiations with a Human point of contact, how is it that the human Central can change its mind after so many years?”

“Humanity isn’t a centralized organism. I’m a separate entity, and so was the one who spoke to you. There is no the Central for humans.”

“There’s an incongruency. We must determine truth.” Within a few moments, Prince Wastik was ushered into the Central’s chamber, escorted of a Hunter carrying a massive metal mace.

“Hello, Wastik.” I said cordially.

“Hello, Captain Bit.” The Prince whistled through his teeth. “Is there a problem with this outcast?” He asked, then added in Galactic standard. “I’m surprised that you had the courage to come here. You can see my plan unfolding, can’t you?”

“This man is the outcast. He’s dangerous and cunning. He’s using you for his own devices.”

“This is the Human Ambassador. This is the true representative of the Central. We’re to share Earth with the Human Race. We were told that there would be some resistance by outcasts such as yourself, but that peace would be the inevitable outcome.” The Central whistled.

I looked at the Central, then at Wastik. He smiled cunningly. “The Central doesn’t understand Galactic Standard, and your precious Hunter friend is in a decontamination cell – and has no link to the central consciousness. He will stay separated for the good of the collective, until he dies. You've been a problem to me for quite some time. But there's nothing you can do now to save your precious Earth, and when all is done, my allies will rise up and crush the Scandivat Collective like the bugs they are – reclaiming Earth for the Elves."

"This man is insane," I played on my flute. "If you could only understand what he's doing." I could not allow him to harm them further.

I continued my explanation. "Two sentient species cannot successfully coexist on one home world as separate populations. We can share other worlds, but not home worlds. Wastik knows this and he intends to use you to destroy the local humans and others of our kind who don't fit into his quest for power. Then his allies will crush your kind, reclaiming Earth in his name. He's using you."

The Central clicked a series of commands, and two Hunters stepped onto either side of me. "Escort the outcast to her ship. I'll not tolerate her lies."

The Hunters were on either side of me, sharp claws exposed. I had to think fast. I drew Jupe's flute from my case. I bowed to the Central, as I would to Tester, leaving the flute at his feet. The Central stared down at the flute, uncomprehending of my actions.

"I'm sorry we couldn't agree." I whistled my good-bye. "There may come another. His name's Jupe and he can help you to heal your world. He was injured by the same blast that damaged your people. This is his flute, and he'll play it for you, should you let him. I'm sorry, but I can't allow harm to come to Earth or to your people. I must have word with this man."

I put my flute in its hip case and yelled out Wisdom's name. My armor fell away. I shifted to angelic form, and with a snap of my wings, jumped backward and rammed a stiff shoulder into Prince Wastik's solar plexus. I dragged him into Otherspace, where I could torture him for his cruelty. But Otherspace was dark, and I found myself stuck, unable to move because of shifted laws. Prince Wastik giggled insanely as he broke free of my weak hold.

"That was stupid. This was the reason I structured the colony propulsion systems the way I did. No chance of angels getting in my way." He laughed at me, his soft fingers stroking my face; finishing with a back handed smack. “The angels created Transcendence in Otherspace, making it the bright and beautiful place that it is – but you’ve been in it so long you can’t deal with the shift in laws that occurs when Realspace bleeds into your home dimension, resulting in Mixedspace and mixed laws.”

He punched me in the chest – right between my breasts. Like an insect trapped in amber, I couldn’t move. I was wracked with pain. The laws of Otherspace and Realspace were chaotically shifting and merging in this Mixedspace, and it would take time to learn to function and exist in such chaos. For now I was trapped. Prince Wastik could move, I merely had to discover his secret.

“Oh, I know you’re trying to figure out how it is that I’m not trapped. It’s simple, really. I had a lot of time to practice and perfect my moves in this Mixedspace. The first time I created the sub-teselar field, I was trapped for nearly a century in Mixedspace. Anybody can learn anything, given a century. I know its rules and incongruities better than anybody – I created this space.”

I stopped trying to move for a moment, looking into the distance. Worse than being in fog, I could not even see particles of mist. It was just an endless twilight, a plane without even the substance of thought.

“You’re not trying hard enough, Captain Bit.” He punched me in the gut, knocking the wind from my lungs.

Anger rose up within me, I couldn’t even figure out how to spit at him. I gasped for air.

“Do you have any idea the pleasure I’m feeling right now? Can you imagine what it feels like to kill somebody slowly, to work them over and watch them suffer?” He said.

If I were Tiffany I would’ve had a witty comeback. If I were Tester or Wisdom, I would’ve torn his head off and used it as a planter. But, being Bit, I could only struggle against the different laws of Mixedspace as he kicked me in the ribs and face.

“It was like this with the first angels who were too stupid to get out of our way. A few of them tried to stop me, tried to save their city. It was more of a challenge to kill them, however, because unlike you they actually possessed intelligence, and were able to adapt to Mixedspace. But what can I expect? You are, after all, only a child.”

"Stop gloating, and get it over with, you bastard." Blood trickle down my face; I could taste it on my lips.

"I like to gloat. It's fun. I have every intention of making you an example for anybody who might try to cross me in the future." Wastik punched me in the head, and I let out an uncontrolled yelp.

Wastik must have sprained his hand, because he rubbed his wrist for a moment. Just to prove he wasn't hurting too badly, he struck me again.

"We both know that only a very fortuitous circumstance brought my power about. If it weren't for two critical mass asteroids at the edge of the Scandivat solar system, the Scandivats' colony would have no need of a new home. Wasn't easy, pushing those asteroids out of their unstable orbits and spinning their incredible mass so they would strike each other and the Scandivats' colony with enough force to create a thermonuclear detonation. It took months of calculations."

"You're so smart." I said condescendingly. "At least you managed to tell me what part was broken. It's you, Wastik. Since you're the person responsible for breaking the universe, I'll have to fix you." Anger boiled in my blood, hot and intense.

"Like to think of it as upgrading, really. You know, remove the useless mash and make a few enhancements to the new ones. I knew that the angels and the Governor of the Forever Children would try contacting the Scandivats' colony, and send a Forever Child as an ambassador. I had to keep that from happening twice."

"So you killed Jupe and my parents, and the Governors before her."

"Oh, I did more than that. It took two asteroid strikes to kill your precious Forever Child and wipe out the old Central. I think the replacement is a grand example of ignorant youth, don't you? I slaughtered the Governors and the Elite Guardian Angels, leaving only the bureaucrats and the children to resist me."

I was shocked, and it must have shown through my beating. He looked at me, as if he had said something he regretted. Then he smiled wickedly, his eyes dark slits without a hint of sincerity.

"I'm sorry, I guess you didn't know that you're the last angel. You hadn't heard about that, had you? I'm afraid you can't call on angels for

help now. Without the Guardians, your bureaucratic race is frozen in place." He looked at me, his eyes feral. "The only Humanity that will remain is mine. My Elves will rule the world and humans will be a thing of the past."

"Not if I can help it." Genesis burst through a hole in the dark.

The local Otherspace brightened, and I felt my strength returning. It gave me a chance to collect my wits.

"How'd you get here?" Wastik asked, turning on Genesis. I kicked him in the butt, sent him spinning.

"Hurry Governor. I can't keep this place stable for long. We have to take our chances in Realspace."

Wastik recovered from my assault and he looked angrily at Genesis and me.

"I'll kill you both." He materialized a sword, ready to slice me in two.

The earrings started to glow, then fizzled, and I felt part of me tapped and drained by their effort. I was still too weak to defend myself, but Genesis jumped straight into Wastik's blade. The Forever Child was no fighter, and his wings were slashed to pieces in seconds. Genesis was left drifting in the center of his own blood splatters. The look of pain on his face was more than I could deal with, and my concern turned to anger and fear. White searing strength rose up from my soul. Genesis faded from sight, leaving Wastik and me alone once more.

Otherspace became Mixedspace once again, but my helplessness didn't return. I'd remembered to make a pocket of Otherspace around me, skin-tight and strong enough to force back the chaos. I was glowing with golden energy, Otherspace energy trickling from every cell of my body, and my strength returned to me. The earrings resonated and added their power to my protective field, and when I turned to face Wastik, he crouched down cautiously.

"You'll pay for what you've done." I said.

Reaching for my sword, and not finding it, I flew straight at Wastik, catching his blade with the flat of my palms. With a hard twist, I snapped his blade free, and sent it spinning into the Mixedspace void. I pounded him with both my fists. My tiny claws slashing cuts deep into his cheeks, his throat bled openly from a cruel swipe of my hand. Catching a punch and wrapping my legs around his waist, I twisted his arm until his wrist snapped at the joint. Still holding his arm, I pushed away, took aim with my knee and broke a couple of his ribs.

My hand locked around his throat and I hissed at him in anger. "You've killed enough."

He vanished from my grip before I could finish his wretched little life – not even his blood remained behind.

"You'll not escape me." I said. "Your cowardice won't go unpunished."

Genesis reappeared, unharmed. "Sorry it took me so long to get back. Where's Wastik?"

"I nearly had him, but he got away." I flew to Genesis and took him in my arms. His wings were misshapen and missing pieces. "What can I do?"

Genesis smiled at me. "This is an illusion. Wastik could never do me any permanent harm."

"I heard his conversation with you as I was working on a way to block off the sub-teselar radiation. If what he says is true, then young Jupe's in serious danger. If the Scandivat world dies, so does Jupe."

"So Jupe must still be alive." I looked at him, my eyes wide with terror.

"For now. I'll see you again. Take care, my friend."

The last of the Otherspace faded, Genesis vanished from my arms, leaving me alone in sub-teselar Mixedspace. Then the world flashed once, and I found myself on the *Persimmon*.

"Are you two safe?" I asked, falling to one knee. The *Persimmon* was in full combat, and obviously damaged. My mind reeled in pain.

Tiffany took me in her arms, ignoring the blood. "We're not out of trouble just yet. What happened to you?"

"Wastik is doing all this so he can rid himself of the humans on Earth. He hurt the colony; he's the piece that breaks other pieces. He must be fixed, along with the damage he's caused."

Tiffany held me close. "Can't fix a dark heart." She wiped the blood from my face with a handkerchief.

I put my head on the crook of her neck, about to cry. "Then I'll have to kill him."

Under Kotian's command, the *Persimmon* used its plasma cannons to pierce a hole through the colony defenses and fled into undamaged Realspace. We took more abuse in our retreat. The Scandivat, like so many wasps, attacked us from all sides, trying to draw us back to the colony. But Kotian would have nothing of it. I was too injured to take command, so Tiffany helped me to the medical cot and strapped me in.

The *Persimmon* fought onward, leaving a path of destruction in her wake. I hoped that none of the Hunters would be killed during our escape. As soon as the sub-teselar fields weakened sufficiently to allow it, the *Persimmon* fled into Otherspace, and I was taken to my quarters and treated for my wounds. I had two pieces of the puzzle – one that didn't fit, and one that had been shoved into the wrong place, but I still had only a rough idea of what the full picture would be.

Within my stomach was a lump that felt as big as my fist. Memories of the fight flooded my mind, traumatized me, really. Had Wastik stayed, he would have lost, but I was certain he wasn't using his full power on me. I didn't want to have to kill anybody, but Wastik wasn't giving me many alternatives.

Knowing the source of destruction, and knowing what I might have to do to end the suffering, it all made me sick.

Chapter 18

Mamma held my head in her lap until I fell asleep. She must have left me once I conked out, because when I woke up she was gone. We were drifting aimlessly in Otherspace. I didn't bother to get dressed – life on a ship could be so tedious. I walked around the ship, looking for my parents, and found them both working on damage done during our escape. The ship looked like it had seen better days.

"What's our status?" I asked through swollen lips.

"Sixty hours in Otherspace, and we're almost done with repairs." Kotian said. He looked at my face and ribs, my legs and back – still badly bruised from the beating Wastik had given me. "I think you should be in bed. You're lucky there weren't any internal injuries."

"When I get hold of that man, I'll teach him the right way to treat a woman," Tiffany said, shaking her fist to accent her emotions.

"Oh Mama, you worry too much." I said, thankful that she did. "Have the Elves begun evacuation of Isastan?"

"Yes dear. By order of King Lotus, all loyal Elves and fairies will be stationed in orbit around Earth. When told about Prince Wastik's involvement with the genocidal attack on the Scandivat Collective, most of Prince Wastik's allies have turned against him. Those few who didn't were quick to fly to the collective – a paltry dozen ships. The Elves will act as the final defense against the Earth's conquest."

"Final defense? Who else could possibly rise to defend the primitives on Earth?"

"You have quite a following. The Galactic Unified Guard and the Galactic Antislavery Coalition will be at the edge of the system to act as the primary buffer, regimented inward, all the way to Jupiter's orbit in four structured fronts. If it comes to war, they'll buy us at least three weeks," Kotian said, his hands moving in description.

"I take it I've been out of it for awhile," I said, holding my head.

"Three days and four nights in Realspace time, and you need to take it easy. You're still healing." Kotian said.

My ribs still ached, and I had to admit that the pain of moving made me feel a little woozy. I sat down, letting my breath out. "I'm really not made for this kind of life."

"We know dear." Tiffany said, her hands buried in an access hatch. "We found something that might cheer you up a little. A diversion from your harder tasks."

"Yeah, what's that?"

Kotian smiled. "Having beaten you so badly, Wastik wasted no time in trying to add insult to your injuries. He sent an encrypted trans-teselar transmission to Lenitia's most cutthroat slave runner. It seems that the Scandivat Collective is going to purchase human slaves for integration into their colony."

I smiled. "And it would be a real thorn in his side if Captain Bit threw him a little party."

"Yeah. There should be no more than two cruisers present, and we figured it might give you a chance to thwart some of his plans."

"I'll do more than that." I thought, rubbing my ribs. "When's this great ordeal supposed to happen?"

"We're on course for interception now. We'll be meeting them just two days out of the Lenitian Central System. We'll be vulnerable to their law enforcement, so we'll have to move in quick and scramble back out." Tiffany said, secured an access panel, and patted *Persimmon* affectionately. "There you go, big girl, all fixed up. You ready for a little action?"

The *Persimmon* chirped an affirmative, and I felt a little of my strength come back.

"Let's go get 'em." I giggled mischievously.

Persimmon hummed into Otherspace, and I set my mind to performing one of my secondary tasks: abolishing slavery from the galactic community.

The *Persimmon* broke out of Otherspace with weapons locked and tethers firing. Prince Wastik's ship fell prey first, struck by four steel cables. The tethers locked solid, and the Scandivat ship was caught by the power of the lines. I cheered as Kotian aimed the other end of the tethers and fired them into the Lenitian ship, thus pinning both ships together.

I opened communications. "This is Captain Bit, pirate superior. Surrender to your destiny."

Prince Wastik answered in person, seated in a throne much like his father's. His hand was tightly bandaged. I smiled savagely, remembering the popping sound his wrist made as I snapped its bones.

"Oh, poor baby. Did you bruise your noble hand while we were rough housing the other day?"

"You broke my wrist." Wastik said, vehement.

"I know, and it was fun. We set those tethers strategically. If you try to escape, it'll tear both your ships apart." Tiffany said.

I was mildly surprised to see Commander Barrot, transmitting on a second channel. "Barrot, I'm so surprised to see you on a slave ship. Weren't you working in law enforcement last time I talked to you?" I was more than sarcastic, having him at my advantage.

"Slavery isn't illegal on Kottana. It's a side job." He said. "If I get free of these tethers, I'll give you a little lesson in law you won't soon forget."

"But you won't get free of those tethers. I don't like people who try to trick me, Commander Barrot. The child you sent me to capture is safe now."

"The boy was worth a year's salary to me. Had a special buyer set up. You cost me, girl." Commander Barrot smiled at me, as if hiding something.

"And firing on us will cost you more. I'll put the *Persimmon* to ramming speed and cripple both your ships in the process." I said.

"I thought you liked to be in control, Wastik. Why are you letting this human do all the talking, and why human slaves?" Kotian said, his tone a near balanced mix of curiosity and loathing.

"Upon seeing how Bit resisted me, I decided that the strong human frame might serve the needs of my hospitable hosts. Commander Barrot keeps his private stock on Lenitia. We were merely meeting here to make financial arrangements."

I sensed derision in his voice. It made me feel uneasy. "I really do wish you'd try to escape into Otherspace." I said. "We both know what'll happen to you if I get you on my turf."

"You'd like that, wouldn't you?" He'd timed his stalling perfectly. My ship's warning alarms went off, and enemy ships materialized out of Otherspace.

Wastik leered at me. "You really surprise me, littlest angel, falling into a trap like this one. Just like your kind – gullible to a fault." He cut communications, and I turned back to Kotian.

"What's going on?" I asked.

Tiffany grimaced. "Twelve high speed fighters, Lenitian combat design. Closing in fast from all sides. They've dumped a teselar beacon; we won't be able to pull the entire ship through to Otherspace. No slaves on any ships, we walked into a trap, I'm afraid. We're going to have to fight this one out. I really don't think we stand a chance."

"Raising shields, readying weapons." Kotian's hands were a blur of light across the weapons console.

"Get us around and ready for a fight." I said.

Tiffany's hands flew across two keyboards, and her face betrayed a decision made deep down within her.

I looked around the bridge, trying to think. "*Persimmon*, why didn't we detect them sooner?"

"They're police craft equipped with inertial dampers and sub-teselar cloaks, closing in perfect unison. They were well hidden." *Persimmon* said.

"Papa, can we blast our way free?"

Kotian smiled, studying thousands of strategies that the computer was busy calculating. "They haven't left any openings, and they're superior in arsenal. It's hopeless."

"What?" I didn't believe him. "There's got to be a way. We fought our way out of the Scandivat's grip."

"Darling, the Lenitians have superior technology. The Scandivats don't." Kotian looked at me, his eyes aglow with a power I couldn't comprehend. "Listen to me, baby. Mother and I've already died once. We came back for this moment. You need to escape into Otherspace, fly away. Use your angelic powers and get out of here. We'll give them a bitter fight, and buy you some time. If we get out of this alive we'll find you. If not, we'll always love you."

The *Persimmon* shuddered under the combined assault of three ships. Soon the two tethered ships were cut loose and added their own firepower to the pot. Tiffany wasted no time in retaliating, two of the fighters were forced off course, and Kotian plotted a high-speed maneuver that would put the *Persimmon* at the heart of a combined attack.

"Get into Otherspace, dear, it's your only hope."

"I'm no coward." I said.

Tiffany looked up at me; Kotian had gotten us through the center of the battle with little damage, and was turning the *Persimmon* around for another strike. The center rapidly shifted, putting the *Persimmon* back into jeopardy.

"You're our only child. We expected a possible trap, so we took measures." Tiffany said, diverting energy to the shields and weapons.

"This is our true time."

"Go." A voice hissed in my head. I looked around; thinking it might be Tester.

When I turned back, Tiffany's eyes bore straight into mine. "I could never give you anything but life, we were always poor. You returned that favor by giving Sparrow and me a little extra time together. Now let us do our job and protect our only daughter. Let us live or die doing what we should have been doing all along – protecting the one thing that made our lives whole."

"No. . ." I said.

"Go." The voice repeated itself, almost hostile.

I went. Whether it was Tester's voice, the voice of destiny, or my own cowardice, it no longer mattered. Mother and Father behind me, I ran to the engine room. I couldn't get safely off ship without some help from the *Persimmon*.

"*Persimmon*," I said, trying not to cry, "focus an Otherspace pocket around me, and project me as far away from this mess as you can."

"Yes, Captain. It was an honor working with you."

I felt myself shift into my angelic form, my body blown into Otherspace. My body was pulled back into Realspace by the power of the teselar beacon. I kept my angel's body, immune to Realspace, watching helplessly from a distance. The teselar field kept me from escaping completely – I'd have to get out of range of it to slip into Otherspace.

Nobody could've expected my body's expulsion through the teselar field to leave a glowing ion trail, but it did, and the enemy would notice it, even in battle. The ships were visible in the distance; each lit up clearly every time they fired their weapons. The light either dispersed or pierced through a thin bubble of energy around each bird-sized vessel. I looked along the path I left behind, an arch of light dispersing rapidly into the vacuum.

Wastik's ship broke away from the fray to come after me. *Persimmon* sat still, pinned in position by the remaining four ships. She had destroyed the rest. She wasn't even flying now, her reserves were probably depleted, and she lay in space, putting round after round into the remaining enemies. I flapped my wings, but the teselar field kept me in Realspace, and my wings only caught the solar wind. I would have to try to break the power of the teselar beacon before Wastik's ship came within weapons range.

My heart caught as I realized that the *Persimmon* was too damaged to help. Wastik's ship was closing in fast, and death wouldn't come slowly this time. Wastik's weapons charged to full, targeting me. My body field, emanating from my psionic synapses, could keep air around me and thus protect me from the void, but it wouldn't protect me from a focused plasma blast. The stones, amplifying my power, could protect me in a fistfight. I doubted that any of my powers could protect me from Wastik now.

The *Persimmon* stopped firing at its enemies, dead in space and I knew I would be next. I didn't have time to close my eyes and wait for the inevitable, wait for the *Persimmon* to be taken and stripped of its resources. I would be dead long before that, once Wastik got his shot off. I stared down the plasma cannon, a dark black square that slowly brightened as it charged for the strike.

The *Persimmon* blew up with such an incredible force that the ships nearest to it were vaporized in the flash. The thermonuclear wave spread out from the center as one massive sphere, and I closed my eyes and curled into a fetal ball, wrapping my wings around my body instinctively. My head swam in the pure light, and when I opened my eyes, I could see only devastation and debris.

The *Persimmon* was gone; no evidence remained that it had ever existed. "Mother." I yelled. "Father. I'm not worthy of such devotion."

I lay in the fetal position, my wings flexing out just enough to set me adrift. Wastik's ship was nowhere to be found, but the remains of the Lenitian ships made my body shake. They were little more than skeletal remains of once great fighting ships. Most of the ships had been vaporized in the blast. Those that remained were slagged metal frames, still molten in the aftermath.

Tiffany and Kotian's faces were superimposed on the blast in my memory, their souls freed forever by the terror. There would be no restoring life to them now, I doubted they would come back even if I could bring them. The bell around my neck should have been resonating in response to the death, and when I looked down at it, I saw why it lay mute.

Something in the blast or in its nature had caused it to shatter. Perhaps it had protected me from the blast. I could only theorize the full power of the lost talisman. I pulled the thong from my neck and tossed it into space. The teselar vibrations died down just after the blast. I could've left at any time, but instead I drifted in Realspace for untold hours, in a stupor.

I couldn't cry, I had no more tears to shed. I felt no remorse. My mind shut down completely. I could have floated forever, the Otherspace bubble constantly replenishing my air supply. But I had a war to stop, now more than ever. After several minutes more, I shifted into Otherspace, and once there, the tears flowed. I felt a soft hand on my shoulder, and when I turned I was looking into the animal eyes of a strange but familiar face.

"We have to go to Isastan's fifth moon."

"Why?" I asked, my head still in a fog.

He smiled at me, suddenly shy. "It's time for you to meet some old friends." His pale face and powerful eyes were familiar to me, but my scattered brain, pushed to its limits by stress and loss, couldn't quite place him.

It occurred to me that this cat-eyed Elf was astonishingly attractive. I mumbled something incoherent.

"How fast can you transcend Otherspace?" He said. "Without wings I am kind of slow."

I felt forever lost in those bewitching eyes, each a shining disk of gold. I put my arms around his strong chest and flapped my wings powerfully. His Elfin ears and milk-pale skin gave me pause as he looked up at me.

"You were at the ball, weren't you?" I said, memory finally serving me.

He smiled back at me, hanging limp in my grip. "Yes. I came here by order of the King himself."

"You never told me your name," I said.

He remained silent, looking toward our destination. Elfin minds are very different from their angelic and human counterparts. The result of culture, I've been told. Still, I found it rude that he didn't tell me his name, especially after admitting that he knew mine. I carried the nameless Elf through Otherspace, the sky blue as day, but with no sun in sight. A dot grew rapidly into a person as I approached it. An Elfin lady dressed in a formal gown waited for me in Otherspace. Carrying a scepter with a fist-sized jewel at its top, she also had a crown speckled with diamonds, emeralds, and a single blood red ruby seated at its center. She put her long fingers around my hands.

The pale-skinned Elf turned to vapor and dispersed, leaving the woman myself alone in Realspace. Within a moment I found myself in human form, surrounded by well-dressed women who immediately started measuring my proportions and scribbling down notes.

"What's going on here?" I said.

"Your clothes were destroyed in the explosion. With a formal ceremony to attend, what little you're wearing just won't do." The woman with the ruby crown answered.

I looked down at myself, then back up at the Lady. Her face was perfectly symmetrical, and her body a pear shaped epitome of grace and balance. Her skin was white as ice; her eyes were black as pitch.

"I don't seem to have any clothes at all."

"How very observant of you." Her voice was so absent of emotion that I had no way of knowing if she was being sarcastic or not.

"Just what is this function?"

"I'm the Duchess Maizo, head seamstress of the eminent King Lotus. By order of the King, you're to choose a suitor."

My jaw dropped. "What?" I exclaimed, pushing one of the Elfin maidens aside to face the Duchess straight on. "I'm no subject of the laws of the Elves. I follow no king." Nobody was going to put me through another one of those formal ceremonies, if I had any say in the matter.

"I'm sorry that you feel this way." She snapped her fingers, and the tailors finished their measurements. "But the choice, in this instance isn't yours, and because of recent events, you're now subject to the King's will."

My head dropped. "And who filed the paperwork making me an Elfin citizen."

"No paperwork was filed." The woman put a hand on my bare shoulder, spun me around, studying my body. "A request was made of the King, and he granted it."

"Who made this request?" I asked.

The woman said nothing. Within twenty minutes, a full uniform had been crafted and tailored, specifically to my needs. The white silk blouse looked more feminine than my other uniform. Upon close inspection in the mirror, I realized that my human form had matured a little. The pants, made of black and baggy cotton, accented the silk well. My soft suede shoes were the exact same shade as the pants. Once dressed, King Lotus entered from the left corridor, his lightly pigmented skin and ancient looking eyes glistening with pride.

"You truly are beautiful, aren't you?" He turned me full circle, "A dashing and beautiful pirate."

"Thank you, sir." I said. "Now can you please tell me why I've been brought here. I may be an Elfin citizen, but it'll be a dark day in Otherspace before I bow to you."

"Nobody's asking you to, dear." He said, chuckling. "By Goddess, an Elf hasn't bowed to his King in nearly seven centuries. I officially outlawed it at my coronation, three decades ago."

"So what's all this news about me having to choose a husband?" I asked.

"Guess I'd better fill you in." He took me to a set of chairs and we both sat down. "At the last Choosing, while you were busy eating countless trays of food, in what I guess was an attempt to burst your stomach and thus commit suicide, your mother and father approached me with a request. It seemed odd at the time, but I'm respecting the request made to me. Your mother asked me that if they should die, would I please take you as one of my daughters.

"At first I thought of refusing. I told her I would think about it, and give her an answer when the ceremony was closing. A King having a pirate for a daughter is practically unheard of, and I hardly knew what kind of pirate you were. When you jumped between the bride and groom, ready to lay down your life for both of them, my decision was made.

"Due to the proximity of the Scandivat colony, our time's limited. We have to combine three formal occasions into one. You're an Elfin Princess now, and must be ceremonially linked to me as a daughter. As is tradition, Elfin Princesses choose their life's mate at sixteen. You are now sixteen, as your mother indicated your birth date in our discussions at my daughter's time of choosing. Of course, supplies are limited, we won't have nearly as much food for you in this ceremony."

I blushed. "I was upset is all."

"The final ceremony's your wedding," King Lotus said, sounding excited.

"Hold it. Stop the star cruiser, and check with the navigator. What did you just say?"

"You're sixteen, it's time to choose a life's mate." King Lotus, crossed his arms, as if defensive.

"I really don't know anybody well enough to marry them." I insisted, trying not to look like I was pouting.

"That's my concern, not yours. I've spared too much time for you already, and I've other matters to attend to. It'll become apparent as the hours commence and the celebration begins." King Lotus rose, squeezed my hand affectionately, and started to leave.

"Answer one question. I know you figured out my parents were dead. That didn't take a genius, it was probably transmitted all over the galaxy by the Lenitians as they popped open the bottle of bubbly and celebrated their victory. But why is this going on now, in the middle of a war for the survival of the Human Race?"

"Your parents made a request, and I'm seeing to its fulfillment. The ceremony will be three hours long. May you enjoy it as much as I did at your age."

After he left, I paced back and forth. "Why me?" I grumbled. "First I'm an angel, then a human, I became pirate, now I'm supposed to be an Elfin Princess."

"It isn't too difficult, dear." The Duchess said.

"Yeah," Uruza said, from behind me. "If I can pull it off, anybody can."

"You know, you looked a lot older than sixteen when I saw you."

"Elves mature quickly, and then don't age for a long time. It's hereditary." Uruza said.

"Where's Fluff?"

She smiled. "Men aren't allowed in the woman's sewing room. He's roaming around. It's a pity you missed the wedding. I'd hoped, after you saved our lives, that you'd stick around long enough to be invited."

"Things are weighing a little heavy right now." I said.

She led me into the ballroom. I took a moment to take a good look around the room. Pillars of stone rose up to a ceiling I would have to use my wings to touch, and the floor was of the blackest polished basalt. Besides the tapestries, the room held little appeal for me. I looked at one, with a knight whose eyes were like a cat's. He looked a lot like a new young friend of mine, only this knight was much older and wrestling with an angel. Despite the dark symbolism, the tapestry seemed playful.

"That's the Knight Wheaton, last of the Paladin Elves. He wrestled an angel for thirty days straight to gain the knowledge of Transcendence for my people, and grant us the right to leave Earth and start our life on

Isastan. Some say he's the Champion of the Elves, some believe he championed for the future of the humans. It just depends on who you're talking to." Uruza explained.

"Thirty days? If I were the angel it would have been over a lot quicker." I looked closely at the angel in question. "But it had to be Wisdom."

Always the prankster, Wisdom wouldn't give anything up without the situation becoming in some way ludicrous. I felt myself about to cry. For the first time ever, Uruza expressed something akin to a human emotion.

"What's wrong?" She asked. "A hero shouldn't cry."

"I'm not a hero yet." I said, trying not to sob. "It's just that everybody I care about is gone."

"Heroine, pirate, Princess, and angel. Someday even more. Be proud of your actions."

I looked away from the tapestry. "Let's get these festivities under way."

Uruza slammed her hand onto my back. "Come sister, let's go into the pack of wolves and tame them."

I tried to fathom the Elfin phrase, but the picture it created terrified me, so I put it aside. It took me very little time to realize that Elves, as a culture and a race, could be harsh. As I stood there, it finally sunk into my head that my parents were dead. Captain Reed, my only remaining friend, was a prisoner of his own people. Prince Wastik had seen to it that every person I ever cared about was either dead or dead to me.

Yet in the middle of all that turmoil, King Lotus became my father. Arranging my mate, my marriage, and giving me a new family, King Lotus knew full well that when the ceremony was over, I'd have to leave, with or without my husband. MY duty was obvious. I would have to infiltrate the Scandivats' colony again, and put an end to their attack on Earth. And that would mean leaving everything King Lotus had given me behind. The Elves, I tell you, are harsh. But sometimes harsh is a good thing.

Chapter 19

I looked around the ballroom, trying to take in every detail. The room seemed bigger than before, and more crowded than I remembered it. Though I knew nobody around me, they all greeted me by sight. Civilians bowed to me in courtesy; officers saluted me as if I was one of the ranks. There was significantly more food on the dining tables scattered at the edge of the dance floor, perhaps in response to my last visit.

The ceiling was one massive slab of white marble supported by pillars of hard green jade. The pillars were set with widened bases into recesses in the building's foundation. The entire floor of the chamber seemed made of a solid slab of transparent, golden flecked stone that looked and felt like amber, though not even a thousand trees working overtime could have produced so much sap. All were polished so well I could see my own reflection when I looked for it. It seemed odd for me to have missed so much detail the last time I'd been at the ballroom.

The King sat at his throne, carved out of a pillar of the same flecked amber as the floor, trimmed with jade and white marble. He stared past the crowed, and I absently followed his gaze. An entire wall of the building was a well-polished window. The window looked out onto the beautiful gardens of Isastan's fifth moon. Isastan and the other four moons were all visible through the window.

I brought my attention back into the ballroom. Lights hung at random heights like distant stars. Tapestries lined an amethyst wall opposite the glass one. Sometimes two could be hung on one panel of polish stone; sometimes one was so large it took an entire segment of wall for itself. I worked my way closer to the tapestries, entranced.

I found myself lost in their complexities. "This place is beautiful."

I said to Uruza.

"The Elves ecostructured this moon and built the dance hall in honor of their home temple on Earth, lost to the expansion of humankind into what is now known as the Middle East. It is the highest dance hall in the Elfin kingdom, both literally and figuratively. Only great people may attend these formal celebrations, beyond Isastan's clouds." Uruza seemed to be looking for somebody.

She waved to Fluff, and he came to her side. He'd grown since the last time I saw him, and still he was probably three inches shorter than Uruza. He wore the uniform of an Elite Military Officer of the Elfin High Forces. Uruza seemed proud of her husband, doting over him.

"I missed you so." He said, saluting me.

"What are you doing in a Combatant uniform?" I said.

Uruza smiled. "Fluff's the Adjutant in charge of the fourth rank of Earth's Defense Corps."

"Oh." I looked away.

A drum beat three times, echoing through the hall, and Uruza smiled at me. "It's time to meet with father."

Taking me by the arm, she drew her sword, clearing a path. If somebody wasn't paying attention, Uruza would simply smack them with the flat of her blade on the rump, forcing them aside by humiliating them. We walked for what seemed an eternity through the crowd. The entire dance hall probably spanned five hundred yards along its outer walls.

When we reached the King's side – several minutes later – the Elfin court shouter announced my name. I would call him a screamer, but his voice was controlled and almost musical, despite its volume. Not much he said made sense, until he got to my name, which apparently had no translation into the Elfin tongue. Everything he'd announced previously he then translated into Galactic Standard.

"The great and mighty Pirate Captain Gracie Bit Alderman has come forward today by order of the merciful and just King Lotus, Lord of all Elfin kind." Uruza gave the man a quick look, and he saluted her, then surrendered his shouting position.

Where the man had been controlled and melodic, Uruza's was the voice of a drill instructor, concise and disregarding. "Today we Elves of the high and noble clan of Lotus accept, by order of the Great Spirit and request of her parents, Gracie Bit Alderman into the Family of the Lotus. I ask any man or woman who challenges this sacred acclimation to come forward and face me, the greatest warrior of the Lotus Clan, in armed or unarmed combat."

The crowd was silent for a length of time. I couldn't even hear breathing, except, of course, my own.

The King rose from his throne and extended his hand to me, expecting me to take it. I did, instinctively.

"As was prescribed, we've allotted the sacred three minutes for any complaints to rise. Behold now, my daughter, Gracie Bit Alderman Lotus, first pirate of the noble family of Elves."

Cheers shot out across the crowd, and I was swept away by my reception. "Why are they cheering me so loud?"

"You'll find out soon enough. The first eighteen people in line will get to express the reason for their exuberance." Uruza said. Still at my side, Uruza's sword was back in its scabbard. I wondered where her kid was, but didn't get a chance to ask before the thought flitted out of my mind yet again.

The entire Elfin, alien, and human mass broke into a distraught and chaotic ramble as out of thousands, eighteen fought to be first in line. Strangely, not only was nobody seriously hurt, but if it even looked like a child was going to get in the way, the nearest person sacrificed his or her struggle to line up by taking the child out of the throng. If somebody fell, they were helped up, patted on the back, and carried aside. It took five minutes for eighteen people to line up.

The first person to come forward had tears in her eyes. It was a rare sight for an Elf to be crying, so I wondered how I could possibly have inspired such emotion.

"My boy was kidnapped by Lenitian slavers, and your name was on his lips when he fell out of Otherspace into my arms. I've since heard a hundred tales of families reunited with lost loved ones because of your actions." She kissed my cheeks, then moved quickly on.

Others past, saying nothing but thanks for all my efforts with the Scandivats. Then one man paused, a man who didn't strike a memory anywhere in my mind. His eyes filled with respect that somebody far beyond my years deserved. He shook my hand over courteously, almost too shocked to give his thanks. When he did speak, it took him considerable effort to get his words out.

"I was a Lenitian Slave Disciplinary Guard. You raided my ship, managing to capture all of us and bring harm to nobody. You might remember me, I was beating an unruly slave when you burst in on me. You were upset. I thought, by the look in your eyes, that I was going to die.

"Instead you shoved me into Otherspace with the slaves. 'Contemplate Honor,' you said. I did, floating in Otherspace for Lord knows how long. Instead of returning to Lenitia, I found myself on Friol, and my life began anew." He kissed my cheek, his breath soft against my ear.

The last in line was Fluff. His left eye was nearly swollen shut, probably from an elbow to the cheek. He had to fight with all his cunning to get even the last place. I didn't want to hear anything he had to say. It still hurt, even after so long, to think of him as Uruza's.

"I owe you my happiness. Thank you for saving Uruza's life. Thank you for the sacrifices I am told you have made in defense of my honor and my life." He kissed my forehead and left me.

My gaze drifted to Uruza, but she was distant. She followed Fluff to the dance floor, leaving me with her father, my father. I studied them for a moment, fighting a dizzy spell. The King startled me half out of my wits.

"He may not remember, but he cannot forget." King Lotus said.

I felt the room start to spin, and I reached out awkwardly for support. King Lotus took me by the elbow and hand and helped me sit for a moment. The musicians had started playing, and the men and women were dancing. When my senses came back, I realized I was sitting in the King's stone chair. I looked up at the King, apologetic, rising and regaining my senses.

"I hate those thrones," King Lotus said. "Have any idea how cold that stone can get?" We laughed together, and he looked around the room. "So many suitors, and I must carefully choose nine. This is the ceremony where you're supposed to ignore everybody around you, and yet be the center of attention at the same time. A difficult task, but I'm sure that you'll manage. Now go away. I'm busy."

I walked to the center of the dance hall, ignoring the people who danced around me. Oddly, they got out of my way. Men winked at me, women glared at me in dark envy, and I ignored it all, studying the tapestries on the far wall.

"Some of those tapestries took two centuries to complete." Genesis said, startling me.

I hadn't noticed him; I was so caught up in the festivities. His wings had healed, and he wore a simple cloth wrap that covered his chest, the back between his wings, and everything down to his knees on both sides. It looked a little like a kilt, and a little like a toga. A belt kept it in place. He snapped his wings back and forth, flaunting.

"Had to shed my old ones and grow new ones. The design is different, but do you think they're just as beautiful?"

"Yes, of course." I said. "Is there any chance you might become one of my suitors?"

"Child, I'm eons past my prime." Genesis giggled.

I pouted for a moment, then thought better of any emotional attempt at manipulation. "Yeah, I understand." I winked. "The wing patterns are beautiful."

Honestly I couldn't see a difference, but if my orange skinned friend could, who was I to argue? He left me then, and mingled with the crowd. I saw no men with the flowers. It was like they were hiding from me. Nearly forty-five minutes past and then the drum beat nine times, and nine young men gathered around me in a circle that suddenly felt tight as the collar of my uniform. They were nine men, but there the similarity ended.

It wasn't in my nature to treat anybody like cattle, so I couldn't walk around in a mood like Uruza had. Three of the men were human, three fairy, and three elf. I tried to put myself in their place. The event must be dehumanizing for them. I wondered if male suitors went through the same event. I doubted it. Clearing my mind, I decided it was time to focus.

I walked toward the King, bringing myself to the man at the top of the circle. A human, he smiled at me nervously. His face was attractive; he seemed curious and afraid. He wore a uniform I had grown accustomed to – The Galactic Unified Guard. They were supporters of the Antislavery Coalition. The crowd was full of them, some on duty, some part of the festivities.

"Who are you?" My voice sounded more like Uruza's than I expected.

"Strike Sergeant McCatherly. I'm in the Alpha Division of the Galactic Unified Guard." The man said, smiling.

I kept my smile small, and moved on. I wondered what I was supposed to be finding in these people. The Elves were rumored to soul link, could I? The next man was a young merchant who worked for King Lotus by traveling across the galaxy in search of exotic building materials. I had to stifle a yawn as he shifted his discussion into the technical aspects of his job. Fortunately, he kept his conversation to a few brief sentences, or I might've had to rudely cut him short.

I talked with two more Elves, one more human, and all three fairies, all of which were about half my height and never spent any decent part of their lives with their feet on the ground. Their wings buzzed endlessly as they spoke. My last choice stood with his head down, as if afraid to look at me. I figured that unless he stole my heart completely, I'd have to settle for the larger fairy; he and I were of about equal intelligence, though I think he was just slightly smarter.

I looked at the last Elf for the longest time. He kept his face hidden by his posture. I took his chin in my fingers and gently pulled his face to mine. It was the very young man with deep golden eyes. His eyes were like Wheaton's, from the tapestry, his face as smooth as mine.

"You never did tell me your name." I said to him, letting my hand drop away.

His eyes studied me, and he licked his blood red lips nervously. "You never asked."

I thought about it. I had never actually asked him, I had only implied indirectly my desire to know his name. Elf minds could be so literal – yet another flaw of a culture so structured by harsh and often ludicrous traditions.

"I'm asking you now." I said.

"Eohl Level Wheaton. An artist and metaphysical scientist." He bowed slightly. "Nothing I've done can compare to your accomplishments."

I giggled, covering my lips. "All of these men are three years older than me. How old are you?"

"Only thirteen." He said.

"What kind of art do you do?" I wondered.

"A little sculpture. I paint, too. I really like to write poems and stories."

"Quite the Prodigy. Must be super smart." I took his hands, testing their softness.

He smiled. "I am. But it's lonely being smart. It would be nice to have a lot of friends."

My eyes darkened with sorrow for a moment. "The price of popularity is high. So what do you think, could you and me make this happen?"

"I think so."

Still holding his hands, I drew him close, and put my forehead against his. "There is too little art in my life." I kissed him.

He seemed surprised for a moment, then melted into my embrace. I don't think he'd ever kissed a girl before. His eyes closed for a moment, and when he opened them, I could see their slits dilate. I took him to the center of the circle of men, saying nothing.

King Lotus' smile seemed genuine. "Is this man to be your husband?"

I could feel a love for him like none other that I had felt before. It wasn't stronger than my love for Fluff, nor did it replace him. It was different and equal, really. I wouldn't have given it up, even for Fluff.

"Yes."

King Lotus jumped from his chair and walked to us, taking us both in a hug. "Guards, take the groom away and get him some decent clothes. The wedding is in an hour."

Three male tailors approached Eohl, grabbed him by the elbows and carried him from the ballroom.

"Father, what just happened?" I asked.

"The ceremony is designed to help make choosing a mate easier. It works because a father knows his daughter, in this case because your father and I spoke long and hard about you while we were both dead. I picked nine from the crowd who would serve and cherish you for who you are, not just what you've done. Your heart found the one who loved you as much as you loved him. It's a type of magic that predates even the Elves." He took up a glass of wine and handed it to me.

I gazed into the amber wine, trying to think. "I've a planet to save. I don't want to leave a widower should I die in this mission."

"Your husband will be going with you." He said, sipping his wine.

I let my head drop, suddenly worried. "Maybe I should have chosen more wisely."

Uruza slapped me on the back, cheering. "There's no wiser choice. He is a strong lad, smart and true. I grew up with him, and he's never let me down."

"Oh . . . But we're at war, and he's an artist."

"No my dear child. Humanity's at war, and you have to put restore peace." King Lotus put his empty wine container on the arm of his throne. "Now let's go and dance together, and kill the hour with a cheery disposition. Save war talk for after the wedding."

He dwarfed me, being a tall, strong, and heavyset man. The King danced as gracefully as my mother had when she was teaching me. As we danced, I listened to the King talk in time with the music.

"Oh, my daughter, we're truly upon a golden age. When this is over, Humanity will know a wonderful peace."

Genesis fluttered patiently near the King's ear. "Might I please have a dance with my dear friend?"

"When the song is over." The King said irritably.

We danced until the song ended, and then I danced with Genesis. Uruza danced with me through the third song.

"So, are you having fun?" Uruza said.

I giggled. The wine I had so recently taken a sip of was flushing my cheeks and making me feel giddy. "Yes. How often does this happen?"

"Every day, though few as lavish as yours. Though there are indeed less reasons to celebrate, we find ourselves celebrating even more." Uruza dipped me down, then spun me around.

Before I expected it, the song was over. The drum beat two times, followed after a long pause by a third, flat beat. Uruza led me back to the throne, through the crowd, the flat of her sword again beating a path past the onlookers yet again. Flushed from dance and wine, I tried not to giggle as I saw my future husband waiting impatiently before the King. Eohl was wearing a suit unlike any I'd seen before. It was a cross between a fashionable tuxedo and a military uniform.

We had the same suede shoes, and his uniform used the exact same black and white cloth that adorned me. A sash that matched his eyes was wrapped around his belly. His hair was drawn back in a queue. He wore gloves of thin white cotton, and a sword hung at his side. All the skin below his collar was concealed. The ceremony was unlike any other in the galaxy – except, perhaps, for the ancient traditions of Earth.

They asked me in Elfin tongue if I would protect my mate, and serve his needs. I agreed, of course. They asked him the same, and he agreed. We drank from the same glass of wine, and then turned to face the Priest, who adorned us with silver crowns. The crowns were composed of simple silver wire with no jewels to adorn them. The curves of that interwoven wire were the crown's only ornamentation. Eohl took my hands, his fingers shaking nervously. The ceremony ended with the most wonderful kiss.

The festivities continued for another hour, music and drink, food and laughter merging in glorious harmony. Then the drums started beating again, at a faster tempo. People left the chamber. King Lotus left us alone, but I could see a concerned look on Eohl's face. He took my hand and started to lead me away from the crowd.

"What's wrong?" I asked.

"The Scandivat advance assault force has come a little early, probably to try to get at you. We'll all be going from the celebration to battle, I'm afraid."

I tried to clear my head, and the wine wasn't helping. We walked down an amethyst hall to a single ship, looking like an apple seed tossed among the apples. As I walked closer, Genesis dropped down to my side, the smile gone from his face. He helped me get out of my clothes and into a new uniform. Genesis strapped a flute to my side, followed by a sword, and a pistol.

"These were Level Ringbreaker's. He never had to use them. Just like he never had to use the jewelry he left you." He put his hand into Otherspace and handed me a wood wand that's once living roots now held a red ruby in their knobby grip. "Your angelic memory has many rituals stored in instinct that will help you use this wand. If that bastard uncle of yours escalates the battle to the cosmic, don't hesitate to use it on him."

I tried to make familial connections. "You mean Wastik, right?"

"Yes dear. You only have a few minutes, so leave. Once you're gone, the Scandivats should take the bait at the edge of the solar system and be on their way. We'll be guarding your retreat." Genesis shifted into Otherspace.

I walked through the hatch of the ship, and it sealed tight behind us. The ship was smaller than the *Persimmon*, but the tactical display betrayed technological superiority. Eohl sat down in front of the weapon's console, hands and feet flying over controls.

"If you could take navigation, I'll handle the defenses." I jumped into the tight cockpit, flipping switches, bringing the ship's systems online.

"You're a gunner?" I asked, surprised.

"Four years of military service is a requirement of all physically healthy Elves. Being a prodigy, they pushed me into service much earlier than others. I had no intention of being a grunt for four years, so I took fighter training and was promoted to the King's First Aerospace Assault Force as a weapons master."

He keyed in a series of security commands, and two lighted spheres dropped from the ceiling, suspended by unseen forces. The orbs seemed to lock magnetically to my hands, and buttons on either side were triggers for propulsion. One orb moved vertically, the other horizontally. Dropping my hand, I triggered the forward thrust button, and then pulled the orb straight up.

We rose slowly off the port pad, and I took us carefully out over the moonscape, trying to get used to the controls. I found that I could control the ship by twisting and manipulating both orbs, and within a few minutes, I was able to control acceleration and deceleration. Restraining belts automatically snapped around my shoulders as Eohl brought the last of the fighter's systems on line.

"We're ready to retreat. Raising shields, weapons activated. Engines are at maximum." Eohl said.

The sky was speckled with Scandivat war ships, and it took all my skill to get us through the wave without running into one. They didn't fire on us. They were more interested in the supplies they hoped to scavenge from Isastan's surface. Thousands of ships escaped into Otherspace, us among them.

"We need to get into Otherspace. Where are the phase controls?" I asked Eohl.

Eohl raised his hand to adjust his new silver wire crown, one hand still working the keyboard. "I'm working on it right now."

I fidgeted, using my whole body to fly the ship between the wall of enemy ships. "What's taking so long?" I said, "I'm not what you'd call an ace pilot."

"We can't do a straight jump, we have to build up a pulse charge. So keep us in one piece until that happens."

Otherspace bloomed around us, and Eohl thanked God under his breath. The Scandivat ships were like transparent ghosts around Otherspace, though they shouldn't have been visible at all.

"What do you make of it?" I asked, awed as we flew through a Scandivat ship.

He studied the sensors closely. "Otherspace is deteriorating rapidly. Soon it'll be nothing more than a transition portal for the computers to fly through."

We drifted in Otherspace, with no coordinates set.

Eohl looked into a contoured locker. "The computer managed to shift your clothes safely into a proper compartment." He sounded a little uncomfortable.

I felt my forehead. The crown remained, and part of its design used my horns to support it. "Who made this crown for me?"

"I did." Eohl said. "I wanted you to always feel beautiful. Pity we don't have time for a honeymoon."

I frowned. "Was a little rushed wasn't it? We have to get to the colony one more time. If I can talk to the Central, I'm almost certain I can convince him to turn around and go home."

"How are you going to do that?" Eohl wondered.

"By eliminating the key problem."

"Wastik. . ." Eohl thought aloud. "He's a tough metaphysicist. He merges will, magic, and technology all into one when he fights, and he may very well be insane, from what I've heard. I don't know that I can counter his attacks, should he start to weave his web of power."

"I'm not asking you to. This battle's between Wastik and me."

"You're my wife. I should protect you."

"I didn't ask you to marry me, I chose you."

Eohl stared at me in disbelief, his eyes filled with hurt feelings. "You think I would've been at that ceremony if I didn't know there was a chance of us being together? It was my choice to attend. If you think you're going into the bowels of hell without me, you're out of your mind."

My anger flared a little, and my eyes glowed red in response to that rage. "I'll not let another man die helping me fulfill what's so obviously my destiny." I looked away, through the port, into space.

"As you noted when you chose me, I'm not a man yet."

I grumbled under my breath, then looked at him, making my voice clear. "Set course for the Scandivats' colony." When he was done, I drew his lips against mine. "If you die, I'll destroy every last Scandivat in existence, Prince Wastik, and any of his allies."

The smile on his face faded, and he turned away, staring through the opposite portal. We both looked in opposite directions for several minutes.

The computer beeped, breaking our silence.

"We'll be at the edge of the sub-teselar field in an hour. Are we going to try to go in peacefully, or are we going in blasting?"

"This may be a fool's errand, but I'm not suicidal. We're going to take the path of least resistance. The Central's still young, and he's probably working under Wastik's coercion. Besides, I'm certain that my presence will draw Wastik out again. Only this time, I intend to trap him in Realspace and finish him."

I closed my eyes and let my mind drift, wondering if I could. Finish him, that is.

Chapter 20

Tester materialized before me. I reached out for her and she took my hands in hers. They weren't real, since I was in a waking dream, but they felt real, and that made the moment a precious one.

"I've missed you." I said, trying not to cry.

Tester squeezed my hands, and seemed to be thinking. After several seconds, she spoke to me. "Have you found the broken piece?"

"Yes, and the person who broke it. The world of the Scandivat Collective must be healed. They must be brought home. I won't fail you. Not like I failed my girl."

"You didn't fail her, you saved her. If you only knew her destiny before your intervention." Tester hugged me close. "You can't fail, because you are doing your best."

I smiled, then lost that little piece of happiness. "I wish I could bring my Mama and Papa back."

Tester's face became very serious. "I feel bad for having put you through so much, being as young as you are. After they died the first time, I took the souls of Tiffany and Kotian into my heart and protected them. I told them about your plan to retrieve them. I explained to them about your duty to them. Someday you would have to die so that they could fulfill their destiny and save the Human Race.

"Your girl and her husband surprised me. Rather than let you die, both of them chose instead to pass their destinies onto you. You have to fulfill a task originally designed for two people – but you're not alone. You've a new family now, and a good husband."

"I don't want Eohl with me." I said, pouting.

"You're afraid that the boy who is going with you will die like your parents did. Until the broken part is fixed, cruel and unnecessary death is inevitable. I have to leave not, honey. Every word costs the Scandivats' colony precious time they might need to save their home world. I love you."

"I love you too." The vision turned to daydream. I slowly opened my eyes.

Eohl was staring at me, his entire body tense. "It's about time you woke up from your little trance. We're out of Otherspace. Think you might want to get dressed?"

"Why are you blushing?" I asked, then looked down, and turned kind of red myself. I put my clothes on, making sure everything was just right. The Scandivats hailed us just as I was buttoning the last button at the top of my blouse.

"Identification of ship and occupants unknown. Identify or be destroyed."

Putting my flute to my lips, I played back my answer, trying to sound as formal and unemotional as possible.

The response was slow in coming. "Please enter portal nine and prepare to visit the Central."

The contact broken, we followed a small, automated ship to portal nine. It proved to be the same portal we had been forced to land in previously.

"That was easy." Eohl said in low tones.

I knew that the apparent ease of entry was a deception. "Sure you won't stay here? I can make arrangements."

"We're a team now. You'll need somebody to keep Wastik busy so you can speak with the Central." He looked at me with those strange eyes, smiling savagely.

"Do you think you can beat him?"

"He'll slaughter me."

I rubbed the crown on my head. "Let's go." The hatch opened to my touch.

An Alpha Hunter met me at the door. Small and deadly, the little Hunter eyed me curiously. "You've left your weapons behind, very good. Identify the new item on your head. It seems purely ornamental."

"It's an Elfin wedding crown. This is my husband – my mate." I paused, trying to create a word that could explain to an alien mind a human concept. "Our wedding was interrupted by the Scandivat Hunter party sent ahead to scavenge for food."

The Alpha Hunter, linked to the Central, continued speaking. "Mate's good – the Central's relieved. Please travel to the Central's chambers. We have many questions."

"We're worried that Wastik might be a threat to us." I whistled to him.

"You'll be safe regardless of the outcome of our decision. Wastik was wrong to threaten you."

The hours we walked were relatively quiet ones. Eohl's eyes scanned everything he passed. He seemed to be trying to absorb every detail into his mind. We milled through Scandivats as they planted seeds and collected their ripe fruits. He picked up a fruit that had fallen, studying it as we walked, then handed it to a passing Scandivat, who chirped in seeming joy and took the fruit on its way.

We were taken to the chamber with none of the search procedures that had been given us before. The Central seemed different somehow. Still small, his head now had a ridge of scales starting at the third eye and ending at the base of his skull.

"Welcome," the Central whistled. "You left me a strange present before, one that triggered memories."

I smiled. "You have questions. I've requests. I'd be happy if you would ask your questions first."

"Why are you and Wastik enemies?"

"Because he feels that Humanity should be only of one kind. It might compare to having only Hunters, or only Scandivats, it might not, but he wants zero diversity in genetics. He wants us to be one pure strain. He wants to accomplish this by killing those who aren't part of his pure strain. I'm not part of his strain, and thus we're enemies."

I stopped playing and he motioned to a set of chairs. "Sit, pirate and mate. Please enjoy our hospitality."

I sat in the soft chair, suspecting that they had made it as we walked up here.

"Where'd you get this flute?" In his hands, Jupe's Flute looked almost natural – though his hands and lips were too alien to play it.

"It was found in the crater at the heart of your old hive." I said.

"We're losing our trust in Wastik. Our race memory was damaged by the holocaust. We no longer understand nor can we interpret Human Galactic Standard. Though we had translators once, that technology's lost to us. But there are incongruities in Wastik's words and behavior. He speaks of the humans and Scandivats' colony sharing the Earth, then talks only of destroying those few oppressors that stand in our way. Advance parties show that nearly seventy percent of the Human guardian Forces have put themselves between primitive Earth and us. We could easily crush these forces, but what of the planet bound primitive humans. They're most dangerous of all. I'm certain that the Hive will not be able to beat seventy percent of the Human Guardians and take Earth's surface from the massive number of humans stationed there. Wastik disagrees." He paused. "There's also the great incongruity."

"Please define this incongruity," I whistled.

"It's twofold. The first incongruity was the declaration that he was the one who helped our hive and is stored so lovingly in the memories of the Scandivat Collective's last Central. Yet his actions are opposite. He doesn't help heal the Scandivats, he doesn't touch me, or even make me feel all that good. He doesn't show compassion or give the Scandivat Collective any of the emotions recorded in the race memory. He therefore cannot be the part who made us whole." The Central paused.

"The second fold of incongruity is in his words. He told us that the drive he installed for us was working at its maximum velocity. We trusted him until he gave us instructions on increasing the colony's speed. Those instructions did not include physical modifications to the drive system or the colony.

"This flute was the third incongruity. Wastik admits to having never seen it or even knowing how to play it. Race memory recalls that this was the means by which the part that made us feel whole spoke to us. Just as you do now. Such similarities make us wonder if you might not be the part that made us feel whole."

"I won't lie to you and say that I am. His name was Jupe, and I'm his caretaker. I've never met him. But the flute was his, and it was found on your world. It's why I'm here now, to try to find him and ensure his safety." I looked at Eohl for a moment, wondering how the Central would respond to my next comment. "Your collective can have my ship. Use the technology so that you can speak with the humans you encounter in their language. I think that you'll be surprised."

The Central stood up, suddenly concerned, reaching for a mace that I had believed was part of a support strut for the wall. "The Hive is in jeopardy."

"What is it?" I asked. The entire colony vibrating in response to what could only be explosions.

"Wastik has been observing us, and now he is angered. He is trying to get to me. I'm not strong enough to defeat him. I can't kill him. He is killing Hunters, slaughtering my kind, but I can't kill him." I reached out a hand, putting it on the Central's shoulder. I could feel his terror. I drew my hand back so I could play my flute.

"We'll stop him. Move your people out of the way, put up no resistance. You'll have to trust me, because to deal with him I'll be unable to talk to you. You need the fastest of your race to help my mate get back to our ship."

He held the flute so naturally, this Central, as if it were part of him. His fingers tittered across the holes anxiously. I saw something in him with my mind's eyes, a connection was made, and for a moment I felt like a genius.

"You're Jupe, and you don't even know it." I said in standard, not wanting to confuse the Central under such stressful conditions.

I turned to Eohl, kissing him good-bye. "Go to the ship, and get back with my wand as fast as you can. I'll hold Wastik as long as I can. I have a plan, and I need my wand here to pull it off."

The Alpha Hunter carried Eohl away from the Central Complex, and I readied myself for a confrontation.

"The Hunter Reed. Is he still alive?" I asked.

The Central whistled an answer. "He's still alive, in stasis. He was unable to adapt to the new thought structure. I couldn't kill him."

"Set him free and bring him here." I said. "It's time for him to fulfill his duty to the Hive."

My heart beat loud and slow, ringing in my ears. I could only hope that my intuition on these matters was sound. An explosion signaled the deterioration of one of the synthetic stone walls. Within moments, Wastik burst into the room, a blaster in his hand. His eyes were insane with rage. He looked at me with hate, then he pointed his blaster at me. The Central lay slouched behind his throne, shaking with fear.

"I'll kill you and imprison him." Wastik said. "I've had enough charades. I can keep him hostage from his own people, and force them to destroy the people of Earth."

"You've got to get through me, first." I said.

"That shouldn't be a problem."

He fired his blaster, giggling with glee as I jumped away from the charged rounds. The weapon was relatively simple in design. A magnetized steel round was blasted through a super conductive coil, then through a powerful static charge. The end result was a tiny packet of plasma that could shear a limb from the body or leave a gaping hole in its wake.

I ran across the Central Complex, hoping that his shots wouldn't kill any of the Incubators. The Central was already moving them out of the way, their wormy bodies slipping slowly to the edges of the room. The Central had dropped his mace, and I tried to lift it, but it was too heavy for me.

"Very smart, little girl, using the Central as a shield. You know I can't hurt him until Earth is crushed under his forces."

I hadn't been using the Central as a shield, but I wasn't going to let Wastik know that. He fired a shot at the throne, startling me, and I crouched down lower, looking for my next cubby to hide in. I pulled my shirt off, and pushed my pants past my feet. Once undressed, I focused and took on my angelic form. With wings I'd have more places to hide, and faster reflexes to fight with.

I grabbed the mace again, and this time found it light enough to swing. His boots clicked on the ground as he walked carefully around me, unable to see me from my hidden place. I crouched down, my muscles shaking with anticipation. I began to have serious doubts about my abilities at about the time Wastik's boots stopped clicking.

What am I doing? I wondered to myself.

I wasn't a fighter, nor was I faster than a blaster shot. I'm really not bullet proof either. I saw his boot as he walked slowly around the complex and I shot up and forward, flapping my wings in a hard surge. With all my strength I brought the mace down on his foot. He nimbly jumped out of my range. Missing his foot, the mace shattered the floor, chipping out a hole in its wake. Wastik got a shot off before I could swing the mace again. The shot hit my wing straight on, and I was knocked against the far wall.

As an angel I had some built in defenses, it would take more than one shot to injure me. I shook off the blow and dove down, retrieving the mace, then threw it at Wastik. He ducked, but the mace glanced across his shoulder before shattering the wall behind him. I could see blood where the dull blades of the mace had ripped open his flesh.

Wastik snarled and fired round after round in my direction. With speed and grace, I flew around the room, one step ahead of his rage. His blaster was glowing red-hot now, and he'd changed power clips twice. Frothing with rage, he fired his last round. The coils burned out; he tossed the blaster aside. He picked up the mace I had thrown at him, and held it in a sinuous grip. I hung from the rafters for a moment, resting. A mace was something I could deal with, so long as he didn't hit me directly. I dropped down, spreading my wings.

"You can't beat me Wastik, not with that weapon."

"I intend to kill you, not beat you." Wastik said. "This isn't a school yard brawl, girl."

He lunged at me and I got a grip on the mace. He broke it free and swung again. Energy wrapped around me, protecting me from the blow, the stones in my earrings glowing in my defense. My soul felt drained. Uruza's fear of the stones was now expressing itself in full glory. Wastik's own dark magic sizzled in response to the light of the stones. Dazed but unharmed, I fluttered backward, catching the mace with my hand. He was stronger than I was, and it took all my strength to keep him from shaking me loose. "Those stones can't protect you forever."

"You can't fight forever."

"Neither can you." The mace resonated violently, burning my hand, and I was forced to let go and jump back. The mace had a cold blue energy surging through it. "You think that I would ever let you have an advantage. I have on my person the one thing that weakens you."

"It must be the ignorance in your head." He suckered me, catching me in the ribs. The stones only took the edge off the blow that time. I fell to my knees, wondering if any bones were broken.

He swung the mace into my back, knocking me to my belly, then went completely crazy. I was pinned to the floor with each blow, and each blow added another bruise to me. The stones in my ears could not keep him from slowly killing me, they fed off my will, and my will was getting pretty dim. I knocked his legs out from under him with a snapping kick, and then flashed the knife-edge of my hand across the bridge of his nose. The damage was minor, and only blinded him for a second. I took flight, hiding in the rafters, biding my time.

The Central watched helplessly while I fought to catch my breath. This battle was taking too long. Wastik was stronger, faster, and seemed just as strong as he had been from the start.

"You can't hide from me forever, girl. You'll come down, eventually."

Hunter Reed slunk into the room, hissing at Wastik. "Take the Central, get him away." I yelled down to Reed. "I'll take care of Wastik." I dropped down onto Wastik's head, ripping at his eyes with my claws. Dropping the mace, Wastik grabbed my feet, placed conveniently on his shoulders, and tossed me across the room, into a far wall. I bounced off the wall, hit the ground, and bounced twice more, and lay still, aching.

"Oh," I moaned. "That was stupid."

When I looked up, Wastik was standing over me. "I'm not stupid enough to go after a full grown Hunter, but since he's abandoned you, I can finish what I started."

Blue fire erupted around the head of the mace, and he slammed it down onto my skull. I cross-blocked, curling into a ball, with my wings wrapped protectively around my upper body. He hit me repeatedly, kicking at me for spite, and I felt almost nauseated from all the abuse.

Something snapped inside of me, and fear was washed away.

A new power rose, the power of somebody at the last edge of desperation. I pushed myself to standing, looking straight into his eyes. My skin, a shade darker from all the bruises, took on a golden glow, and I put my hands together in prayer, my wings half bent as I brought my thoughts into focus. I sent out a blast of pure white Otherspace energy into his face. He fell back, the blue flame around him extinguished.

The battle of force, which I would have lost, became a battle of wills. His Mixedspace laws fought with my Otherspace principals. My psychic force was pushed back, then fluxed forward, dispersing his will in all directions. My hands worked patterns in the air, and he threw his mace straight at my face. It breached the field, but not my fingertips, which I threw up to catch the mace. I held it in front of my face, my fingertips now stronger than chords of steel, and tossed it aside. A Hunter returned, merely an observer, and I knew that things were about to get ugly.

"Well, well, we have unwanted company." Wastik reached out with his mind and drew the mace back, then tossed it straight at the Hunter.

I jumped in the way, and paid for it. The sound of bones crunching filled my ears, and I lay there puking bile. Breaking a wing is like a cross between having your head bashed in and using a fork to rip your own internal organs out. I lay there, fluttering in spasms, my wing shattered, and along with it, my will. When I looked around, the Hunter was nowhere to be found.

"I knew you'd defend him, it's in you're nature, since you're a guardian. Now look at you, unable to fly or fight. Such a pity, your sense of duty." Wastik gloated, working me into a corner as he talked.

I dragged myself back, terrified. Not just my wing, but also my arm had been broken, and my will fizzled around me in weak little spurts. I hissed at him as he drew closer to me, the mace hanging in his grip. He limped, at least a little more injured than his words implied. His left ear was missing its point, one of his eyes was swollen and bruised, and his hands were burned from the effects of the stones on his skin. His face was shredded with minor cuts.

"The Central's chamber will be your grave, little girl." Wastik said, raising his mace.

Having backed into a wall, I let my head drop, and waited for the inevitable.

He swung the mace down once more, but it never struck home. I looked up from my curled position to see Eohl standing over me, his hand holding the blue tinged mace in a single fisted, milk white grip. His own body glowed golden red, and he tossed me the wand I had left on the ship. Wastik slapped Eohl with his empty hand, but Eohl tore the mace from his grip.

Having done all he could, Eohl fled the mad man, jumping like a cat across the debris that littered the Central's chamber. He didn't get far before Wastik caught up to him, slamming him in the back. He took the mace back from Eohl and turned away.

"You can't beat me, you throwback." Wastik said.

"No, he can't beat you, because it isn't his destiny." I said. "But I can." I took my human form, raised the wand, ready to use it.

Wastik turned from Eohl, and as Gracie I was fresh for a fight. The wand started to glow, and then fizzled out.

"Oh, brother, now what?" I moaned, trying to keep from being slaughtered by Wastik. I ran, shaking the wand, dodging his swinging mace with every ounce of clumsy human skill I could muster. I yelled at the wand as I jumped and ducked, scrambling frantically away from Wastik.

"We're being chased by a really big psychopathic Elf, you crazy wand. Genesis said you'd help me."

Then I realized that Genesis never told me exactly what the wand was for.

"Elves and Forever Children, damn you all for your ambiguity." I yelled, trying to keep out of harm's way.

Eohl yelled at me, "Can't you use it?"

"No way. It's not a weapon. I think it's for fixing broken parts." I said. In my human form, Wastik would be able to slowly beat me to death, just as he had done to my angel form. He was simply too strong for me to beat him in a muscle fight. Wastik chuckled, feeling his advantage.

"That wand is just a useless piece of wood. Metal, heavy and hard. Now there's something useful to me." He swung the mace at my face.

I ducked and dodged, one step ahead of him, trying to keep alive and find a way to stop Wastik. Though there were weapons on the ship, if I shouted to Eohl to get them, Wastik would finish the boy and take them for himself. Fortunately, the central hadn't forgotten me, and therefore the Scandivat were on my side. Hunter Reed burst into the room, grabbed Wastik by the mace hand, tossing his massive Elfin body into a pile of rubble.

Whistling in his native tongue, his words were heavy with wicked sub-tones.

"It's over." He said. "I've merged, I'm one, and my people will resume their true journey. We're going home and starting over."

Wastik looked at me, at Eohl, at Hunter Reed, and finally at the Hunter Alpha force that worked its way cautiously into the room. Wastik was cornered.

"I think it's time for you to go home as well." I said, ready to see him into prison.

"Damn you all." He whispered turning on the Hunters, his mace at ready.

There were too many Hunters for him to hope to win. Working together, Eohl, Reed, and me could have stopped him. With seven Hunters added to the mix, he wouldn't leave the Central's chambers under his own will. Wastik responded almost predictably. Feeling trapped, he chose to fight rather than surrender. He tossed the mace straight into the face of one of the Hunters, and would've killed her if not for Eohl.

Eohl's hand shot out, and the mace stopped cold, hanging in the air. Eohl fell to one knee, drained by his action. Captain Reed took up the mace and faced Wastik. Wastik knew that if he continued to resist, the dangerous new Central would crush him into pulp.

"Damn you all." He repeated in a harsh splatter of spittle. He raised his hands, slashed out a series of sharp edged symbols in the air around him, and everything turned pitch black.

Chapter 21

The pain returned almost instantly. I looked around, but there was nothing to gain bearing on, and vertigo set in. This wasn't Realspace, where there was always something, namely matter, to focus on. In Realspace, one was never without either light, or essence. I wasn't in Otherspace, where thought and dream replaced matter and therefore distorted time and reality. This was another type of space entirely, a space where there was only energy in its purest form.

My eyes couldn't adapt to such a place – the energy wasn't visible, but I could feel it pulsing around me. There was nothing physical except me, beaten almost to death, and Wastik, with his twisted mind working its bitter magic. The wand hung loosely from my good hand. The only point of consciousness in the entire void was Wastik.

"Where am I?" I wondered.

Wastik's hands glowed, and he seemed to be looking for something. He too floated in nothing. "We're not in the dark matter heart of some hideous black hole, if that's what you're thinking. You aren't in Otherspace, though you don't need to breath here either. This is Zerospace, a quantum singularity of the absolute present. It is the plane where the sum resultant of every calculation in every universe nulls out." His giggle was a sickening mix of anger and loathing. "Now all I have to do is change that sum in a very special way, and chaos will reign."

He began working his dark metaphysics, his hands flashing with his wicked will. I could feel the Zerospace shift violently in response, and knew that I would have to do something to keep him from accomplishing his goal.

"A few more shifts, and both Earth and the Scandivat Home world will be turned to pure energy. That energy will flood Otherspace, so that Zerospace can restore its true sum of nothing."

"This is really going way over my head." I said. "But it sounds like you're going to destroy things."

"Earth and the Scandivat Home world will be destroyed, and Otherspace with them. You're really such a simpleton."

"Hey, I've only lived a measly sixteen human years." The wand tingled in my hand. "But you've destroyed your own soul, and that destruction flowers out from you. I can still stop you."

There was no gravity, no air, no pressure or lack thereof. My wounds didn't bleed, and my wing didn't ache from the occasional eddy or breeze, I was in a cocoon of true nothingness. I found that I could focus in this Zerospace quite well, and that for every move that Wastik made, each a part of his ritual of destructive calculation, I could counter and return the space to its true sum of nothing. In this magical battle, Wastik couldn't win. My instincts in the use of magic were right on.

Then it got personal. Seeing that he couldn't keep me from reversing his work, Wastik's energy ripped through me, and I was knocked farther away. Strangely, it didn't matter much. In a space where there's nothing, there can be no distance. It hurt for all of a millisecond, and then my own energy, combined with the full power of both earrings and the focus of the wand, forced his energy back. Light erupted for the first time in perhaps a thousand million years in the dark of Zerospace, illuminating Wastik and me in its dull blue glow. That light was mine. Wastik's will wasn't light. It looked like a pool of viscous black oil. It sucked at my energy, tried to overpower it, and fizzled.

Hanging limp in Zerospace, I focused my power through the wand, forcing his raw energy back onto him. In Zerospace this wouldn't be a battle where a physical blow could break the will of an opponent, or even weaken it. In Zerospace, it would be a battle of raw will and wit. Space shifted, gaining a new dimension of darkness. I had to strain under his hatred.

His dark will licked closer to my skin, trying to work its way into me, but my own power forced it grudgingly back. Without even a vectored gravity, all I could do was try to overpower his will, to fill him with my energy, but I still had no idea what this would do.

Focusing all my energy forward, I pushed through an opening in his defenses and got him straight in the heart. His will went wild, spreading out through my light like a swarm of angry bees. Then the blackness fell back into him. He was knocked back by the blackness, writhing in pain. His body turned white-hot for a thousandth of a second, then exploded with the force of a hundred suns. Every last bit of his dark energy was gone, and so was he.

After the battle, all the energy I had been using circled back into the wand, and with the exception of my presence, nothingness was restored to Zerospace. Where it had been frightening before, the blackness now felt more like a friend. But nothing, not even an absence of pressure and gravity, could get rid of the pain that tormented me, the pain of crushed skin and muscle and bone.

Drained and weak, aching everywhere, I closed my eyes for what felt like an eternity. When I opened them, I was still in Zerospace, still in pain. My heart pounded in my chest, aching. I looked around for the longest time, wondering where the door was.

There wasn't much to say about Zerospace. I ached more now that the fight was over, and that was compounded by an absence of imagery and sensory information. I could get into and out of Realspace and Otherspace, and even the mixture of the two. But I had never been in Zerospace, and I had no idea how to leave.

"Father, Mother." I whispered.

The silence of Zerospace was complete. The sound would carry forever. I wondered how fast sound traveled in a plane with properties like Zerospace.

The answer rung through my head. "I am here."

"I want to go home." I said, coughing. "If I don't leave soon, I think I'm going to die."

"I'm working on it now. I won't let you die." Where normally Tester's voice was harsh and scolding, now she was loving and compassionate. “There are but a few resultant forces to balance before you can go home.”

“I’m scared, mama.” I said, trying not to cry.

“Don’t be. You’re in the very womb of creation, at the point where everything, including you, first came to being. You are in the infinite present. You are in the dream of God. We’ll always love you, child.”

I closed my eyes, trying to ignore the pain. When I opened them, I was with friends. I fell forward, gravity reminding me of my injuries.

Eohl looked down at me, obviously unsure as to how to handle an injured angel. “Can you turn into a human? We have to leave.”

I tried to shift, but it was a total failure. I fell forward, and managed to gasp. “No.”

“She goes nowhere.” Reed said.

Eohl looked defiantly at him, ready to fight the whole colony to see to my safety.

Reed calmed him with a gentle posture and soothing words. “If you try to move her now, you’ll kill her. We’ll take care of her. We are friends. You can help by staying out of my way.” He stopped whistling and his Scandivats worked around me, moving rubble away.

Several Hunters, working with hundreds of different organic tools and creatures, built a soft bed under me without moving me from the Central’s chamber. Somebody put a blanket over me, and in the warmth of it, I fell into a healing sleep.

For a while I thought maybe I was still trapped in Zerospace and that I had dreamed my return. I had slept so hard that it required a great effort just to pry open my eyelids. When I did, I was still with friends. Still an angel, still too weak to change my form, I didn’t try to move anything, because everything hurt.

Eohl sat next to me, working on something thin and wiry. “Eohl. What are you doing?” I wondered, half awake.

“Your crown got trashed in the fight. I’m making you a new one. I’ll be done soon.” My arm was in a sling, and I knew that my wing was bandaged to my body. “Reed woke you up because there are some people here who need your advice.”

I looked around, my balance lagging behind my sight. King Lotus and another of several delegates stood over my bed. “The Scandivat have surrendered to us, what should we do with them? If you tell us what to do, your friends will listen to you."

I stared at King Lotus in disbelief. "Take them home and help them fix their world. Is that all?"

The King looked behind him, but I couldn't see that far. "See, we should show mercy." He looked back at me. "Don't worry, dear, I'll see to it your orders are carried out. Will we have to deal with Wastik again?"

"Not in this lifetime."

He left me, and I slowly moved my head back to focus on Eohl. "I think I'll go back to sleep now."

They came and woke me on many occasions, asking me questions that I hardly remember answering. Then, after Eohl threatened to punch the King, Reed sealed the colony from visitors, and I finally got some serious sleep. I don't remember waking up for a long time, but when I finally did, Eohl was gone. I could make out my surroundings. I was crouched forward, in a cushioned chair. I felt a little stronger. I held my head up and looked around.

I could see the sky through a massive, dull glass barrier. The ground below looked like three feet of darkened amber. Hexagonal pillars of stone rose up to meet that single piece of once molten glass. On a hexagonal table set near my good arm, the new silver wire crown Eohl had been working on glistened beautifully in the light. Only this crown had three small, bright green emeralds set right in the center of it.

"Where am I?" I asked.

Reed answered me in galactic standard. "You're in the new Central's chamber. My home."

"There are no Incubators here," I said, surprised.

"I thought you might find them displeasing. Besides, I've scattered the incubators around the main colony, so that there will never again be a threat of complete colonial decay, as was caused by the Great Impact. There is somebody who's waited for you to wake up, a Forever Child named Jupe. He wants to ask you something. He's lost his voice, but we're working on restoring it to him."

Jupe looked out shyly from behind the Central. "I'm here now, the world is healed." He played on his flute. "I want to stay."

"This is your home. You are their child." I said.

Reed translated, I don't think he would have understood me otherwise. He ran away, happy with the answer, playing his flute as he ran down the hall.

With Jupe gone, I had Reed's attention once more. "How long has it been? It must have taken a long time to build this new colony."

"Been two months. You were very close to dying when you came back from your fight with Wastik, now you're very close to being fully healed." Reed set a sensor pad on my hand, retracting his claws. He seemed pleased with the information it gave him. "We were all worried about you. Eohl paced endlessly through the Hive, and I diverted as many resources as were needed to keep you safe and alive."

I lay my head back, looking up through the glass. "How did you make a single piece of glass that big?" I asked. It spanned a quarter mile in every direction from me, and looked to be a hundred feet thick.

"We didn't. It's the crater from the asteroid impact. The heat of the asteroid melted a layer of dirt into glass. We did a scan of it, determined it was stronger than our stone ceilings, and saved ourselves years of restoration work by adapting it to our new home.

"The Medic class was very professional in healing you. Your wing isn't fully recovered, nor is your arm, but the bones are mended. We were going to wait until tomorrow to take your sling and wing bandage off, but if you promise to be very careful, we can take it off a day early."

"Believe me," I said, "I am in no condition to do much of anything."

The bandages came off, and I flexed my arm and wing, working the tight tendons out with slow and careful consideration for the pain it caused. I had finished putting my bodysuit on and was just putting my wedding crown back on my head when Eohl rushed in to greet me. He held my hands, and the Central Reed left us to talk alone.

"Hello. I missed you I love you." He said in one great huff of excitement.

"Fill me in. What happened while I was away?"

"Earth is safe, the Elves are home. Though Otherspace has been somewhat restored, the angels have left it for Realspace. The angels are now citizens of Isastan. Of course you have the honor of being the King's youngest daughter, as well as a hero. What's best is there's peace between the Elves, humans, and the Scandivats.

"King Lotus followed your words explicitly. The Scandivat Race will rebuild any damages they have done to Friol and the Isastan home world. In return they will become part of the galactic community. So, have you tried changing into a human yet?"

"Why do you ask?" In reality, I felt no desire to. My angelic form was at least a month from full recovery.

"Just try it." He said.

I did, and looked down at my dark human form, then shifted back to my angelic form so that I could continue to heal. "So, what's the big deal?"

"All the angels lost their wings." He said. "You may be the last angel in all the Human Race."

I laughed. It sounded preposterous. "Lost their wings? Then they've left Otherspace for good."

"The angelic Council decided that all angels should be as other humans – without Otherspace alterations."

"Don't expect me to shed my wings any time soon. I actually use them." I smiled wickedly, and flapped my wings, slowly rising off the ground. It took very little effort, because I'd lost weight while healing. But I didn't have enough strength to take any long flights.

"Be careful. You could still hurt yourself." Eohl said, putting his hands on my waist to keep me hovering.

I knew better, but I set down to humor him. "As soon as I'm cleaned up, we're going on vacation."

"That sounds nice, though we'll hardly have time for it." Eohl said. "But King Lotus has made a direct request that as soon as you're ready, we're to be greeted as heroes in the highest hall of Elfin heroes so that you may be officially honored for your heroics, and then seen off on our honeymoon."

A honeymoon. I smiled at the thought. "Let's get out of here."

Though my angelic form was healed enough to fly, I took human form so I could walk with Eohl back to the ship. We flew into Otherspace directly from the colony, and arrived on Isastan's fifth moon after but a few hours of travel. In the cramped space of the cockpit, I dressed in my best uniform, and stepped into the amethyst docking bay.

King Lotus greeted us as we exited the air lock. "My daughter and son-in-law." He yelled, taking us both in a massive hug.

It was such a gentle act, as if we were both made of glass. After setting us down, he quickly adjusted our crowns and made sure that we looked just right. "I hope that the Scandivat Race treated you well enough during your recovery."

I nodded, smiling, but before I could say anything, he continued, "At first we thought they were holding you prisoner, but Eohl set us straight, before war broke out. As you slept and recovered, we followed your suggestions for peace exactly. I made a treaty, then established trade. They have construction and design techniques so superior to our own architecture as to make most of it obsolete. And they're learning our agricultural techniques, and applying them to their world laws. Well, I've chatted long enough with the hero of three planets. Please, please, enjoy the festivities."

The ballroom was much as I remembered it; only today the sky could be seen even beyond the glowing orbs of light, and its blue-green mother, Isastan, swallowed half of it. The entire roof, which had been pitch black before, was now crystal and transparent, making the room brighter than it had been last time. The gold-flecked amber floor glowed under the added light, the people looking like they might be standing on a map of the galaxy rather than on a dance floor. The gardens were in bloom, but so many people failed to notice just how wonderful a sight it was.

Grandfather Jodiah saw me first, and started a rhythmic clapping that was soon taken up by every person in the hall. When the drummers joined it, their massive wood and leather instruments beating to the time, I thought the chamber would never know silence again. I'm sure there is a sacred number of drum beats associated with greeting a hero and her husband, because the drum and the clappers stopped on the same beat.

That silence filled me to my very being. It was so complete that every breath I took sounded too loud. Every move I made seemed like an avalanche. If I had been in angelic form, a wing stroke might have sounded like a hurricane. I was just beginning to feel uncomfortable, when King Lotus started his speech.

Chapter 22

King Lotus stood on top of his throne, dressed in gold silk pantaloons, cape, and blouse, with his gold crown tilted on his head. He had a silver goblet in one hand, and a pair of freshly brushed black suede boots. His voice carrying, despite the size of the room, King Lotus was a man of incredible volume. Despite this, there was no echo, and the crowd listened intently.

"People of Isastan, the angelic Council of Nine, and family and friends from all over the galaxy, today we glorify the actions of my youngest daughter and those who helped her on her way. The full story is ours, because her actions saved us from certain war and probable destruction. For everybody to see, a tapestry has been built up by the Scandivat Race to our requested specifications, in thanks for her help in saving them from extinction."

Eohl took my hand and guided me around. The tapestry unrolled, a glorious creation of Scandivat ability combined with Elfin artistry. I had to get closer to see what lay in the background. The images were like ghosts. Kotian and Tiffany were there, their faces illuminated by an explosion just beginning. Fluff was on the tapestry as well, with Uruza in his arms, frozen in a permanent embrace.

If one looked at the explosion, one could still make out the *Persimmon* at the center of the blast, and it was obvious that in moments the ships surrounding her would be destroyed. At the edge of the blast was me, in my angel form, curled into the fetal position and surrounded by a shield of golden light. All this behind the big fight between Wastik and me, his stolen mace no less menacing in the picture.

Eohl was in the tapestry as well, and Central Reed. The tapestry clearly implied that I would be victorious, despite my crushed state. As I looked, there were three more faces on the tapestry, faces I could not quite remember. Then my memory triggered. The Forever Children who had given me the gifts all stood around Jupe, who played to them on his flute.

"I asked that we not to be included." Genesis said, having flown up next to me. "All we did was give you the things Governor Ringbreaker had willed to the next governor. There was never any risk to us, we helped out where we could. You made the greatest sacrifice. Governor Ringbreaker had one more gift for you, a ring of keys to his many homes. This one is most suiting to your honeymoon, I'd think."

He pulled a rusty skeleton key, dangling from a string, out of an Otherspace pocket. There were symbols on the circlet, three of them, each more rusted than the last.

"This is a key to his cabin on Earth. It's yours to keep now." Genesis vanished, I stared at the key for a moment longer. I turned away from the tapestry, waiting for King Lotus to push the ceremony forward.

He nodded and continued. "Let's all remember this day, and those who died ensuring that it would be as glorious as it was."

For twenty-seven drumbeats we remained silent, then the festivities broke out and the silence was stolen by a chaotic combination of voices, celebration, and music. As I walked by, a few people smiled at me but nobody seemed to want to destroy my time with my new husband. We sat at a table and talked about our plans for the honeymoon.

After about an hour, King Lotus and Grandfather Jodiah sat down with us, and promptly started arguing over the key spots in the galaxy known for their romantic atmosphere. The archangel Joseph of the Council of Nine took a moment to interrupt our conversation. I hadn't ever met the Council of Nine until now, and I wasn't impressed by what I saw. He asked when I was going to shed my wings. I laughed at him, probably a very rude thing to do in public.

"Why, Sir, I'll never shed my wings." I returned my attention to King Lotus and Grandpa's friendly argument about the best hotels and resorts in the galaxy.

"I'm afraid that the Council has decided –"

King Lotus looked up, his voice as loud and resonant as a bass drum. "My Daughter, kind sir, has made her decision. We discussed this before, and I told you that her decision would be final." He returned to his conversation, leaving archangel Joseph to sputter in surprise.

"Sir, you are but a King . . ."

"I am the King of the world you're living on. Remember that please, when we speak again."

"All Kings answer to the Council of Nine." Joseph said, "As was written in Elfin lore nearly two eons past."

Jodiah stood up slowly, smiling. "Why, archangel Joseph, are you trying to pull rank?" He patted the hilt of his sword, his other hand rested on his blaster. "I don't listen to any Council not voted into appointment by my people."

This thing was getting way out of hand, all I wanted to do was plan my honeymoon in peace, and now this stranger was insisting that I shed my wings. I had no intention of following his request. I liked to being able to fly. I liked the ability to move as fast as any space ship through Otherspace. I wanted my freedom.

"So long as one person holds the power to shift between the realms, there is a threat of imbalance. You must understand the importance of this transition."

"I really wish you would just leave me alone." I said, rubbing my temples, a headache coming on.

Eohl pushed his chair out with his knees, his hands firm on the tabletop. In response three of the Council of Nine moved in close, ready to back their leader.

"Gentlemen, this is a celebration, a festive occasion. You are upsetting my wife and I wish you would stop." Eohl said, his voice surprisingly firm.

"If she doesn't abide by the decisions of the Council, she must be punished." Archangel Joseph said, his arms crossed sternly.

"You know, when I was a kid visiting Transcendence, I felt like a speck of dust and couldn't really tell why. Now I know, the higher angels are a bunch of over-inflated snobs." I said, taking Eohl's hand and rising to leave. "We're out of here." I walked back to the ship, an entourage of angels, guards, and friends seeing us off.

"You're a part of our order, and must live by our laws." Archangel Joseph insisted.

"She's my daughter, and protected by the laws of the Elfin Kingdom." King Lotus said.

"Her rights as a citizen of Friol are protection enough." Jodiah half yelled, undoing his pistol strap.

Sword and blaster, I'm afraid, mostly govern Friol's law. I knew he would use either without a moment's hesitation. I was about to enter my ship when archangel Joseph put his hand on my shoulder to detain me. I looked around me, taking stock of the situation. Jodiah, Uruza, and Fluff already had their hands on their swords. So did seven of the nine angels who had followed me. King Lotus' face was red with rage, and Eohl was ready for another fight in my honor. Genesis sat on the ship, just over our head, his teeth savagely bared. He looked ready to drop into the fray should one develop.

"You're all being silly." I said. "I'm a pirate, and I live by my own rules."

Archangel Joseph let out an indignant breath. "I'm afraid that I've no choice but to order your detainment until the ceremony of transition can be completed and you can be integrated into the new angelic order of Isastan."

I hadn't carried a sword since before the battle with Wastik, but I had no intention of going down without a fight. Shrugging off Joseph's grip, I raised my fists, ready to shift to angelic form at a moment's notice. If the Council lived by their own laws, they'd be unable to fly. As an angel, I could take Eohl into the safety of Otherspace, and we could go on our honeymoon without a ship.

As it turned out, none of the Council seemed to be so set on obeying the laws they exacted on others. There was no way I could beat nine heavily armed feather winged archangels, and I was about to surrender before people started getting hurt. Lightning blew a hole in the roof of the docking chambers and left a black crater in the floor near my feet. The sound of the thunder reverberating off the walls, pierced my ears, and chilled my soul. Everybody stood still, the Council of Nine visibly shaken. Wisdom was there, only he had horns, suggesting that he and Tester were in one form at the moment.

He carefully put himself between the angels and myself. "I really do wish I'd come sooner, Bit. I had hopes that the Council would maintain their integrity in my absence." Tester stepped out of Wisdom's form; two who were also one protected me from the Council of Nine.

Tester lifted Archangel Joseph by the collar and held his face close to hers. "We left Bit here to fix the universe. We trusted that the Council wouldn't become corrupt. It's apparent that you and your fellow Council are less human than I thought." She tossed Archangel Joseph to the ground.

He cowered at her feet, apologizing. Tester shunned, him, turning her back and speaking no further on the matter.

Wisdom lifted Archangel Joseph in a telekinetic grip. When he spoke out, his eyes were playful. "Couldn't help but notice that all of you kept your angelic powers when you had your masses return to the human state. Probably with the justification that if you didn't keep your power, you wouldn't be able to stop somebody should they evolve to the point where they might endanger the greater good." He giggled mischievously. "Well, the rules have been rewritten where angels are concerned. Mark my words, little bureaucrats, you won't be flying for a very long time."

All nine archangels were cowed. The fear on their faces was impressive.

"The rule now is as it was ten thousand years ago. Only those who have earned the right shall have the power of the angels. That includes all angels, and all sentient life in the galaxy. Remember the war? Remember your own bigotry and hatred, and how it nearly cost the angels their lives. It won't happen again, because people with such emotions won't be able to grasp the true power."

Turning back around, Tester seemed to look straight into Joseph's soul, Wisdom released his gentle hold on the man. Her words we slick, like a snake's slither, when she spoke to him.

"If you ever touch my daughter again, I'll do more than clip your wings." Tester dismissed them all with a motion of her hand, and hugged Wisdom, vanishing with a snap of wings and tail.

The Council of Nine lost their wings. I turned away, stopping when I was in the hatch, looking back at everybody.

"The party was great, King Lotus, and the tapestry's beautiful. But for now, I think Eohl and myself need to take some time together."

I stepped aboard the fighter, and sat down in the pilot's seat, Eohl at my right. We jumped to Otherspace as soon as the ship could accommodate us. We were in Otherspace for ten minutes while I ran a diagnostic of the ship's engines. A thought occurred to me.

"What should we name this ship?" I asked.

"You're the Captain. I'm just a weapons master." He admitted. "Besides, I don't know that you would like what I wanted to name it."

"What's that?" I wondered

"The Sparrow sounds right somehow." Eohl said. He misinterpreted the frown on my face. "I guess it is a silly name, now that I think about it."

"No way. It's a perfect name. Computer, nomenclature identification, Sparrow."

"Yes Captain. Sparrow on-line and ready for service. Diagnostic completed." The ship's voice was automated, nothing like the *Persimmon*'s had been. But it was our ship, and would be a fine Pirate's ship, with a few modifications.

"Request coordinates."

"I've an idea." I said, smiling with anticipation.

He smiled at me, his golden eyes dilating with pleasure. "Then let's go with it."

I took off my clothes and quickly stuffed them in a carryon, then walked to the back hatch.

"Hold this." I said, handing Eohl the small bag.

I opened the back hatch onto Otherspace, and felt the Otherspace warm breezes inviting me to open my wings and fly. Taking Eohl in a grip under his arms and around his chest, I jumped forward, and fell away from the ship. The hatch sealed behind us, and the Sparrow waited patiently for us to return. It was programmed wait virtually forever: I had no intention of leaving it so long.

"Where are we going?" Eohl said, as I flapped my wings ever harder.

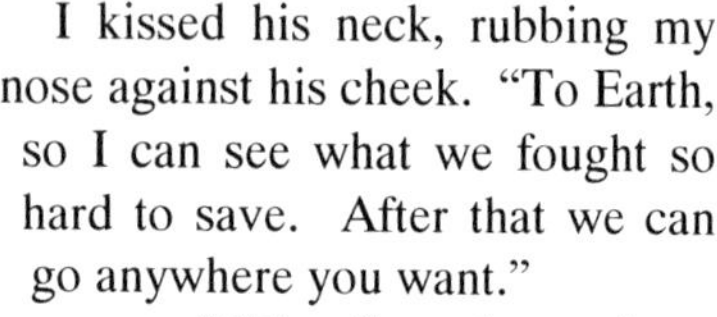

I kissed his neck, rubbing my nose against his cheek. "To Earth, so I can see what we fought so hard to save. After that we can go anywhere you want."

With a flap of my wings, I dropped into a dive, and one of Earth's forests materialized around me.

I landed on a massive tree branch, staring down into the deeper forest. The air was warm and moist from a recent rain, and as I dropped down to the canopy floor, we landed in cool shadows. I found the cabin nearby, and pulled the skeleton key from my carryon. The lock fought for a moment, then clicked, and opened into a small house with wood walls.

It had only one room. The room had a table, a bed, and a cast iron stove set in the center. I opened the back door, expecting to find a closed bath. Instead I found a hot spring for a bath. I smiled at such simplicity. Closing the door, I turned and caught Eohl in a loving embrace, then kissed him gently on the lips.

"Do you think you could stay here for a couple of days?" I asked.

Eohl had been looking around the room.

"Cupboards are full of food, we could stay here for a week, if we wanted to." He said. "Though a couple of days would be good."

I won't talk about my honeymoon much more. Eohl and I traveled all over the galaxy, staying with friends and relatives, and generally having a month long romantic fling. And two months after the honeymoon, I turned up pregnant. Of course I should have been, we were doing what it takes to get pregnant three nights into the honeymoon and pretty much twice every night thereafter.

I felt like it might be a bold new adventure, having a child. Many people were wondering if my child would have wings or be an Elf. Because of the new laws on angelic transformation, the child probably wouldn't have wings. Unless, of course, he earned those wings in a past life. Because of the laws of genetics, I was willing to bet he would have pointed ears, and my eyes.

Eohl and I were given what King Lotus referred to as "the small mansion" as a wedding present from the entire family. The small mansion had thirty bedrooms, an indoor battle room and a library that swallowed one of its four floors entirely. Like all Elfin homes, it wasn't a blemish to Isastan's surface, because it was build completely underground. I insisted on having a private garden and a quick way out from my bedroom, so I could take evening flights and have distant picnics with Eohl.

Everybody spoiled me, including Uruza, who was expecting a second child several months sooner than myself. She was staying with us until her child was born, because it is the duty of the younger sister to help the eldest in delivery. I was actually looking forward to that time, when her baby girl would be born with my help.

Her first born kid, Golun, ran around the house playing pirates and slavers with other children whose names I wasn't really familiar with. Eohl patted my belly almost daily, happy and afraid, just like me.

"I promise," Uruza said, her serious Elfin manner still that of a warrior. "When your time comes, I'll be your midwife." She said it very seriously, as if it were a personal sacrifice.

I smiled at her, surprised when she hugged me. Being surrounded by Elves gave me a different perspective on childbirth. Creatures of pure formality, everything had to have a ritual. I found their sense of duty unparalleled, and the source behind their need to serve was equally surprising. Though they seemed formal, their devotion to their family and love of their friends was the force behind everything they did.

I found it strange because their expression of love was without emotional parallel, and yet they would never express it outwardly. The only thing that really made me wish that I still wasn't pregnant was the Lenitians. They were still a slave economy, and that made it difficult for me to sit around and wait to have my child. With a child to think of, I couldn't go on binges of piracy against the Lenitian merchants. I was in no condition for such games, and when the baby was born Eohl and I'd both be too busy caring for it to be hopping around the galaxy in the name of liberation. Eohl and I spoke of it one evening, when I was feeling a little depressed.

"I wonder how long it will be before my name is forgotten completely by the Lenitians." I said, sipping at a glass of water.

"Probably never." Eohl said.

"Why is that? You know something I don't," I said, putting my head on his arm.

"It seems that you've made a few friends among the pirates. I let word out that the reason the Lenitians have been so lucky lately is that the great and mighty pirate Bit would soon be the gentle and loving Mother Bit. I got an unexpected response. Captain Jonas took up arms in your honor, and agreed to continue your mission for as long as it takes for you to return to the Captain's seat.

"Captain Jonas and his men have been raiding slave ships – using your exact same attack strategy – nonviolent but unyielding. During every attack, they declare they're freeing the slaves 'in service of Captain Bit.'" He giggled mischievously, kissing me.

I was happier than I'd ever been before, confident and successful. Besides the Lenitian affair, there really wasn't much going on in the galaxy, so for now, I enjoyed my vacation. I figured my time in service might even be done. The years past with few concerns. One evening, when my son was old enough, Eohl and I decided to take him into Otherspace for a history lesson. We flew to the remains of

Transcendence, scavenging for memories. As Eohl talked about the angelic wars and how Transcendence had been built from the dreams of the angels, I was temporarily separated and found myself at Wisdom's throne.

Tester and Wisdom were waiting. "I knew you'd find your way here eventually." She said. I bowed reverently, and was rewarded with a hug from Wisdom.

"Enjoy your rest honey. When I need you again, I'll call on you. You are the last angel, after all." Wisdom kissed my forehead and Tester my cheek.

A flash of light signaled the end of our conversation, and when I regained my senses I was in Eohl's arms. He looked concerned. Transcendence began to lose its glimmer, and, with my child in my arms, I turned to Eohl, a single tear running down my cheek.

"Let's go home, dear. This isn't the place I thought it was." Taking his hand, we shifted back to Realspace, Transcendence behind us, and our future ahead.

About the Author

Theron was born in 29 November 1971, and started writing novel length stories when he was eleven. He served 8 years in the US Armed Forces as a member of the Arizona Air National Guard, and is currently the Head Writer for Elucid Press. Published in the areas of fiction, poetry, human rights, activism, and metaphysics, Theron has a knack for picturesque details and complex character development that both entertain and inspire those who read his works.

About the Illustrator

Christy was born in 29 September 1970. She felt the rush of independent commercial artistry at sixteen, when she landed her first contract with a major national corporate entity. Since that time she has been extensively involved in commercial and fine art, and has illustrated several novels. The proud recipient of the 1999 Glyph Award for best book cover design, Christy has proved herself a powerful force in the art world. Christy is currently working on the illustrations for the plume edition of Bit at Large, among other intense and diverse projects.